The Ashburton Reunion

*Two estranged brothers find each other
and two special women to love!*

Orphaned as children, Joshua and Leonard
Ashburton were thrown half a world apart when
Josh's guardian moved to India. Leo remained
in England, being groomed to become the
next Viscount Abbingdon.

Reunited after twenty-five years, both brothers are
happy to be together again, until Josh starts to fall
for the woman almost promised in marriage to his
brother! The two brothers have found each other—
now they need to find the right women to love...

Read Joshua's story in
Flirting with His Forbidden Lady

Available now

And look for Leonard's story

Coming soon!

Author Note

One of the things that initially drew me to writing historical romance was how different the rules of society were two hundred years ago. I loved to imagine how I would react if I were told I had to wait to be introduced formally to someone before speaking to them or that I couldn't be left alone with a man, no matter how innocent the situation. I find it astonishing how much things have changed over the last few hundred years.

When I first started planning *Flirting with His Forbidden Lady*, I was thinking a lot about how our reasons for marrying have changed over the years. In Regency times a love match was a rare thing, especially among the aristocracy, and alliances were often formed without a thought for the suitability of the couple who would spend the next few decades married. I wanted to write about a woman who knows she should marry one man for all the normal, conventional reasons but is tempted into following her heart and pushing against society's and her family's expectations. Beth is that heroine, and I hope you enjoy watching the battle between her sense of duty and her heart.

LAURA MARTIN

Flirting with His Forbidden Lady

HARLEQUIN
HISTORICAL

HISTORICAL™

Recycling programs for this product may not exist in your area.

ISBN-13: 978-1-335-50613-9

Flirting with His Forbidden Lady

Copyright © 2021 by Laura Martin

This edition published by arrangement with Harlequin Books S.A.

For questions and comments about the quality of this book, please contact us at CustomerService@Harlequin.com.

Harlequin Enterprises ULC
22 Adelaide St. West, 40th Floor
Toronto, Ontario M5H 4E3, Canada
www.Harlequin.com

Printed in U.S.A.

Laura Martin writes historical romances with an adventurous undercurrent. When not writing, she spends her time working as a doctor in Cambridgeshire, UK, where she lives with her husband. In her spare moments Laura loves to lose herself in a book and has been known to read from cover to cover in a single day when the story is particularly gripping. She also loves to travel—especially to visit historical sites and far-flung shores.

Books by Laura Martin

Harlequin Historical

The Pirate Hunter
Secrets Behind Locked Doors
Under a Desert Moon
A Ring for the Pregnant Debutante
An Unlikely Debutante
An Earl to Save Her Reputation
The Viscount's Runaway Wife
The Brooding Earl's Proposition
Her Best Friend, the Duke
One Snowy Night with Lord Hauxton

The Ashburton Reunion

Flirting with His Forbidden Lady

Scandalous Australian Bachelors

Courting the Forbidden Debutante
Reunited with His Long-Lost Cinderella
Her Rags-to-Riches Christmas

Visit the Author Profile page
at Harlequin.com for more titles.

For Nic, I miss you.
I hope it isn't another nine months until
we are together again, but in the meantime
here's a book about that special bond
between sisters.

Chapter One

London 1815

'Elizabeth, are you listening to me?'

Suppressing a groan, Beth moved back from the carriage window and fixed her gaze on her mother.

'This is important. Your future is dependent on how you carry yourself tonight. All our futures.'

'I know, Mother.' She tried to keep the exasperation from her voice but it was difficult to summon enthusiasm for a lecture she had received at least four times today alone. Here she was, sitting in a dress they couldn't afford, going to a ball she didn't really want to go to.

It wasn't that she didn't like balls; she loved dancing and socialising and laughing as the night passed in a flurry of excitement. It was this ball in particular she was dreading. Mr Ashburton's ball. The ball during which her mother was expecting her to captivate a man she had barely exchanged a dozen words with.

'Make sure he dances with you at least twice. Be engaging, charming. Show him you will be a good wife.'

'Yes, Mother.' It was easier just to agree than try to protest, to ask how she was meant to show a man she didn't know she would make a good wife.

'And smile. You're pretty enough when you smile.'

Thankfully the carriage stopped before Lady Hummingford could say any more and Elizabeth almost leapt out with relief as soon as a footman stepped forward to open the door. She paused for a moment, looking up at the imposing white façade of Millbrook House, set back from the street behind smart black railings, which framed a neat little garden.

In a few seconds her mother was by her side, hurrying Beth up the steps to the open door and into the house. Already there was a crush of people inside, the noise building as they ventured in deeper from a quiet hum to an almost deafening roar of laughter and conversation. There were guests in the grand hallway, fanning themselves in the unseasonably warm April heat, sipping from glasses of punch and lemonade. Standing at the entrance of the ballroom was a footman ready to announce all new arrivals, and Beth watched as her mother gave their names before she was pulled into the melee of the ball.

'Lady Hummingford and Lady Elizabeth Hummingford.'

It took a moment for Beth to adjust to the heat and the light. Her mother had timed their arrival so their entrance would make the maximum impact, allowing most of the other guests to arrive first. It meant the musicians were already playing and couples already dancing in the middle of the ballroom. Beth allowed herself a moment to enjoy the swirling dresses and quick steps; she loved to dance and appreciated how happy music and dancing made people.

'Where is he?' her mother murmured, frantically searching the ballroom for their host.

'Good evening, Lady Hummingford, Lady Elizabeth,' Miss Culpepper said as she sailed over to them. This might be Mr Ashburton's home and his name on the invitation, but Miss Culpepper would have been the one to oversee some of the finer details that were essential when organising a ball. She was a distant relative of Mr Ashburton's, elderly and childless, who had stepped in when Mr Ashburton had been orphaned at a young age and volunteered to raise him. She was known throughout society as a bit of a dragon, never afraid to say exactly what she thought and disapproving of most she came across.

'Miss Culpepper. What a fabulous ball. A success even so early in the evening.'

'Thank you, Lady Hummingford, you are too kind.'

'Is Mr Ashburton close by? We would like to give him our regards.'

'I'm not sure where my dear great-nephew is at the moment but I'm sure he'll return to the ballroom shortly.'

Beth stretched her neck up as she caught a glimpse of a tall, dark-haired man on the other side of the ballroom. Mr Ashburton was easy to pick out over other people's heads—he must be at least six feet tall, perhaps even more, and his hair such a dark brown it was almost black. He disappeared again almost as soon as she caught sight of him and Beth tried to push away the feeling of relief.

She wanted to get married, wanted to be a wife and start a family, wanted a house of her own to run, away from the interference of her mother. She'd conversed with Mr Ashburton twice for no more than a few minutes each time. Apparently he didn't attend many society events, didn't seem to be in London all that often, not that Beth would know as they'd only made the journey to the capital a couple of weeks ago themselves. On the two occasions they had talked, both over a year ago now, her impression of him had been that he was a serious man, dedicated to running the estates he would one day inherit. He didn't smile much, didn't laugh much, but he seemed pleasant enough. There were plenty of worse candidates for a husband. The issue was more that when she looked at him she didn't feel *anything*. No racing of her heart, no difficulty catching her breath, no delicious tingling of her skin. Beth didn't expect love at first sight but she was certain there should be something, some sign of attraction or, at the very least, a feeling of companionship when faced with the man she would be spending a lifetime with.

Miss Culpepper had moved on to the next guests, so Beth and her mother weaved their way deeper into the ballroom.

'I think I saw Mr Ashburton.' She slipped her arm out of her mother's and turned to walk away.

'I'll come with you.'

'No,' Beth said a little too quickly, pausing a moment and giving a reassuring smile before continuing. 'I think I should speak to him alone.'

Her mother eyed her for a minute before finally nodding. 'Remember how important this is. Annabelle's future is at risk too if you don't secure this match.'

As always when her mother reminded her of her debt to her sister Beth felt a little nauseous. Annabelle was one year younger and the sweetest girl in the entire world. Beth had to make a good match and marry a man with enough money to support not only herself but also her mother and younger sister. They were living off goodwill and the influence of the Hummingford name, but their lines of credit were one by one being cut off and if Beth didn't marry soon they would be facing financial ruin.

'I know, Mother.'

Lady Hummingford let go of Beth's arm and quickly Beth slipped away before she could change her mind. She would go and seek out Mr Ashburton, but not just yet. She needed a few minutes to collect her thoughts, to convince herself she could do this. Mr Ashburton would make a perfectly tolerable husband—who was she to want more, to wish for something that only happened in stories?

Weaving through the ballroom, Beth smiled and greeted people as she passed but didn't stop to talk. Instead she made her way to where the French doors were thrown open and stepped out onto the terrace. The air was marginally cooler outside, but not cold enough for Beth to need anything on her shoulders. Many of the other guests seemed to have had the same idea, with little groups gathered along the length of the terrace. Spotting the stone steps that led down into the garden, Beth checked that no one was watching her and made her way into the darkness below. She'd just find some-where to sit, somewhere to contemplate her future for a few minutes, away from the crush of the ball, and then she would summon some enthusiasm for hunting down Mr Ashburton.

Joshua Ashburton stepped out of the carriage and paid the driver, not taking his eyes off the striking white façade of the house in front of him. It was large, espe-cially for a town house, easily the largest in the street. Even before he took a step towards the house it was apparent that there was some sort of gathering or ball going on. There was a swell of music from inside, mixed with the hum of dozens of voices talking all at once.

He hesitated, wondering whether to stop the car-riage he'd arrived in before it trundled off down the street, contemplating if it would be easier to go away and come back tomorrow. Twenty-five years he'd waited for this moment, another day surely wouldn't make any difference.

He knew logically it wouldn't make a difference, but still he couldn't seem to turn himself around and walk away from his brother's house.

'Perhaps just a peek inside,' he murmured to himself. He didn't need to march in and declare himself, didn't need to disturb his brother's party. Five minutes, just to get a sense of who his brother was. They had exchanged letters over the years, but you couldn't get a real insight into a person from their letters alone.

Josh started towards the front door but stopped be-fore he reached the steps. There was a little pathway by the side of the house, no doubt leading to the back garden, and he could see the gate was very slightly ajar. Quickly he changed course and headed down the path, pushing open the gate and making his way into the garden. The music was louder here and as he rounded the corner of the house he could see the terrace filled with guests and the open doors to the ballroom. People seemed to be enjoying themselves—there was laughter mixed in with conversation and he could see the rhythmic movement of couples dancing inside.

The garden was large, as befitted a property like Millbrook House, and from what he could see of the interior it was richly decorated. From the letters that crossed the ocean every few months he knew his brother had bought Millbrook House a few years earlier, wanting something of his own in London even though he much preferred the countryside. By the size and grandeur of the house it would seem Leo was doing very well for himself.

'Good for you, Leo,' he murmured. Never once had he begrudged his brother his good fortune, never once had he wanted to change places. Leo might have been raised by the relatives with the money and status, but Josh's upbringing had been filled with love and adventure and he knew you couldn't put a price on that.

He'd almost seen enough. Tomorrow he would return and enjoy his reunion with his brother, but tonight he would go back to his rented rooms and leave Leo to his ball and his guests.

As he turned he tripped over something sticking up from the grass in the darkness, stumbling slightly and feeling a jolt of pain shoot through his ankle. He managed to catch himself, cursing quietly as he regained his balance. He limped over to a nearby bench, bending down to massage his ankle. Thankfully it hadn't even been a proper twist, a couple of minutes' rest and it would be more or less back to normal, perhaps with just a little twinge here and there.

He sat back, stretching his legs out in front of him and looking up at the starry sky.

'Oh.' Beth heard the exclamation escape her lips before she could stop it. She'd spotted a bench to the left of the garden, hidden from view of the terrace, and made her way over only to find it already occupied.

'Good evening.'

She peered through the darkness, her eyes still not completely adjusted after leaving the bright light of the ballroom. It was Mr Ashburton. She just about managed to stop herself from rolling her eyes. Of course he would be here, the very man she had decided to actively avoid for a few minutes and he was sitting in her refuge.

'Good evening,' she said, standing awkwardly, not knowing whether to join him on the bench or turn and head back towards the house.

She looked at him. She couldn't profess to know him well but there was something different about him tonight. Normally he held himself so stiff, so upright, but here he was lounging on the bench in the most relaxed manner. He even looked up and smiled at her.

'Won't you join me?'

She glanced uncertainly over her shoulder. Her mother might have encouraged her to spend time with Mr Ashburton, but even she would balk at the idea of being alone with him in the darkness of the garden.

Anyone might have a similar idea to her, wanting to escape the crush of the ball for a few minutes, and come upon them.

Still…there was something about the way he was smiling at her that was making her heart beat a little faster in her chest. Before she could talk herself out of it she circled around him and perched on the other end of the bench.

'It's a wonderful ball,' she said, falling back on mundane conversation to carry her through until her nerves settled at least a little.

'Is it? I'm glad.'

'You haven't seen for yourself?'

He shook his head and Beth wondered if it would be rude to ask why he would throw a ball and then hide out here in the garden. Perhaps he'd just received some bad news or he was developing a headache. Perhaps…she shook her head to stop her imagination running away with her and focussed again on the man next to her.

'I can hear though. The music, the laughter, it certainly sounds like a success.'

Beth tilted her head to one side and listened to the sounds of the ball for a moment, catching Mr Ashburton watching her with those sharp eyes of his.

'It does, doesn't it?' she agreed.

'Surely if it is such a success you should be in there dancing, Miss…'

Beth blinked. He couldn't have forgotten who she was. They'd been introduced, admittedly a year ago now, but surely he remembered the woman he had promised to marry.

She swallowed the indignant outburst and smiled at him stiffly. 'Lady Elizabeth.'

'Lady Elizabeth.' There wasn't even a flicker of recognition in his expression.

For a moment she closed her eyes. What if her mother had got it all wrong? Lady Hummingford was convinced Mr Ashburton had all but agreed to marry Beth before their father had died five years earlier. Lord Hummingford had spoken of some debt owed, a service he had provided Mr Ashburton, and the promised outcome had been that Beth would marry the wealthy and successful young man if she wanted. In her parents' minds it hadn't been an engagement, but it hadn't been far off. The whole point of this season, all the money they'd spent renting rooms they couldn't afford and buying dresses on rapidly reducing credit, was to remind Mr Ashburton of his promise and persuade him there was no benefit in waiting any longer.

'I needed a little air, a little space to think.'

'And where better to do it than under the stars?' he murmured, looking up. Beth followed his gaze and for a moment was captivated by the twinkling stars in the dark sky above. 'I've always found I think best in the open air. I find something calming about looking up at the stars above us and realising I'm a very small part of a very big world.'

'You find that comforting?'

He looked at her, shooting her a grin that lit up his face and made him look young and carefree. Beth felt something tighten inside her and she had to force herself to focus on his reply.

'Strange I know, but I like the thought that I'm just

one of millions of people. If I'm having a bad day there will be thousands having a worse time, and if I'm having a good day there are thousands sharing it with me.'

'I've never thought of it like that. I like it, it's philosophical.'

He gave a little self-deprecating shake of his head. 'I had far too much time on my hands during the voyage from India. It seems to have resulted in me sharing the thoughts that should perhaps stay locked in my own head.'

Beth laughed. This wasn't how she'd expected her conversation with Mr Ashburton to go. In public he was always so upright, so formal. She wasn't sure if she had ever even seen him smile, but here he was laughing and relaxed and making a joke at his own expense. Beth almost enquired about his voyage from India, she hadn't even been aware he'd been out of the country, but before she could ask he had posed his own question.

'What did you need space from?'

'My mother,' she said before she could censor her words.

'Ah.'

'I know she means well,' Beth said quietly, 'but sometimes the weight of her expectations can be a little stifling.'

He regarded her for a few seconds as if weighing up something in his mind. 'What you need is a distraction.'

She blinked, surprised as he stood abruptly and held out his hand. For a moment she just looked at it, not moving.

'Dance with me. I promise you'll find it distracting.

I enjoy dancing as much as the next man, but I'd watch out for your toes if I were you.'

Hesitantly she placed her hand in his. It was madness, but it was as though he'd hypnotised her. Slowly she stood, checking over her shoulder, looking at the flickering lights on the terrace to check if anyone could see them.

'We shouldn't…'

He moved a little closer to her and she felt the warmth of his breath as he whispered into her ear. 'Sometimes it's good to do something forbidden.' The words conjured up a host of illicit images and she felt fierce heat begin to creep through her body.

'What if someone sees us?'

'We're hidden by the bushes.'

She allowed him to pull her gently into position and, as if he had signalled the musicians they were ready, the music began to swell in the ballroom. It was a waltz and it only took three steps for Beth to know Mr Ashburton had lied. He was an accomplished dancer, holding her in a way that made her feel as though she were floating just off the ground. She glanced up, taking a moment to study his features in the darkness. Even now there was a hint of a smile on his lips. He was an attractive man with a strong jaw and dark eyes that contained a sea of warmth. Perhaps this arranged marriage wouldn't be so bad, if he *had* actually agreed to marry her.

Beth let herself get lost in the moment, pushing away all conscious thought to enjoy the pressure of his hand on the small of her back, the sway of their bodies in the darkness and the magical feeling in the air.

As the music faded she should have stepped away,

but Mr Ashburton stayed where he was for a moment, holding her close and looking down into her eyes. She felt an irresistible pull, a need to know what his lips felt like on hers, and she could see the same attraction reflected back as he gently placed a finger under her chin and tilted it up just a fraction.

She'd never been touched like that by a man before, never felt the spark of excitement even a gentle caress could send through her body.

'You dance well, Lady Elizabeth,' he said quietly.

Beth barely heard his words, she was too distracted by the heat of his body so close to her own and the naked desire flaring up inside her.

'Thank you.'

She was sure he was going to kiss her, she even rose up a little on the balls of her feet to narrow the gap between them. The moment seemed to stretch out for ever, the anticipation building second by second until she wanted to shout out, to beg him to pull her into his arms.

'Joshua?' The voice came from the darkness behind them, refined and clipped.

Beth stepped back so quickly she nearly tripped over the hem of her dress, only Mr Ashburton's hands on her arms saving her from ending up in a tangle on the ground. She glanced behind her, stiffening as she saw Mr Ashburton emerge from the darkness.

'How…?' She looked from one man to the other. There were two of them. Both tall with dark hair and dark eyes, with the same strong jaw and straight noses. As she looked closer there were subtle differences in their looks and perhaps an inch difference in height, but there was no mistaking that they were closely related. Brothers perhaps, but surely she would know if Mr Ashburton had a brother.

'Leo.' The man in front of her, the Mr Ashburton she had almost kissed, took a quick step forward and embraced the other man.

Beth was still trying to catch up, her mind whirring as she realised why Mr Ashburton had seemed so different, so relaxed. The man she had been sitting with, Mr Joshua Ashburton, was not the man she was promised to in marriage.

'Lady Elizabeth,' Mr Leonard Ashburton said, giving her a stiff, formal bow. 'It seems you have met my brother.'

'Indeed,' she managed to utter.

'I didn't want to disturb your ball,' Mr Joshua Ashburton said, clapping his brother on the back. 'My ship got in earlier than expected and I couldn't wait for our reunion, but when I saw you were entertaining I thought I wouldn't burst in on your evening.'

'Instead you thought you'd dance with Lady Elizabeth in the garden.' The words were delivered without much emotion but Beth felt the heat flood to her cheeks. She'd hoped he hadn't seen anything more than two people standing together in the garden innocently conversing, but it was apparent he had caught at least a little of her indiscretion.

'I should leave you to get reacquainted with your brother,' Beth said, stepping quickly away.

'Thank you for the dance, Lady Elizabeth.'

She swivelled, catching Mr Joshua Ashburton's eye, and felt the undeniable pull of attraction.

Unable to do anything more than nod, she picked up her skirts and moved as quickly as she could without actually breaking out into a run.

Chapter Two

'You truly wish to accompany me?'

Joshua threw his head back and laughed at his brother's quizzical expression. It had only been a day and a half since his reunion with his brother after twenty-five years but already it felt as though he knew the man sitting across from him as well as if they'd never been parted. He had been six years old when they'd lost their parents, with Leo eight, and the serious, pensive little boy had grown into a serious, pensive man.

'I've got three months in England,' Josh said, tapping his fingers on the arm of the chair. 'Then who knows how long it will be before I can come back again? I don't want to waste a minute.'

'It won't be a fun afternoon.'

'You don't know that.'

'It is tea with the mother of the girl I promised to marry and then have dragged my feet ever since. It is *not* going to be fun.'

'Who is this girl?'

Leo regarded him for a second before answering. 'You've met her. Lady Elizabeth.'

The image of her swaying closer to him, blue eyes locked on his, lips parted in that way that hinted she wanted to be kissed, flashed into his mind.

'Lady Elizabeth,' he murmured, savouring the memory. 'She seemed pleasant enough, why the delay in marrying her?' Pleasant was an understatement. Everything about her had been alluring: the sweet scent of roses in her hair, the feel of the curve of her waist under his hand as they danced, the way her cheeks had flushed every time he'd looked at her.

His brother sighed, running a hand through his thick hair, the same gesture Josh knew he himself favoured when he felt stressed.

'I haven't even asked the girl. It was an arrangement between myself and her father. I owed him a debt of gratitude for a…favour he performed for me. In return for his service I promised to marry his daughter when she was of an appropriate age.'

Josh was intrigued about the favour but knew not to push his brother on something he seemed so protective of. 'You must be quite the catch, for him to arrange the marriage like that.'

Leo shrugged. 'When Lord Abbingdon dies I become the ninth Viscount Abbingdon and inherit all the land and money that accompanies the title.'

'And Lady Elizabeth is the daughter of an earl?'

'Indeed. But an impoverished one. Her father was concerned she might be forced to marry someone in trade, someone wealthy but not titled, who could prop up the flailing family fortunes. In me he saw money and a title—the best he could hope for.'

'You sell yourself short. So why the delay?'

Leo closed his eyes for a moment. 'In truth I do not know. I need to marry, it is a stipulation of Lord Abbingdon's will. Of course the title and property will come to me no matter what, but he has threatened to give whatever money he can away if I am not married by the time he dies.'

'A little unreasonable.'

'He tells me it is bad enough that he hasn't got a son of his own to inherit, but after you and I there is no one even slightly suitable to inherit the title, or so he says. Hence the stipulation I must be married.'

'Is there someone else you wish to marry?'

'No. And I'm sure Lady Elizabeth will make a good enough wife. It is just I barely know her.'

'Then we must remedy that.'

Ten minutes later they were strolling through the streets, enjoying the sun on their faces and the warm breeze that reminded Josh of the days just before the monsoon back home.

'What about you?' Leo asked as he lifted his hat to a group of young women who all chorused good afternoon when they passed.

'What about me?'

'Is there someone you plan to marry, someone you hold in high regard in India, or are you looking for a wife here?'

'Good Lord, no. I love India, I can't imagine living anywhere else, but I am well aware it is not the life a well-brought-up Englishwoman would necessarily wish for. I fear I'm destined to be a bachelor my entire life.'

'You have to go back?'

'Yes. I have to go back.' He had to, but he also wanted to. England was a pleasant diversion, the chance to get to know the man walking next to him in person rather than through the letters they had exchanged throughout their lives, but it was a short interlude, nothing more. His real life was waiting for him back in India, the shipping business, the transport lines, the hustle and bustle of the docks.

'Very well.' Josh was beginning to become accustomed to his brother's stoic acceptance of everything he was faced with. He couldn't imagine Leo becoming incensed or enraged, instead just nodding in that calm way of his and moving on.

They paused outside a narrow town house, its paint a little less pristine than the others on the street. There was an air of genteel neglect, nothing that stood out by itself, but next to its neighbours this house just looked as though it needed a little more money spent on it.

Leo approached first, knocking on the door and standing back, waiting until a nervous young maid admitted them and repeated their names as if worried she might forget before leading them to a room on the first floor off a narrow hallway.

'Mr Leonard Ashburton and Mr Joshua Ashburton,' she said, dipping into a clumsy curtsy as the men passed her into the room.

Josh's eye quickly swept the room looking for Lady Elizabeth. It was a reflexive action, one he couldn't control. He just wanted one glimpse of her, to take the sight of her in one more time before he resigned himself to the fact she was as good as his brother's fiancée.

She wasn't there. Getting up to greet them was a slender woman in her late forties, no doubt Lady Hummingford. He could see a few similarities between her and her daughter, but Lady Elizabeth was fair where she was dark, and petite where her mother was tall.

'Alice, inform Elizabeth we have guests. Please sit down, gentlemen, my daughter will join us shortly.'

Josh sat, looking around the room. It was small but neatly decorated, although there were no personal touches, no paintings on the wall or figurines on the mantelpiece, and all the furnishings matched a little too well. If he wasn't much mistaken these were rented rooms, and cheap ones at that. It would seem his brother was correct about the Hummingfords' financial struggles.

'Mr Ashburton, I wasn't aware you had a brother. It is a pleasure to make your acquaintance.'

'The pleasure is all mine, Lady Hummingford.' Josh inclined his head. He hadn't been brought up in these circles. Mr Usbourne, his guardian, was a kind man, a wealthy man, but he wasn't a member of the aristocracy. Society in India was limited so Josh socialised with a mixture of people, but the rules weren't quite the same there. Luckily he was a quick mimic and only had to observe how his brother behaved to be able to emulate him perfectly; still the formality felt a little stifling.

'Will you take tea whilst we wait for my daughter?'

'Please.'

'Very good.'

* * *

Elizabeth started nibbling on the edge of her thumbnail as she regarded herself in the mirror, only conscious that she was doing it when she caught sight of her hand raised up to her mouth.

'He's just a man,' she repeated to herself for the hundredth time. Mr Ashburton, Mr *Leonard* Ashburton, had sent a note the day before to ask if he could call this afternoon. Her mother had been buzzing around with nervous energy ever since and Elizabeth had quickly retreated to her room. The solitude had been a relief, but it had meant she'd spent the last twenty-four hours worrying about the encounter.

Top of her list of concerns was that he had seen her entirely inappropriate behaviour in the garden at his ball when she'd danced with his brother in the darkness, and had come to declare her a harlot, not fit to be his wife. Second on her list was exactly the opposite: that he might have decided to stop dragging his feet and that he was coming round to tell her they would be married within the month.

There was a soft knock at the door. Alice opened it and poked her head through the gap.

'The gentlemen are here, my lady. Your mother asked for you to come down.'

'Thank you, Alice.' Beth smiled at the maid, trying to put the nervous young girl at ease but she had already dropped her eyes to the floor and was starting to withdraw. 'Wait. Gentlemen? Is there more than one?'

'Yes, my lady.'

'Who are they?'

Even before Alice spoke Beth knew the answer. She

remembered the feel of Mr Joshua Ashburton's hand on the small of her back guiding her around their private outdoor dance floor and the hammering of her heart as the music faded away and he kept hold of her for just a moment longer than he really should. Even now she could feel the warmth that had suffused her body, that tiny spark of pleasure at just being close to him.

'Mr Ashburton and Mr Ashburton,' Alice said, and before Beth could ask any more she slipped away and clattered down the corridor.

Beth closed her eyes and let out a long breath. She had no idea what both men were doing here. There was absolutely no reason for Mr Joshua Ashburton to call on her and her mother. Quickly she tried to suppress the flicker of excitement she felt. She needed to focus her time and energy on his brother, not allow herself to be distracted by Joshua Ashburton's mesmerising smile and good humour.

Checking her reflection in the mirror one final time, she flashed a smile to check it didn't look too forced then left the sanctuary of her bedroom and walked downstairs.

The house they were renting whilst in London was small and even as she descended the stairs to the first floor she could hear the murmur of voices in the drawing room.

As she entered the conversation stopped and all eyes turned to her. Both men stood and she was struck again by how similar they looked. They both were tall with broad shoulders and hair so dark it was almost black. They both regarded her with rich brown eyes, set on either side of a straight, narrow nose. Despite all the similarities she could tell which brother was which immediately. Leonard Ashburton looked at her with a serious expression on his face, greeting her formally. His manner was cool and restrained and she was struck with the impression that he worked hard to maintain an unreadable façade.

His brother, Joshua Ashburton, was the complete opposite. He smiled broadly as soon as Beth came into the room, his eyes lighting up as she turned to regard him. He actually took a step towards her as if about to take her hand or some other equally intimate gesture before catching himself and stepping back again.

'Good afternoon, Lady Elizabeth,' Leonard Ashburton said as they all sat down. Beth's mother was trying to signal something with her eyes, but Beth couldn't work out what so quietly ignored her.

'Good afternoon. It is kind of you to call.'

'You remember my brother, of course.'

Beth felt the heat rising up into her cheeks as she was forced to turn and acknowledge Joshua Ashburton again. He was sitting back in his chair in a relaxed manner, one ankle propped up on the opposite knee.

'I hope you don't mind me accompanying my brother, Lady Elizabeth.'

'Of course not.'

'Mr Ashburton was just telling me how his brother has only recently arrived from India,' Lady Hummingford said.

India. Beth allowed herself a moment to imagine a country so different from theirs. She'd read books about it, poured over the pictures in the big atlas her father had kept in the library at Birling View. It sounded so exotic, so exciting, and his recent return explained both why she wasn't aware of Joshua Ashburton's existence and the hint of a tan on his face.

'You must be thrilled to have your brother home, Mr Ashburton.' Beth forced herself to address the man she was meant to be promised to, even though she wanted to study the man sitting next to him.

'Indeed. Although his visit is only brief. We must make the most of him whilst he is here.'

Beth allowed her eyes to flit to Joshua Ashburton, to find his attention fixed squarely on her. He even smiled when her gaze met his. Beth felt a guilty flush and quickly turned her attention back to Leonard Ashburton.

He seemed a man of few words, content to sit in the awkward silence that was beginning to stretch out ahead of them whilst Beth floundered for a topic of conversation.

'I understand you spend much of your time in the countryside, Mr Ashburton.'

'I do.'

She waited a moment but it became apparent he wasn't going to expand on his answer. 'Do you have a country residence or do you stay with family?'

'My great-uncle has a few properties in Sussex and Kent. He is an elderly man, infirm of body although still very sharp of mind. I run the estates for him now and live in one of the smaller properties just outside Tunbridge Wells.'

'Oh, Tunbridge Wells is such a delightful town, so stylish,' Lady Hummingford gushed. 'We've often taken a small diversion on our way to London to spend a night there.'

Beth's childhood home, the only home they owned now their London house had been sold a few years ago and the two other estates inherited along with the title by a distant cousin when their father died, was just outside the little town of Eastbourne, looking over the white cliffs and rolling hills. She loved living by the sea but knew it was another thing she would have to give up as a married woman.

'Where do you live, Lady Elizabeth?' Mr Joshua Ashburton asked.

'We have an estate on the south coast, near Eastbourne. I enjoy rural life, although I can't deny a stay in London is very diverting.'

'Lady Hummingford, perhaps I could have a word with you in private,' Mr Leonard Ashburton said abruptly.

Beth's eyes widened. This was the moment he revealed his intent. Either she would be rejected as an unsuitable wife for a future Viscount or he would be discussing a proposal.

'Of course.' Lady Hummingford looked serene, as if this weren't what she had been working towards for the last year. She rose, the smile just visible at the corners of her mouth, and Beth watched as she and Mr Leonard Ashburton left the room to take a stroll around the garden. Her mother glanced back, making sure the door was left wide open, but she was too keen to talk to Mr Ashburton to protest that Beth was being left alone with a gentleman.

The silence only lasted for a moment after they left,

then Mr Joshua Ashburton swapped seats so he was sitting directly next to her. They were still separated by the arm of the chair, but it felt a little inappropriate.

'Lady Elizabeth, we meet again.'

'I feel I need to explain—'

He held up a hand. 'No need.'

'There is. I wouldn't normally behave like that.'

'You didn't do anything wrong, Lady Elizabeth.' She had the irrational urge to ask him to call her Beth. It was how she thought of herself, even though only her sister ever called her Beth out loud, but she wanted to hear her name slip between his lips, uttered in his perfect English with just a hint of an accent she couldn't place.

'I shouldn't even have been alone in the garden, let alone stopped to dance with you.'

'These rules you all live by,' he said with a rueful shake of his head.

'The rules of society?'

'Why should you feel guilty for spending a pleasant few minutes alone with someone else? It wasn't as though anything inappropriate happened.'

Beth thought of the hand on the small of her back, the way their legs had brushed together as they danced. She felt her pulse quicken as she remembered the moment the music had stopped and his finger had tilted her chin up so their lips were only a few inches apart. They might have been saved from crossing the line by the arrival of Mr Leonard Ashburton, but that didn't mean Beth hadn't behaved scandalously, both with the action of straying into the garden unchaperoned and in her thoughts and wishes in that moment before they'd been interrupted.

'Although…' he said, a mischievous glint in his eye. 'I do suspect you wanted me to kiss you.'

Beth spluttered. It might be true, but a real gentleman wouldn't point out a little indiscretion like that.

'I did not.'

'You did.'

'I thought you were your brother,' she muttered.

'That I do believe,' he said softly, leaning back in his chair as if he didn't have a care in the world. 'But it was *me* you wanted to kiss.'

She stood, needing to put some distance between herself and the man in front of her. Even now he had some sort of pull on her. She found it difficult to look away, difficult to be pragmatic.

The drawing room looked out over a small garden and Beth took a moment to collect herself, looking down at the figures of her mother and Mr Leonard Ashburton strolling side by side below.

'Why are you here?' she asked suddenly, spinning round.

'I am merely accompanying my brother.'

'And why is he here?'

'To see if you and he will be suited.'

'Suited?' Beth repeated to herself. She glanced out of the window again, wondering whether it really mattered if they would be suited. Her mother certainly didn't think so; her mind was on survival rather than Elizabeth's future happiness.

'Marriage is for life,' Joshua Ashburton said quietly. 'It seems sensible not to rush in.'

Elizabeth tried to let go of some of the tension she was holding in her shoulders and came and sat back down, choosing a chair further away than her original one, ignoring Mr Ashburton's smile as he watched her sit.

'Tell me about India,' she said after a moment's silence.

'What would you like to know, Lady Elizabeth?'

'Anything. Everything. I've never travelled further than Sussex, would you believe?' She gave a little laugh that was meant to be self-deprecating but even to her ears it sounded pitiful. She'd grown up reading of all the wonderful places across the globe in her father's library, but neither of her parents had liked to travel and by the time she was old enough to gain a little independence they had no money to waste on frivolities.

'I live just outside a little town in the Bengal area of India. It is about twenty minutes' ride from the sea, set in leafy green hills. The sea down below is the most brilliant blue you could imagine and the beaches are made of powdery golden sand.'

Beth closed her eyes, trying to imagine the scene he was describing but it was so different from anything she had ever seen it was hard to summon the image.

'India is hot, much hotter than here year-round, although it is a different heat in the different seasons. Just before the rains come there is an unbearable humidity and when the first cloud bursts it is a welcome relief.' He smiled at her. 'As you can see, I love my country. I could sing its praises all day long.'

'You think of India as your country?'

'Of course. I've lived there since I was seven. This is the first time I've been in England as an adult.'

'I didn't realise.' She tried to work out why the Ashburton brothers would have been separated and raised half a world apart.

He was reclining in his chair again, looking more at ease in her drawing room than she did.

'And you're only here for three months now?'

'I am. My guardian is getting old, he wants me to take over the business. He's stepping down in nine months so I've got to be home for then. I almost didn't come—three months is such a short time after half a year at sea—but it isn't as though there will be a good opportunity for me to leave once I take over.'

'What is your guardian's business?'

'Shipping and transport. Do you know how much is made in India and shipped all over the world? It's a rich and bountiful country and we run one of the biggest shipping companies in the east. We transport goods all over India, as well. There're some whispers about building a steam railway and we want to be at the forefront of that. I know some pioneers are using steam locomotives to transport goods in mining and I wonder if it could be used on a wider scale. Can you imagine a steam locomotive that travels the breadth of India, transporting goods across the country?'

'It sounds like a big responsibility.'

He shrugged. 'It's what I've been brought up to do.'

Beth felt a sudden pang of jealousy. She'd been brought up to marry and bear children, nothing more. Once that was accomplished her purpose would be fulfilled. It was a bleak thought.

She cast around the room for something to distract her, her eyes settling once again on the window. It seemed cruel that her fate was being decided outside without her presence.

'You look nervous.'

Beth blinked. Mr Joshua Ashburton certainly didn't seem to mind stating things exactly as he saw them.

She started to deny it and then caught herself. She was allowed to be nervous; it didn't mean she wouldn't do her duty and marry the man her mother was selling her off to. Suddenly feeling very tired of it all, she allowed herself a little honesty.

'I don't know your brother, Mr Ashburton. We've conversed three times, four if you count today. I don't know if he is a kind man or not, I don't know if he will love me or beat me or ignore me. Yet it is my duty to marry him, if he will have me.'

'I can't claim to know my brother well,' Joshua Ashburton said slowly, a frown on his normally smiling face, 'but he is a good man, Lady Elizabeth, an honourable man.'

She nodded. From what she had heard about Leonard Ashburton she thought it was probably true. People painted him as a serious, hard-working man who didn't have much time for fun, but there were no whispers about malice or cruelty. That she should be grateful for, but she felt as though she shouldn't have to be pleased that her future husband wouldn't beat her.

'He also wouldn't force you into a marriage you didn't want.'

Beth felt the tears rising to her eyes. It wasn't Leonard Ashburton doing the forcing. She knew her mother would never let her turn a wealthy and soon-to-be-titled gentleman down. They were in too much debt for that.

'I don't have the same freedoms you do,' she said in a voice no louder than a whisper. Beth knew she was sharing too much with this man she barely knew, but it was as though he had hypnotised her. He was so easy to talk to, to share things with, that she wanted to let all the family secrets spill out. She wanted to tell him of the debts and the more and more frequent refusals of lines of credit, and of course the more personal debt she owed to her sister, the reason Beth had to be the one responsible for all of their futures and not just her own.

'No,' he said after a moment of silence, 'I suppose you don't.'

Before she could say any more she heard her mother's voice grow nearer as she and Leonard Ashburton returned inside.

Her mother was beaming, and as she entered the room she lay a featherlight touch on Mr Ashburton's arm. It seemed the negotiations had gone well.

Beth summoned a smile, feeling sick as she waited to hear her fate.

'We must be going. Lady Elizabeth, it was a pleasure seeing you again. I look forward to our stroll around the pleasure gardens tomorrow night.'

'The pleasure gardens?'

'I suggested the idea to your mother a moment ago— the Vauxhall Pleasure Gardens are beautiful at this time of year. Lady Hummingford confirmed you are not otherwise engaged.'

Allowing her innate social manners to take over, she stood and allowed Leonard Ashburton to kiss her hand before he turned and left, leaving her in the dark as to whether they were engaged or not.

She was so shocked she didn't register Joshua Ashburton until he was right in front of her. He picked up her hand from where it was still held out in front of her and brought it to his lips, brushing the most gentle of kisses on her skin. All the time his eyes didn't leave her own and she felt a flurry of excitement deep inside. Too soon he had pulled away and Beth was left holding her hand to her chest, feeling the thump of her heart through her skin and trying not to show how flustered one tiny kiss on the hand had made her.

'What did Mr Ashburton say?' She tried to pull her focus back on to the important matter in hand as the two men were shown out by the maid.

'He proposes a courtship, a trial of sorts, to see if you will be suited. He remembers his promise and if all is well between you at the end of six weeks the wedding will be arranged.'

Six weeks. It was no time at all. Six weeks to convince a man she didn't care for that she would make a perfect wife. Six weeks to convince herself this was for the best.

Chapter Three

The sun was barely up when Josh left Millbrook House. It was cool with the streets in shadow, but the watery light of dawn was already beginning to hint at the glorious day it would soon become.

He loved the early mornings, often choosing a stroll over the hills or down to the beach back home instead of another hour in bed. There was something magical about discovering a place before many people were up and about, something wonderful about walking through an empty street or through quiet countryside whilst everyone else was still abed.

It was only his fourth day in England and he felt as though he had so much to see and do. Three months was no time at all to catch up on a lifetime missed out on with his brother, and he was curious about this country where he had been born too.

Leo was the same as he had been as a child in many ways, although many of his qualities seemed amplified. He had been a serious boy, but now there was a gravity about him that exceeded how he'd been as a child, and

Josh sensed a sadness too. He hadn't probed too deeply but he felt as though his brother didn't much care about his future happiness and was far too focussed on duty.

Take the example of his proposed marriage. Leo was hardly interested either way. He felt he needed to get married and he was the sort of man to honour a promise made, so Lady Elizabeth would be an adequate solution, but he was going into it without a thought for his or Lady Elizabeth's future happiness.

Josh found himself pausing at the thought of Lady Elizabeth. She'd looked even more beautiful in the daylight. He'd felt a pull when they were in the same room together, as if he needed to be close to her, even though he knew they should only exchange pleasantries at a suitable distance. The urge to sweep her into his arms for another waltz had been almost overwhelming and he'd felt such sympathy for her as she'd revealed just a little of her frustration at her lack of control over her own future.

'She'll make a good wife,' he murmured.

She was poised and graceful and everything a future viscountess should be. Even if she and Leo were poorly matched. At the thought he felt a surge of disloyalty. It wasn't his place to feel anything for Lady Elizabeth except perhaps a brotherly regard if she did one day become his sister-in-law. Once again he remembered the vitality and sparkle in her pale blue eyes and had to push away the knowledge that brotherly regard was *not* what he felt when he thought of her.

Strolling through the wrought-iron gates of Hyde Park, he had to step back a few paces as three young men on horseback came speeding past. They looked like grooms, up and about early exercising their master's horses. Josh watched them trot down the wide avenue and join a few other young men on horses before he took one of the smaller paths into a quieter part of the park.

He had been walking for about ten minutes, following the ornate signs for the Serpentine, when he heard a murmur of voices. There was something about the tone that put him on edge and he quickened his pace to get a glimpse of what was round the corner.

'Get off me,' a high voice shouted, followed by a low and ominous chuckle.

'Just one kiss, that's not too much to ask.' The man's voice was refined but slurred and even without seeing him Josh knew he was drunk and out of control.

'Let me go.'

'She's a fighter.'

'Anyone would be if faced with the prospect of kissing your face,' one of the companions slurred.

'Steady on. It's not that…' There was a deep groan, the sort emitted when a man was hit in his nether regions.

Josh broke out into a run, rounding the corner and almost barrelling into the three men standing there, one hunched over and still moaning. His eyes flicked quickly across the scene. All three men looked to be in their cups, drunken and tottering, but still a menacing sight for the petite young woman who they surrounded. She had her back to him, struggling to get free from the grip of the largest of the group. The men were well dressed, although unkempt from a night out drinking, which made him think they were gentlemen, in birth if not behaviour. That was a relief at least. Most working-class men would know how to fight at least a little. Bar brawls taught you how to punch to do some real harm and he didn't fancy facing three men who knew how to handle themselves.

Josh didn't even shout a warning, knowing surprise was his best weapon. Launching himself at the closest man, he crashed into his back, sending him sprawling onto the ground. Without pausing to take a breath he swung a punch at the second man, hitting him squarely on the jaw and feeling the force of the impact jar up his arm. The man's head snapped back and he stumbled, blinking with disorientation and clutching his face in pain.

The third man was the one holding onto the woman's arm and Josh had to manoeuvre himself to make sure he didn't catch her with his elbow as he pulled back to deliver another punch. He'd lost the element of surprise but the man's inebriation worked in Josh's favour as he stood there open-mouthed for a moment before attempting to hit out. Josh dodged the poorly aimed punch and delivered one of his own.

'Get out of here,' he growled, watching intently as the men eyed him up before two of them turned back to pull on the third man's arm. Josh's eyes met his and for a long moment they stared at each other, before the man allowed his friends to guide him away.

Josh watched them go, making sure they didn't change their minds, before he turned to the woman shaking beside him. As she looked up at him he was shocked to see Lady Elizabeth, dishevelled from the tussle but still looking radiant in the morning light. Her cheeks were wet with tears and she had a red mark on one where it looked as if one of the men had slapped her.

'Did they harm you?' He watched as her eyes focussed in on his momentarily, widening as she recognised him.

'Mr Ashburton.'

'Are you hurt?' he repeated. She seemed dazed, in shock, and not able to concentrate on him. Her eyes kept flitting from side to side as if searching for her attackers. 'Lady Elizabeth.' He placed a hand gently on her arm and at the first touch she flinched away, but as he slowly increased the pressure just a little it calmed her. She was shaking under his hand but after a few seconds her eyes came up and met his again and this time he could tell she was starting to relax just a fraction.

'No, not hurt.' A hand flew to her cheek and she touched the red mark, wincing as she did so.

'They hit you?'

'Yes.'

'Did you know them?'

She shook her head, looking down at her crumpled dress and beginning to try to straighten it.

'Come and sit down, tell me what happened.'

Allowing him to take her by the arm, Lady Elizabeth followed as he led her out to a more open area of the park. He reasoned they would both feel more comfortable if they could see who was approaching from all directions without any bushes or trees to hide a lurking figure.

As they sat his knees brushed hers and for a second they both stiffened at the contact. Lady Elizabeth moved away quickly, perching on the very end of the bench so there was a good foot of space between them.

'Thank you,' she said quietly, her eyes coming up to meet his. Under her scrutiny he felt his pulse quicken and he had the urge to close the space between them, to sit so his knees touched hers, his hand rested on her thigh.

'You don't need to thank me.'

'If you hadn't been there…' She shuddered as she trailed off.

'Don't think about it.'

Lady Elizabeth glanced down, frowning as she saw his bloody knuckles.

'Your hand is hurt.'

Josh hadn't even noticed the blood. He remembered a jolt of pain as his fist had connected with the second man's jaw, but in the heat of the moment it had been pain soon forgotten.

'It's nothing. It will heal in a couple of days. What happened, Lady Elizabeth?'

She was silent for a little while and Josh began to wonder if she was going to answer him.

'I always wake up early, well before anyone else in the house. At home I ride along the cliffs for an hour or so before breakfast, but we couldn't bring the horses to town.' She smiled faintly and Josh wondered if the poised Lady Elizabeth was in fact almost as out of place in London as he was. 'I just wanted some fresh air.'

'Forgive my ignorance in the ways of London society, but I thought a young lady always took a maid or chaperon with her wherever she went.'

'I'm supposed to whilst in London, but do you know

how suffocating that is? Never to be alone?' She shook her head. 'I won't make the same mistake again. I knew I should have stuck to the main path or perhaps not come into the park at all, but it just looked so beautiful in the morning light.'

He had thought the very same thing as he'd entered Hyde Park through the main gates.

'I think those men were on their way home. They smelled as though they'd been drinking all night.' She gave a little shudder at the memory.

'They grabbed you?'

'Yes. Pulled me around a little, tried to…touch me.' She paused and then looked over at him again. 'I'm very glad you came by when you did, Mr Ashburton. I don't think I've ever been so scared in my life.' Lady Elizabeth gave a little humourless laugh and clasped her delicate hands together in her lap, her knuckles turning white under the pressure. 'I suppose that sounds pathetic, as if I've led a very sheltered life.'

'Three men attacked you, Lady Elizabeth. I would be worried if that hadn't scared you.'

'You were very quick to dispatch them.'

'They were drunk. I doubt I could have been so effective against three men if they had been sober.' He was being modest. Josh led a physical life in India; he might be in line to inherit the business very soon but his guardian had insisted he get to know each aspect inside out, which had involved working each of the different jobs for a period of time. His muscles had grown strong under the Indian sun and his reflexes fast as he'd worked the machinery in the workshops. 'Would you like me to walk you home?'

'That would be kind, thank you, but not yet. If you have a few minutes to spare?'

He couldn't think of anywhere else in the world that he wanted to be more right now than on a bench in Hyde Park with Lady Elizabeth.

Beth could still feel her hands shaking every time she relaxed her fists. For a moment, before Mr Ashburton had arrived, she'd thought she was about to be dragged into the undergrowth and taken advantage of. Perhaps the men would have come to their senses before that, but their judgement had been clouded by the alcohol that was making them stagger and she had felt real fear.

In many ways she'd led a very sheltered existence. She could remember trips to London when she was young, always short-lived as her father hadn't been keen on leaving her sister home alone for too long, but her mother had insisted Annabelle wasn't to come with them. The trips had stopped when her father had fallen ill, and then a few years later he'd died and most of the properties had gone to a cousin, a male heir. They'd kept the house in Sussex and the London town house, but soon even that had to be sold to pay for upkeep on Birling View. Since then she'd lived a quiet life at home with her mother and sister, untroubled by the outside world.

'Come take a stroll with me. It is turning into a glorious morning.' Mr Ashburton stood and offered her his arm. She hesitated for a moment, then stood and placed her hand into the crook of his elbow. 'I've never been in a park like this before,' he said quietly, 'with the carefully planned rolling landscape and trees planted to draw the eye.'

Beth followed his gaze and looked out over the park from their vantage point. It was beautiful and as they started to stroll she felt some of the tension she had been carrying start to ease.

'Actually that must be a lie,' he said with a broad smile. 'When I was a child we spent much of our time in London, but do you know I can't remember a jot of it? I was six when I left, and, although I can remember the people, the places are all a complete blank.'

'Why did you leave?'

'Our parents died. Mother first and Father soon after. Congestion of the chest, so I'm told.'

'I am sorry.'

'Thank you. It was a long time ago but I do often wonder what life would have been like if they'd survived.'

Beth glanced up at him, marvelling at the easy, open way he spoke. Most of her acquaintances were stiff and formal, even when amongst friends, but Mr Ashburton spoke freely, giving away little parts of himself in the conversation.

'Why did you go to India?'

'Whilst Leo stayed here?'

Beth nodded. It was an odd arrangement, the two brothers separated after their parents' deaths.

'They struggled to find anyone to look after us. We have no close family, no one young at least. Miss Culpepper is a great-aunt or something of the sort, she's the closest relative, and then there's Lord Abbingdon—he was a widower and did not want the burden of someone else's children.' He paused for a moment as he led her down to the edge of the Serpentine and chose a path that continued by its edge. 'In the end Miss Culpepper agreed to take Leo—he's the eldest, of course, the heir. Luckily for me Mr Usbourne stepped in and offered to take me.'

'Mr Usbourne was not a relative?'

'No, a friend of our father's. He tells me he held back at first because he knew he was off to India, but when no family would take me he and his wife were secretly pleased. They couldn't have children, and they loved me like a son from the day they picked me up.'

Beth felt a pang of sympathy for the little boy Mr Ashburton had been, orphaned, with only his brother left, and then told no one wanted to take him in.

'Don't feel sorry for me, Lady Elizabeth. I've had a good life, better than most. Leo might be the heir, the one chosen to stay, but I grew up as part of a family.'

'And you haven't seen your brother since you left England all those years ago?'

He shook his head. 'Twenty-five years is a long time. We write, of course, but there is only so much you can learn about someone from a letter.'

The park was still quiet, with the odd couple strolling in the distance; they had this stretch of path by the lake completely to themselves.

'Thank you,' Beth said quietly.

Mr Ashburton turned to her and gave her a puzzled look.

'For distracting me. I know it was your intent, and it has worked.'

He smiled, his eyes crinkling at the corners just a

little. Beth felt the need to take a deep breath, as if there weren't enough air to sustain her in the immediate vicinity.

'Happy to be of service, Lady Elizabeth.'

'I should be getting home. Would you be so kind as to escort me?' She didn't want to leave; if she could have her way she would continue strolling round Hyde Park with Mr Ashburton all day, but soon her mother would rise and Beth knew if she wasn't home by then she would have to endure another lecture about how she should behave, and that would not include leaving the house at daybreak for a walk unchaperoned in the park.

'Of course. Now, how do we get out of here?'

They both looked around for a moment, disorientated by the different paths they had taken. Beth didn't want to go back the way they'd come, that would mean passing through the area she had been attacked in, and so she pointed for them to continue the way they'd been walking.

'I'm sure there will be a gate this way.'

They continued to stroll through the park, eventually coming upon a gate that allowed them back onto the streets. It didn't take long for Beth to orientate herself once they were back on more familiar territory and within fifteen minutes they had turned the corner into Egerton Gardens.

'Thank you,' Beth said as they paused at the bottom of the steps that led up to the house.

'You're welcome, Lady Elizabeth.'

Beth waited a moment longer, unsure why she was hesitating. He had delivered her home, just as he'd said he would, and now here they were. Really there was nothing more to say, nothing more to wait for, but wait she did, unable to break the force that seemed to hold them together.

Looking down at her shoes, she took a deep breath to steady her nerves and stepped in a little closer to Mr Ashburton at exactly the moment he did the same. Their bodies collided with a soft bump and Beth felt the taut-ness of Mr Ashburton's muscles beneath his clothes. His arms came up and steadied her, holding her firmly just above the elbows until he was sure she had regained her balance, and even then he lingered a little longer.

Beth's heart was pounding, her body overcome with an unfamiliar heat, and she had the urge to rise up onto her tiptoes and brush her lips against his. Even as she had the thought she knew it could never be, but her body swayed closer to him rebelliously.

She saw a flash of something that looked very much like desire in Mr Ashburton's eyes before he dropped his hands from her arms so quickly it was as though she'd burnt him.

'Goodbye, Lady Elizabeth,' he said, taking a step back.

She couldn't reply, not trusting her voice to come out as anything more than a squeak. Instead she nodded briefly and hurried up the steps, only allowing herself to breathe once she was inside the house with the door closed behind her.

Chapter Four

Josh paced in front of the unlit fireplace, aware of the tension in his shoulders and the minute clenching of his jaw. He knew exactly why he was worked up but he didn't want to admit it to himself. In half an hour Leo would leave for his evening with Lady Elizabeth. He would spend the next few hours strolling through Vauxhall Pleasure Gardens with Lady Elizabeth on his arm, discussing the world and the future.

'Stop it,' he murmured to himself. It wasn't right for him to feel this dash of jealousy. Lady Elizabeth was promised to Leo and he had no right to think of her as anything more than his future sister-in-law.

Leo walked into the room, holding a letter in his hand and frowning deeply.

'Is there a problem?'

'There could be. Lord Abbingdon has been taken unwell. He's summoned me to his bedside immediately.'

'Do you think it is serious?'

'He's not a young man and the tone of the letter is grave, but I suppose I will not know for sure until I get there.'

'Do you want me to accompany you?'

'No, I'll ride until nightfall and complete the journey tomorrow.' He shook his head. 'Of course, it means I will have to cancel my plans with Lady Elizabeth.'

'I'm sure she will understand.'

'Unless…'

Josh looked up, seeing the question in his brother's eyes.

'Unless?'

'You could go, take Lady Elizabeth to the gardens. It may work better than cancelling. I only have six weeks, after all, to make my decision. You can be my eyes and ears, let me know what you think of her.'

He knew he should say no, he should tell Leo to send a message to Lady Elizabeth cancelling their excursion, but Josh hesitated for just a second.

'Wonderful. I knew I could rely on you.'

'Surely it would be better to postpone. You may be back in a few days and you could take her then,' Josh said as he finally found his voice.

'I trust you, Josh. I know it's a bit of a bore, but it means a lot to me. Thank you.' Leo clapped him on the back and Josh could see his brother's mind had already moved on, probably planning his imminent trip to Lord Abbingdon's country residence. 'I'll try not to be long in Kent, hopefully only a day or two, with a couple more for travelling.' Leo looked at him earnestly. 'I know our time together is short.'

'I'll be here when you get back. There's no rush.'

'I'd better pack. Give my regards to Lady Elizabeth.'

'I will.'

* * *

An hour later he rapped on Lady Elizabeth's front door, listening to the maid's footsteps as she approached and fumbled with the door before opening it.

'Mr Ashburton for Lady Elizabeth.'

'Come in, sir, Lady Hummingford is in the drawing room.'

Josh followed the maid upstairs to the narrow room he'd been shown into the day before when he'd visited with Leo.

'Mr Ashburton, how wonderful to see you again. Elizabeth has been looking forward to this evening all day. She's talked of little else.'

'My brother...' he began, meaning to give Leo's apologies, but at that moment Lady Hummingford continued speaking and Lady Elizabeth also entered the room. Josh's words trailed off as he took in the sight of Lady Elizabeth dressed for an evening out. She was wearing a midnight-blue dress with silver flowers embroidered across the bodice and along the hem. It had long sleeves, it was only April after all, but the neckline dipped tantalisingly to show the smooth skin of her chest. She was carrying a pale grey shawl, silky in look, again with silver flowers embroidered along the edge.

Josh saw her eyes narrow slightly in confusion as she looked at him. Her mother might have no idea that it was the wrong Mr Ashburton standing in their drawing room, but Lady Elizabeth did.

'I'm terribly sorry, Mr Ashburton, I know I was meant to accompany you and Elizabeth this evening, but I have come down with the most awful headache,' Lady Hummingford said, a pained expression on her face. 'I have arranged for our good friends Mr and Mrs Wilson to meet you at the gardens and act as chaperon, if that is acceptable?'

Now would be the perfect moment for him to reveal he wasn't Leo, he wasn't the man meant to be in their drawing room, but just as he opened his mouth to speak again Lady Elizabeth gave an almost imperceptible shake of her head. Josh clamped his lips together.

'Of course, Lady Hummingford. You must rest,' he said, doing his best impression of Leo.

'We should leave, Mr Ashburton.' Lady Elizabeth took a step towards the door and Josh followed, offering her his arm once they were downstairs.

'Have a lovely evening,' Lady Hummingford called after them.

Neither spoke until they were in the carriage and Josh had given the instruction for the driver to move away.

'Mr Ashburton,' Lady Elizabeth said slowly, looking at him carefully as if to be completely sure as to his identity.

'Indeed.'

'It *is* you?'

'Yes. It's me.' He smiled at her and felt a flood of satisfaction as the colour rose to her cheeks. He hadn't been mistaken; she was glad it was him. 'My brother sends his apologies, he's been called away. Lord Abbingdon has been taken unwell.'

'Nothing serious, I hope?'

'Leo won't know until he is there. Let's hope not.' He paused, leaning back and looking at Lady Elizabeth for a few seconds before continuing. 'You knew it was me straight away?'

She hesitated and then lifted her eyes to meet his. 'Yes. You look quite similar to your brother in many ways, but there are plenty of differences too. And there's something about your demeanour, how you come across. I think I'd know the difference between you and your brother even if you were completely identical.'

Her answer pleased him more than it should.

'Yet you stopped me from telling your mother the truth.'

Lady Elizabeth's eyes widened. 'I did,' she said slowly.

'Why?'

'She would only have made a fuss.'

'Cancelled the evening in favour of rearranging when Leo was available?'

'Exactly.'

'And you didn't want that?' He watched the colour deepen in her cheeks as she shook her head.

'I didn't want that,' she admitted, her voice little more than a whisper.

Josh leaned in, closing the gap between them in the small carriage. 'I'm glad. I didn't want that either.'

'You were keen to see the pleasure gardens?'

He smiled. 'That, amongst other things.' He shook his head, knowing he could not go any further down this route, reminding himself of why he was here: purely for Leo's benefit. 'How are you, Lady Elizabeth? Have you recovered from the incident earlier?'

'Yes, thank you. I'm indebted to you.'

'Not at all.'

'I won't be taking any more walks alone in Hyde Park that early in the morning.'

'Nor elsewhere, I hope.'

'No.' She sighed. 'Part of me wishes I could just be back in Sussex where things are more simple and I can walk out alone without fear for my safety.'

'You'll be going home after this season?' He realised his error as soon as he'd uttered the words. If things went to plan for Lady Elizabeth she would never be going home again. She would marry Leo and uproot her life to live wherever he chose. 'Sorry, I didn't think.'

'I'll miss my home, of course I will.' She looked away for a moment. 'It will be my sister I miss the most though. This trip is the longest we've been apart.'

'You have a sister? I didn't realise.'

'Yes, Annabelle. She's a year younger than me.'

Josh frowned; if he wasn't mistaken, Lady Elizabeth was in her early twenties. He couldn't see why her sister wasn't accompanying Lady Elizabeth and their mother for the season in London.

'She didn't want a season in London?'

Lady Elizabeth shifted uncomfortably. 'Mother thought it best she stayed at home.'

Josh nodded, wondering if the finances were so tight they couldn't stretch to bringing both sisters to London for a few months. If that was the case Lady Elizabeth's family badly needed this marriage to Leo and the money and connections it would bring them.

'I'm sure she'll visit you once you're married.'

Lady Elizabeth nodded but it didn't seem as if she agreed with his statement.

'We're nearly at the pleasure gardens,' she said, swiftly changing the subject.

'Have you been before?'

'No, but I can tell by the queue of carriages. It's quite the popular spot.'

'I've been intrigued about these gardens, the spectacle of them lit up at night, ever since Leo spoke about them.'

'How are you finding your reunion with your brother?'

'It is strange, I can't deny it. In some ways it is as if we haven't been separated for over twenty years. He's always been my brother, even if we were half a world apart. Yet...' He trailed off, trying to think of the right way to express the barrier he felt between himself and Leo, the sense that his brother was holding part of himself back. 'Leo was always hard-working, serious, even as a boy, but I can remember his laugh, his love of playing games. I haven't seen that side of him since my return.'

'He's always focussed on his duty?'

'Exactly. And I understand he has great responsibility, he runs all of Lord Abbingdon's estates, takes care of all the family business.'

'It's still early. Perhaps as he relaxes into having you back a little more you'll see other parts of him.'

'Perhaps.' Josh hoped so. He got the sense that Leo was a successful man, driven and ambitious, but he wasn't sure he was happy. 'He will make a good husband though, you have nothing to fear there. He's a good man, a kind man.'

Lady Elizabeth looked away and Josh tried to read the expression on her face but found it impossible.

'We're here,' she said, seeming relieved to change the subject from her impending marriage.

Beth took Mr Ashburton's hand and leaned on him a little as he helped her down from the carriage. Ever since she'd first stepped into the drawing room and re-alised it was Joshua Ashburton waiting for her rather than his brother she'd felt on edge and excitable. She'd seen he was about to explain his identity to her mother and something rebellious had stirred inside her. She wanted to go to the pleasure gardens with him, wanted to stroll arm in arm by the lamplight. In three months she would likely be married and would never be able to do anything so reckless again.

'Do you see your mother's friends?' He had kept hold of her hand as he looked around and Beth did nothing to pull away.

'No, perhaps they're not here yet.'

'Did your mother say we were meeting them inside the gardens or outside?'

'She didn't say.'

They walked slowly to the little kiosk where the tick-ets were sold, but just as they were about to approach a footman in a smart livery hopped out of a carriage and hurried over.

'Lady Elizabeth,' he said once in earshot, executing a deep bow, 'Mr and Mrs Wilson beg your forgiveness.'

'They are well, I hope?' Beth peered around the foot-man to look at the carriage. No one else was emerg-ing—they must have sent the footman in their stead.

'They have received some bad news. Mrs Wilson did not want to let you down, but Mr Wilson insisted they stay in for her health.'

'Of course. Please tell them not to worry at all and give them my best wishes. I will send a note tomorrow to ask when I might call on them.'

'Thank you, my lady.'

The footman hurried back to the waiting carriage and hopped back inside and Beth and Mr Ashburton watched as it sped away.

'All to myself,' Beth heard Mr Ashburton murmur and she turned to see him smiling at her, a hint of mischief in his eyes.

'I suppose we should return home.'

'We could. We probably should.' He looked over his shoulder to the entrance to the pleasure gardens. 'Although I'm told it is no more scandalous to stroll around the gardens than to walk together in the park.'

'In the day maybe.'

'It is still light.' They both looked up at the rapidly fading light.

'You are a bad influence, Mr Ashburton.'

'Half an hour—grant me that. Then I will return you back home, reputation intact.'

Beth glanced at the entrance and then to their carriage waiting a little way down the road.

'Half an hour?'

'I even promise to stick to the main paths.'

'I do want to see inside…'

As soon as she acquiesced he was on his way to the kiosk, asking for two tickets and handing over the money.

There was a small group of people going through the entrance gates but once inside they seemed to disperse and Beth and Mr Ashburton could amble along looking at the gardens as if it were their own private space.

Although she had felt an initial uncertainty about stepping into the pleasure gardens without a chaperon Beth knew she was never going to say no. There was something about Mr Ashburton that made her want to ignore every sensible instinct in her body, to be reckless and rebellious.

'Look, they're lighting the lamps. When it gets dark the lamps will guide the way along the paths.' Mr Ashburton was pointing to where half a dozen workers were making their way along the edge of the paths lighting the lamps that were positioned at regular intervals.

'It must look magical in the dark, lit by just the flickering lamps.'

'Perhaps we could stay until just after sunset. Another few minutes surely won't make much difference.'

'You will get me into trouble, Mr Ashburton.'

'I have an important duty to carry out tonight, Lady Elizabeth, and I need as much time as possible to complete it.'

'What duty is that?'

'Leo has charged me with finding out a little about you, about your character.'

Beth blinked, wondering if she meant so little to the man she was one day to be engaged to that he didn't think he should be having this conversation himself. She felt the sadness descend upon her as she often did when she thought of her impending marriage and the reason she was the one needed to support her whole family.

'You look sad, Lady Elizabeth,' Mr Ashburton said quietly. He looked thoughtful for a moment. 'I know this isn't how a young lady would hope to be wooed.'

'It's not that. Or perhaps it is a little.' She sighed, knowing she shouldn't be showing any of these emotions. Mr Ashburton had just said he'd been charged with finding out a little of her character. Now was not the time to show her doubts or her frustrations with her lot. Yet Mr Ashburton was easy to talk to, perhaps too easy, and she had the urge to spill her deepest thoughts and secrets.

'I know it is the way of the world, the way of our world at least, but when I was a young girl this wasn't how I thought my entire future would be decided.'

'You could say no to Leo,' Mr Ashburton said quietly. He was looking down, as if not to put further pressure on her with his gaze. The words were probing enough.

'No, I couldn't. Not really.' She exhaled forcefully and then added quickly, 'Not that I want to say no, you understand, it is just it feels as though my whole life is being mapped out and I don't have a say.'

'Surely your mother would understand if you wanted to make a different choice.'

Beth considered whether to try to change the subject, but something about Mr Ashburton's open, friendly face made her continue. 'Things have not been easy since my father died. Not easy at all. There is my mother and sister to support and if I am honest it is either finding a husband or seeking employment as a companion or some such role.' Beth laughed but it was without humour. 'And you can imagine my mother's opinion on paid employment.'

'What about your sister?'

'What about her?' Beth couldn't stop the sharp edge coming into her voice as it always did when someone asked about Annabelle.

'Is she looking for a husband too?'

'No.'

'Surely she is also of an age to marry. It would lift some of your burden.'

'Annabelle can't…' she said sharply, then closed her eyes for a moment to compose herself. 'I'm sorry. Annabelle isn't planning on marrying.'

Mr Ashburton regarded her for a moment and she saw the questions in his expression, but he just shrugged in that relaxed manner of his and moved on.

'Forget about duty for a moment,' Mr Ashburton said, holding up a hand to ward off her protests. 'Difficult, I know, but just suspend reality for a few minutes. If you could have any life you chose, what would it be?'

Beth considered. For so long her future had been mapped out, prepared for her. Even before Mr Leonard Ashburton had been proposed as her future husband she had been brought up to be a wife and a mother, to run a household, to raise the children. Her hopes and her dreams had never been asked about, let alone considered when planning her life.

'I'd like to travel, to ride across Europe on horseback, sail around Africa, to journey across the Atlantic and continue on from New York to the west coast.'

'They're big dreams.'

'And entirely impossible.' She shook her head, try-

ing to rid herself of the images of all the places she
wished to visit but most likely never would. 'I do want
to marry, to have children, to do all the *normal* things
expected of me.'

'But perhaps not yet,' Mr Ashburton murmured.

'How about you? You're free, unfettered. What are
your dreams?'

'Not so free. As I mentioned, my guardian is expecting me back home in nine months. He's stepping back
and I will take over running the company. It's what I've
been working towards most of my life, but it is a big
responsibility. There will be no time for anything else
for the next few years.'

Beth nodded slowly. She was being self-indulgent.
Everyone was trapped by their circumstances, the expectations of others and having to put practical consid-
erations above emotional.

They walked in silence for a few minutes, taking
one of the winding paths off the main walkway that led
through a beautiful garden filled with trickling water-
falls and mossy green ferns. To the west the sun was
setting, casting a burnt-orange glow to the sky. There
was no one else in this part and Mr Ashburton led her
towards the fountain in the middle of a little garden that
was surrounded by a low stone wall. He sat and after a
moment's hesitation she did the same, feeling a sense
of calm wash over her as she listened to the splash of
the water behind them and watched the sun dropping
in the sky in front of them.

'It all doesn't seem so bad when you stop a moment
and watch something like this,' she murmured.

Mr Ashburton's eyes were on her and she felt the

already familiar pull, as if she were being reeled in towards him despite Mr Ashburton not moving an inch.

'I always sit and watch the sunset, ever since my first voyage to India twenty-five years ago.'

'You used to watch it on the ship?'

'Yes. I was a very sad little boy then. I adored my parents and they'd just died, and I'd been taken away from the brother I loved and looked up to.'

There was a hint of sadness in his eyes even now and Beth remembered her devastation at losing her own father five years earlier. She'd been much older than Mr Ashburton had been when he'd lost his parents and she'd still felt as though her world was falling apart. She liked that he was so open about his emotions, so willing to show the human side of himself. So many gentlemen were stiff and seemed as if they were keeping everything locked inside.

'My guardian was very kind to me, but he's also a very wise man. He didn't rush my grief, didn't push me to stop mourning my parents. I wanted to be on my own a lot, but each night on the ship he would find me after dinner, take me up to the deck and we would watch the sun set together.'

'He sounds like a wonderful man.'

'He is. He taught me to never underestimate the need for peace and tranquillity in your life. So every night, no matter how busy I am at the docks or with the workers, I will pause to watch the sun set and take a moment to appreciate the good things in life.'

Beth remained quiet for a moment, contemplating his words. 'It's something we do far too rarely,' she murmured eventually, watching the sun start to fall beneath the horizon.

Soon there was just the orange hue left and the rapidly falling darkness.

'Our lives are so different,' Beth said, turning back to face Mr Ashburton to find him watching her. 'You have purpose, an idea of your future, what your life will look like. For a long time I've felt as though I've just been waiting. Yet you are still better at appreciating the quiet moments. How can that be?'

'Natural talent?' He had a gleam in his eye and the hint of a smile on his lips.

'That's something to put in your obituary one day. "He was talented at being still."'

'Perhaps *not* what I'd like to be remembered for.'

'What would you like to be remembered for?'

'I'm too late to be the man who invents the steam engine or the hot-air balloon—perhaps I'll have to be contented to be remembered as the man who brings the steam railway to India. One day the Usbourne Shipping and Transport Company will be at the forefront of the development of a countrywide steam railway network.'

Beth laughed. 'Nothing too ambitious, then.'

'I wouldn't want to stretch myself.'

She wasn't sure how but the distance between them seemed to be shrinking; his hand was almost touching hers where it rested on the stone surround of the fountain and she felt her body edging towards him, as well.

'What would you like to be remembered for?' He held her gaze as he waited for her to answer and, with his eyes fixed on hers, Beth found it hard to think of anything but the man next to her.

'No one has ever asked that of me before. Are wives and mothers remembered past their children's generation, perhaps their grandchildren's?' She shrugged her shoulders, a gesture her mother absolutely hated. 'If I could do anything I suppose I'd like to travel the world and write about it. To become the person experiencing all these fabulous places rather than reading about them.'

'*That* is a good ambition.'

It was getting dark quickly now, the sky turning from orange to black, and behind them the main path was lit up with the twinkling lights of the lamps. It was a romantic location, perfect for couples wanting something a little more private than a night at the opera or sharing a dance at a ball. She glanced at Mr Ashburton. It was his brother she should be here with, but she found she couldn't regret it was Joshua Ashburton who had turned up at her house tonight.

'You look thoughtful.' Their hands were touching now, little finger to little finger, the contact sending warm bolts through her skin.

'I was thinking how glad I am we're here tonight.' She paused and corrected herself. 'How glad I am to be here with you.'

There was a moment where neither of them moved, and then Mr Ashburton's hands were on her face, guiding her lips towards his. He kissed her hard, as if he knew this would be the only kiss they would share, as if the illicitness was driving him on. Beth felt every muscle in her body clench and tighten, and she gripped hold of him, willing him not to pull away. Never had she felt such desire. It flooded through her, threatening to drown her, and only once he pulled away slightly did she realise she hadn't taken a breath for the whole time they'd been kissing.

'I'm sorry,' he said, using one hand to tidy her hair where he must have tangled his fingers in it.

'Don't say sorry.'

He looked at her, and for a moment she thought he was going to kiss her again, but then, with the most serious expression on his face she'd ever seen, he moved away.

'I didn't plan that,' he said quietly. 'I don't want you to think I brought you here to…take advantage of you.'

'I know.' Of course, she believed him. There was an undeniable attraction between them, a pull that was difficult to ignore. She believed Mr Ashburton was an honourable man, just as she was normally a respectable young woman. They'd both been caught up in the moment. He trailed his fingers across her cheek, as if he couldn't help but touch her, and Beth had the urge to sink into him, to feel his body against hers. There was a surge of desire in his eyes and then suddenly he dropped his hand and looked away.

'Perhaps I'd better see you home.'

'I don't want to leave things like this. There doesn't need to be any awkwardness between us.' As soon as the words left her lips she knew they were a lie. She would never feel comfortable in Mr Ashburton's company because she was craving something that he could not give her, something they could not share.

'No awkwardness,' he said. He lifted his hand as if about to touch her on the cheek again, but stopped with his fingers midway between them. Instead he stood and offered her his arm. As she rose and fell in beside him she felt her heart sink. It was cruel that the first man she'd ever felt any attraction to, the *only* man she'd ever felt any attraction to, was unavailable to her. Worse than that, he was the brother of the man she was meant to be convincing to marry her.

Chapter Five

Josh shifted in his seat for the fiftieth time, feeling the guilt gnawing at him. He'd thought about making an excuse to his brother, finding any reason to be anywhere other than the opera house this evening. It might be the sensible thing to do, but to Josh it seemed cowardly, so here he was speeding towards an evening in the company of Lady Elizabeth.

Five days, that was how long had passed since their kiss in the Vauxhall Pleasure Gardens. Five days to dwell on each exquisite moment, and wallow in guilt that he'd let it occur. He'd almost confessed to Leo a grand total of six times, but on each occasion he'd hesitated, knowing it wasn't just his secret to tell. It might change how Leo saw Lady Elizabeth, and, although Josh wasn't enamoured with the idea of her marrying his brother, he did understand she had to marry someone and Leo would treat her well.

'Did the old man appreciate you dropping everything and speeding to his bedside?' Josh tried to distract himself from thoughts of Lady Elizabeth in any way he could. Leo had returned home two days ago, declaring Lord Abbingdon in fine health.

'I'm not sure Lord Abbingdon appreciates anything or anyone.' Leo had a wry smile on his lips but he still looked tired, having ridden for a day each way to visit the old man and then stayed up late working to catch up on what he had missed whilst away on his trip. 'Tell me, did you go to the pleasure gardens with Lady Elizabeth in the end?'

'Yes.'

Leo regarded him for a moment, an eyebrow raised in question. 'And?'

'It was a pleasant evening.'

'Lady Elizabeth seems an unoffensive enough girl, although her mother is a little…persistent.'

'Her mother was unwell. She didn't accompany us.'

'Oh? And she allowed Lady Elizabeth out unchaperoned?'

'She arranged for some friends to meet us at the gardens.'

'I see. So what did you think?'

'Of Lady Elizabeth?'

Leo nodded his head.

'She's a very nice young lady.' He tried to make his answer as bland as possible, aware of Leo's eyes resting on him.

'Anything scandalous? Or annoying?'

'No, although I only spent an hour or two in her company.'

The carriage drew to a stop outside a grand building that people were already streaming into. Josh was dressed in his finest evening wear, but as he looked out of the window he saw he wasn't going to be out of place. The ladies were wearing flowing dresses made of satin and silk and many had feathers or other decorations in their hair. The gentlemen all wore jackets and cravats, some carried canes and all had smart top hats on their heads.

'A place to be seen,' Josh murmured. Society here still puzzled him a little. In India, of course, there was a class system. It was at times difficult to understand and harsh in the unbending division of the castes. The people he socialised with were other landowners, other men of business and their families. The circle was small but the rules much more lax than here in England.

'Do they have opera in India?'

'Not that I've ever seen.' Josh smiled at the idea. He'd been to the theatre many times, marvelling at the bright costumes and complex steps performed by the Indian dancers, but something told him this was going to be an entirely different experience.

They made their way through the crowds into the opera house. Josh had to suppress a smile at the number of people who stared at him and Leo, obvious in their shock at the similarities between the two brothers, one of whom they'd had no idea existed.

He knew the moment Lady Elizabeth stepped through the doors. They were talking to Lord Willingham and his wife, discussing all the new building going on around London, when he caught sight of her out of the corner of his eye. She glided into the atrium, petite and poised, and seemed to suck all the air out of the room. He couldn't help but turn towards her, catching her eye for just a fraction of a second before forcing himself to turn away.

As he rejoined the conversation he felt Leo's eyes on him for a moment, a slight frown on his brow.

'Mr Ashburton, Mr Ashburton,' Lady Elizabeth said with a polite little dip of her head as she came to join their circle. 'And, Lady Willingham, how lovely to see you and your husband again.'

Josh watched as she charmed the elderly couple, marvelling at how easily she slipped into this world. From the little she'd told him about her life she hadn't experienced much of London society herself, but it would seem some things were innate behaviours for someone of her rank. She was attentive and interested in what the couple had to say and he could feel Leo's approval directed towards her as she demonstrated how good she could be in company.

Josh felt a spark of jealousy and quickly dampened it down. Lady Elizabeth had informed him how important it was she marry Leo. He liked her, respected her, and as such he should be pleased she was gaining his brother's approval.

'Shall we go upstairs?' Leo suggested once Lord and Lady Willingham had taken their leave. He offered his arm to Lady Elizabeth and she took it, but not before Josh caught her glance surreptitiously at him. He shook his head, trying to convey that their illicit kiss remained a secret between them.

When they arrived at their box Josh was distracted for a few minutes, taking in the opulence of the theatre and the rows upon rows of well-dressed people settling into their seats. Their box was just to the right of the stage, affording them a decent view of both the stage area and the other guests.

'Would you excuse me for a moment? There's someone I have to speak to,' Leo said, directing his words to Lady Elizabeth. She smiled graciously and watched as he left.

Once they were alone for a moment neither of them moved. Lady Elizabeth's posture seemed unusually stiff and Josh realised she was struggling not to turn to him.

'Lady Elizabeth,' he began but she shook her head.

'My mother will be here at any moment. She was just talking to some friends downstairs.'

'I wasn't planning on saying anything scandalous,' he murmured. He could see the twitch at the corner of her lips as she tried her hardest not to smile. 'Unless you're more worried about my actions than my words.'

Lady Elizabeth stood abruptly, her cheeks flushing with colour. The movement drew some stares in their direction and he saw Lady Elizabeth notice them too, forcing herself to sit back down slowly.

'I meant no offence. I merely wanted to lighten the tension.'

'You haven't said anything to your brother?' She didn't look at him as she spoke and he had the irrational urge to do something to provoke her.

'About?'

'You know what about.'

He normally thought of himself as a chivalrous man, but Lady Elizabeth was still refusing to look at him and he knew they had at most a couple of minutes before either her mother or his brother returned.

'Leo is a very understanding man,' he said quietly.

Lady Elizabeth finally turned her horrified eyes on him and immediately he regretted deceiving her.

'I haven't said anything,' he reassured her quickly. 'Part of me wanted to, but it isn't just my secret to tell.'

'Thank you.' Her expression was serious again and he wondered if she had been worrying that Leo would find out about the kiss ever since the evening they'd spent in the pleasure gardens. She sighed and Josh had the impression she was weighed down by her worries this evening.

'Is something else troubling you?'

'My mother,' she said eventually, tilting her head towards him so no one in the surrounding boxes would be able to ascertain her words. 'She keeps pressing me on where I am with the…engagement.'

'Of course, she thinks Leo took you for a stroll through the pleasure gardens.'

'She thinks he should have had enough time to assess our suitability.' Lady Elizabeth bit her lip and Josh's eyes were drawn to where her teeth made an indent in the rosy skin. For a moment he was completely distracted from what she was saying, imagining instead tracing a finger over her lip and smoothing the frown off her brow at the same time.

'Ah, Mr Ashburton, what a delight it is to see you again.' Lady Hummingford sailed into the box and greeted him. She flashed him her most charming smile as he stood and bowed and he realised she'd once again mistaken him for his brother. She eyed her daughter and seemed to decide it would be a good idea to leave them alone for a few more minutes, albeit with the eyes of all the other opera-goers on them. 'I'm just going to have a little word with Mrs Arlington. I'll be back shortly.'

'Mother...' Lady Elizabeth started, but Lady Hummingford was already halfway out of the box.

'Do we really look that similar?'

Lady Elizabeth smiled for the first time since being left alone in the box with him. 'No, at least I don't think so. There are many similarities between you, especially on first glance, but you don't look identical. At least not to me.' The last sentence was added quietly as she raised her eyes up to meet his.

Josh felt the pull of desire, the undeniable attraction, but there was something more there too. Of course, he found Lady Elizabeth physically attractive, she was pretty and petite and her smile was nothing short of dazzling, but there was more to it than that. He'd never grown close to a woman before, he'd always been too focussed on the business to take much notice of the young women thrust towards him in society in India, but now he wanted to *know* Lady Elizabeth. He wanted to know what made her happy and what made her sad. He wanted to uncover her sense of humour and discover why she frowned every time she spoke of her childhood.

Careful, he cautioned himself silently. Even to his mind it sounded as if he was falling for Lady Elizabeth.

'Tell me how this works,' Josh said, searching for an innocuous subject to distract him from the thoughts in his head. He didn't want to feel anything for Lady Elizabeth, didn't want to complicate his short stay in England with anything unnecessary. Three months and he would be returning to India and she would need her reputation intact to marry.

'How what works?'

'The opera. All of this.' He gestured to the beautiful people sitting in the boxes, the ladies fluttering their fans and deep in conversation with one another, the men often sitting slightly further back and observing the proceedings.

'Can I tell you a secret?'

'Of course.'

Lady Elizabeth lowered her voice and leaned in closer to him. There was still a chair separating them but even so Josh fancied he caught a hint of the rose perfume she used to scent her hair.

'This is my first time at the opera too. Mother made me promise I wouldn't say anything.'

'She worries Leo will be put off by your lack of funds?'

'Perhaps, although your brother cannot be ignorant of how we've struggled since my father's death. I think she worries more I will seem unrefined. It must be unheard of for a young woman of the aristocracy not to have attended the opera by her twenty-second year.' She shook her head with a wry smile. 'Mother made sure I had good tutors, could play three different instruments, speak French and organise wonderful dinner parties, but we haven't been to London for years and there are some experiences the wilds of Sussex just can't give you.' She gave a brief smile and Josh felt a surge of desire as his body inched towards her. He couldn't tear his eyes away from her lips and found it hard to focus on anything but the thought of kissing her again.

'I'm hardly the person to reassure you on the matter of refinement,' Josh said with an answering smile, 'but I doubt Leo would be so shallow. What does it matter to him if you've been to the opera before?'

'One of the main roles as the wife of a member of the aristocracy is to make their husband look good. A wife who isn't refined, who doesn't know when to applaud and when to sit back, that could make the husband look bad.'

Josh shook his head in amazement. He didn't understand the aristocracy. He couldn't imagine deciding who to marry based, not on love or mutual respect or friendship, but on whether or not that person would behave correctly at the opera and dinner parties.

'It *is* important,' Lady Elizabeth said insistently. 'Think about your world, imagine marrying someone who didn't know how to interact with the other landowners or their wives, who made socialising more difficult for you.'

'I wouldn't decide not to marry someone just because she didn't know how to make small talk about cotton or workers' rights.'

He could see she wanted to say more on the subject, but something caught her eye down below. Josh leaned over the edge of the box, following her line of vision, catching sight of the flickering flames just as someone below shouted, 'Fire.' Immediately he felt a rush of energy throughout his body, as if it were preparing him to jump down and tackle the blaze himself.

The fire looked as though it had started at the edge of the stage, where the curtain had billowed and strayed too close to one of the sconces holding half a dozen candles. As they watched the fire flickered for a few moments and there was a second when it seemed as though it might die out, and then suddenly it took hold, speeding up the curtain, sending out thick billowing smoke.

For a long moment all eyes were turned to the stage as if mesmerised by the flickering flames and then the shouts and screams began as people began to panic. Josh knew a fire like this in a packed building with only one main entrance could be a disaster and quickly he grabbed hold of Lady Elizabeth's hand and pulled her to her feet. He'd seen a fire like this before, in one of the warehouses near where their ships docked, and he would never forget how quickly it spread or the devastation it had left in its wake.

'We need to go,' he said, pushing the chairs out of the way and pulling her out of the box. Their box was situated right by the stage and as such they were one of the closest to the fire and furthest from the stairs. Already people were dashing out of their boxes and stampeding along the wide, plush corridor, their politeness forgotten in their panic.

Josh held Lady Elizabeth's hand in his, not caring about the impropriety, just wanting to know she was safe by his side. Quickly they followed the crowd, every so often checking over their shoulders for the flicker of flames.

By the time they'd reached the stairs the fire still wasn't visible on the upper level but black billows of smoke were starting to pour out of the doors to the boxes and fill the corridor.

'My mother.' Lady Elizabeth turned a worried face up towards him. 'What if she hasn't got out?'

'She was closer to the stairs. She will be somewhere in front of us. She's probably outside already.' It was the truth, their box had been further from the exit than any of the others and they were here with the rest of the au-

dience trying to escape, but he hoped Lady Hummingford hadn't frozen in fear as some people did when faced
with fire. He let his eyes flicker over the crowd, hoping
to see her statuesque figure but not able to pick anything definite out just from the backs of so many heads.

Tightening his grip on Lady Elizabeth's hand, he
surged forward, knowing that even if her mother wasn't
outside he wasn't going to let the woman beside him
re-enter the building. He'd seen the devastating effects
of a fire first-hand and knew once Lady Elizabeth was
outside he would pin her to the ground rather than let
her risk her life by going back into the building.

With relief he spotted Leo a little ahead of them,
helping an older lady who was struggling with the pushing crowd and the angle of the steps.

'Why has everyone stopped?' Lady Elizabeth's eyes
were filled with fear as she looked up at him. It was true
the crowd was only inching forward at the bottom of
the stairs, the grand entrance foyer completely packed
wall to wall with people.

'They are moving but the doors are holding everything up.'

Not designed to let people out in an emergency, the
grand glass doors would only let a couple of people
through at once.

Josh allowed himself to glance behind them at the
smoke rapidly advancing. They would get out, he was
sure of it, but not before they had inhaled lungsful of
the harmful smoke. Quickly he took hold of Lady Elizabeth's wrap and began looping it around her chin and
mouth.

'It'll protect you from the worst of the smoke.'

'What about you?' She had to repeat herself a couple of times to make him understand her now her mouth was covered.

'I'm fine.'

They were halfway across the foyer now, swept along in the crowd, which seemed to have grown a mind of its own. Josh wasn't sure they would be able to get out of its pull even if they wanted to. Behind them the doors to the lower auditorium stood open and they could feel the heat of the flames on their backs. The fire had spread from the stage area, devouring the heavy curtains and then starting on the plush-covered seats in the stalls.

Beside him he could feel Lady Elizabeth trembling and realised she'd glanced back too, and he gave her hand a reassuring squeeze.

'We're nearly there, we're nearly out.'

It was thirty more agonising seconds before they were at the front of the crowd and out through the doors into the fresh air. Lady Elizabeth clawed at the wrap at her throat and then sucked in great breaths of air and he felt the fresh air tickle his throat and make him bend over double coughing.

'We need to get you further away.'

'What about you?'

'I have to see that Leo got out.' Even as he said the words he saw the top of his brother's head across the crowd and felt some of the tension he'd been holding inside start to dissipate.

'And my mother. I need to know she's safe.' Lady Elizabeth's eyes were flicking over the crowd, the tension evident. He knew the moment she spotted her mother, saw the relief blossom on her face.

'She's moving in the same direction as us, further away from the fire. You can meet up with her in the street. The crowd will be impossible to get through until it thins a little.'

People were standing around dazed outside and Josh was horrified to realise no one had started to organise the effort to put out the blaze. There were shouts of 'Fire,' and people from nearby buildings had started flooding onto the streets, but as yet everyone was just looking in awe at the smoke billowing from the opera house, seemingly mesmerised by it.

He led Lady Elizabeth through the crowd, making sure she was a good half a street away from the fire before stopping and facing her.

'Are you hurt?' He looked over her, taking in the mussed-up hair and smudge of soot on her cheek. Without thinking for who might see, he raised his hand and gently rubbed the smudge away, feeling the softness of her skin beneath his fingers. He let his fingertips rest on her cheek for a moment even when the smudge was gone, before remembering where they were and what was happening.

'Just a little shaken.'

'You're safe, you're out of the fire.'

He glanced over his shoulder, not wanting to leave her but knowing he had to help put out the blaze or it would be more than just the opera house that burned today.

'You're going back.'

'It takes a lot of water and a lot of men to fight a fire like this.'

She nodded and he saw her visibly square her shoulders and straighten her back.

'Then I want to help.'

'No, it is too dangerous.'

'Mr Ashburton, you have no say whatsoever on what I do. You are neither my father nor my husband and as such I would thank you to keep your orders to yourself.'

'You're not going back near that burning building,' he said, gripping hold of her hand.

'I'm not stupid. I won't go back inside. But I can help with the chain of water. I'm just as capable as any man of passing a bucket up a line.'

He eyed her for a moment, seeing the determined set to her jaw and the steely look in her eye.

'Promise me you'll keep right back.'

'I promise.'

He had the urge to kiss her, to take her in his arms and kiss her without caring who else saw. Josh even felt himself take a step towards her, but quickly he caught himself. This wasn't the time or the place for any romantic gesture and Lady Elizabeth was not the woman he should be bestowing a kiss on.

Chapter Six

The smoke was billowing out of the opera house now, great black clouds coming from the windows and the roof. Mr Ashburton still held her by the hand and Beth found the contact more reassuring than she would like to admit. Never before had she been in a fire, but she knew of the devastating consequences they could bring. Only a few weeks ago a cottage near their country estate had caught fire and now it was a blackened husk rather than the family home it had once been.

'Leo,' Mr Ashburton called, diverting from his original path and leading her over to his brother.

Leonard Ashburton was doubled over coughing, but he managed to straighten as they approached. His eyes flicked curiously to where his brother held her hand and quickly Beth pulled away, coming up short as Joshua Ashburton continued forward to embrace his brother.

'Thank goodness you're safe.'

'You too. I was worried as you were still in the box, closest to the fire.'

'We need to organise a water line.'

'We do or the whole street will soon be in flames. Might I suggest we find your mother, Lady Elizabeth, and she can take you back home?'

Beth wanted to find her mother, to reassure herself that she really was safe and well, but there was no way she was going home when she might be of use, even in a very small way.

'Thank goodness you've not been hurt, Elizabeth.' Her mother pushed through the crowd to the left of them and came and embraced her daughter stiffly. Even after such a horrific experience Lady Hummingford still struggled to hold Elizabeth for more than a few seconds and even that felt uncomfortable and forced. 'Thank you for getting her to safety, Mr Ashburton.'

Beth had to suppress a smile as her mother looked between the two men in front of her, still struggling to tell them apart.

'It is my brother we have to thank, Lady Hummingford. He escorted Lady Elizabeth from the opera house.'

'Thank you, Mr Ashburton.' Her eyes narrowed slightly as they settled on Josh, and Beth could tell her mother was wondering why the *wrong* Mr Ashburton had been the one to play her hero.

Mr Joshua Ashburton nodded briefly, then excused himself and began hurrying back over to the entrance of the opera house. She heard him shout a few words, gathering the men in the crowd close to him and issuing instructions. He looked as if he were born to lead, a natural at giving orders and expecting them to be followed. Beth found herself watching him with interest for a few moments before remembering what was happening and the company she was in.

'I must go help my brother,' Leonard Ashburton said, bowing formally to her and her mother.

'Come, Elizabeth, we should go home. I have no idea where the carriage will be but I'm sure we can walk a little way without too much trouble.'

'I'm not leaving, Mama. Not yet.'

As Lady Hummingford looked at her in surprise Beth squared her shoulders and straightened her spine. If she was going to help she needed to get into position in the human chain, taking her place to pass buckets up and down the line, not stand here arguing with her mother.

'I'm going to help.'

'Nonsense.'

'I'm going to help, Mama.' Elizabeth turned and started over to the rapidly growing crowd centred around Joshua Ashburton. Lots of people had already retrieved whatever containers they had available from nearby buildings and already the first chain of people had been set up, snaking along the street to a nearby public water pump.

'Elizabeth, don't you dare defy me. This is no place for a lady. You're coming home with me.'

Beth hated that she actually hesitated for a moment, hated that she almost nodded her head in agreement.

'No. You go home, Mother. I'll ask Mr Ashburton to see me home after the fire is out.'

Without waiting for an answer she pulled her arm out of her mother's grip and ran forward, inserting herself in the second line that was forming between a woman dressed in a plain woollen dress and a man who kept anxiously looking at the buildings around him.

Beth didn't know where the water they passed up the line was coming from. Perhaps another public pump. She didn't think they were near enough to the river to access that ready supply, but she could have been wrong. The next half an hour passed in a blur of aching muscles and repetitive movements as she passed bucket after bucket of water one way and empty buckets back down the line for refilling.

At some point the horse-drawn carts began to arrive, laden with the firefighting equipment: large tanks filled with water and hand pumps to direct the stream of water where it was needed the most. Between buckets Beth caught a glimpse of Joshua Ashburton striding out to meet the man in charge, and before long their line had been redirected and now they were tasked with filling up one of the great reservoirs whilst the men on the carts pumped and directed the stream.

She wasn't sure how many hours later the cautious cheer began to spread through the crowd as the fire was declared under control. She felt more exhausted than she ever had in her life before, her arms ached, her shoulders screamed in agony every time she tried to move them and her clothes were stuck to her body with sweat. Her once fine dress was without a doubt ruined, covered in soot and dirt, ripped in places and looking as though it were twenty years old, not a mere few weeks.

Beth managed a weary smile, allowing herself to be embraced by the woman who had stood in front of her in the line before staggering over to the edge of the street and sinking down onto a low wall.

'Careful, you look as though you could fall asleep.'
Beth looked up into Joshua Ashburton's smiling face

and managed a weak smile of her own. She realised he must have kept an eye on her the whole time, even when co-ordinating the efforts of all the volunteers, to know where she had staggered to so quickly.

'I've never been so tired.' She wanted to lean against him, to allow him to wrap his arms around her and rest her head on his chest.

'You were incredible. It's been four hours and you never flagged.'

'Four hours? Really?' She wasn't sure if it felt like forty minutes or four days. Shaking her head in disbelief, she looked up at him again. 'I was just one small pair of hands in the line. You played a much more important role than me.'

Mr Ashburton looked as if he was going to protest when his brother came up and clapped him on the shoulder.

'Well done, Josh.'

Leonard Ashburton was as sooty and ruffled as the rest of them, although his upright bearing hadn't changed. His eyes danced curiously over her and she wondered if she imagined the slight tightening at the corner of his lips.

'You stayed to help, Lady Elizabeth.' It was phrased partway between a statement and a question and she wasn't sure if there was a hint of disapproval in his eyes.

'I couldn't leave.'

'And your mother?'

'She went home.' Leonard Ashburton raised an eyebrow but said no more to her, instead turning to his brother. 'You did well, Josh. I think the fire would still be blazing if it weren't for your quick actions at the start.' For the first time Beth saw a softness in Leonard Ashburton's expression. He might be a serious man, a man who didn't often let his emotions show, but it would seem he cared for his brother.

'Go home and get some rest. I'll see Lady Elizabeth home.'

For a moment she thought Joshua Ashburton might protest, but he just nodded and she realised she was silly to hope he would insist *he* be the one to escort her home. It was his brother she was soon to be engaged to, despite the undeniable attraction between them.

'Rest well, Lady Elizabeth,' Joshua Ashburton said as his brother offered her his arm.

She had to resist the urge to look back over her shoulder and instead focus on putting one foot in front of the other as she tried not to lean too heavily on Leonard Ashburton.

For the first five minutes they barely said a word to one another. Beth was so exhausted it took all her energy to just walk without stumbling and she wondered if, despite his stoical expression, Leonard Ashburton might also be struggling to continue.

'You didn't have to stay this evening,' he said eventually when they were a few streets away from the opera house. There were no carriages for hire in the streets at this hour and Beth was starting to accept they would need to walk all the way back to her rented residence.

'I couldn't leave, not when there was a chance I could help, even if only in a very small way.'

She felt his eyes on her and wondered if she had said the wrong thing but found herself too tired to care.

Leonard Ashburton was an enigma, so quiet and hard to read. For all she knew he might thoroughly approve of her defying her mother and joining the water line, or he might think less of her for her unladylike response to the situation.

'I'm sorry I was called away last week. And today our outing was cut short.'

'The fates are conspiring against us.' Beth wasn't sure why she said it—it was hardly the right thing to say to convince the man next to her they should marry within the year. She wasn't normally superstitious, preferring fact and logic to anything occult, but their path to an engagement hadn't exactly been smooth.

Guiltily she tried to suppress the memory of the kiss with Joshua Ashburton. She felt the heat begin to rise in her body and the blush spread across her cheeks. Staying to help fight the fire at the opera house Leonard Ashburton could probably forgive, but she doubted he would be able to move past her kissing his brother.

'Indeed. Hopefully our next meeting will be more of a success. My brother tells me you had a pleasant evening at Vauxhall Gardens.'

She shot him a sharp look, but there was nothing but polite interest on his face.

'It was. Thank you. It was kind of him to accompany me when you were called away. I've never been to a pleasure garden before and the experience was one I had been looking forward to.'

They walked in silence for a few minutes, Beth concentrating on her aching feet and legs, too tired to try to impress the man next to her. Equally he didn't seem overly enthused to use the opportunity to get to know her any better, but she supposed he must be at least as tired as her, if not more so given his active role at the heart of the firefighting.

At her door he waited until the maid had responded to the loud knock before giving a sharp little nod of his head and turning on his heel. It was hardly the farewell of a fond suitor.

Chapter Seven

The atmosphere in the dining room was decidedly frosty when Beth finally rose the next morning. She had contemplated skipping breakfast completely but in the end had decided she would have to face her mother at some point and the ache in her stomach wouldn't be silenced until she ate a few slices of buttery toast washed down with delicious tea.

Her body ached from the exertion of the night before. Beth had thought of herself healthy and strong, back home she walked miles every day and rode her horse at every opportunity, but the repetitive action of passing the heavy buckets of water backwards and forwards had worked, not only her arms, which felt leaden now, but also the muscles in her sides, which pulled as she walked.

Silently she took her seat to the left of her mother, hoping she would at least get a few mouthfuls of tea before her mother began her tirade.

'I am very disappointed in you, Elizabeth.'

The cup hadn't even reached her lips. Beth clenched

her jaw and then forced herself to relax and take a sooth-ing sip of tea before she placed the cup back on the table and turned to face her mother.

If she was wise she would suppress the rebellion that was surging inside her, apologise for defying her mother and promise to renew her efforts to catch Leon-ard Ashburton's admiration.

'We put the fire out,' she said, raising her eyes and holding her mother's cold stare.

'The brave men who manage the firefighting equipment put the fire out,' Lady Hummingford said brusquely. '*You* did not.'

Beth shrugged, a gesture she knew irritated her mother no end, even though she knew it was a child-ish rebellion.

'I was a part of it. A small part, but I helped.'

'You shouldn't have been there. You should have come home with me.'

Beth held her mother's eye, lifting her chin a notch. She didn't want to seem defiant, but she also knew that sometimes she had to stand up for herself. Her moth-er's character was so strong, her will so unbreakable, that sometimes it was much easier to just go along with her opinion, but Beth knew sometimes she had to as-sert herself.

'I thought it important to stay and help.'

'What is wrong with you?' Lady Hummingford stood and began pacing up and down across the tiny room. It only took eight steps to cover the distance from wall to wall before her mother had to turn and start back the other way.

'What *is* wrong with me?'

'It is as if you are not aware how important, how *vital* it is you get engaged to Mr Ashburton in the next few weeks.'

'Of course I know, Mother.'

'But do you? Surely if you know how close we are to destitution, how near to complete and utter ruin, then you would not do anything that may harm your chances of an engagement even one tiny little bit.'

Beth swallowed. She knew they were living on a knife's edge, that the creditors were circling and it would only take one to swoop in and they all would follow, clamouring for the money Lady Hummingford did not have.

'Three months,' Lady Hummingford said, pausing in her pacing. 'Three months until we lose everything. Birling View, all the contents of the house, the horses. Three months, Elizabeth.'

Beth felt her hands begin to shake and clenched them together in her lap.

'How?'

'How? How?' Her mother's voice was rising shrilly. 'Do you have any idea what a mess your father left us in financially? And then all the properties that were entailed went to your damn cousin. The sale of the London house barely covered half of what we owed.'

'I didn't know.' She knew things were desperate. Their finances had been dire for years, but she hadn't realised they were this close to the brink of complete destitution. She'd thought they would have a little longer to settle on a solution.

'No. You didn't. But you do now. Three months, Elizabeth, and you will be the daughter of an earl who is forced out onto the street. We'll be forced to beg your cousin for charity.' Her mother shuddered. Beth knew their cousin, Peter, would come to their aid in whatever small way he could, but he'd also been marred by their father's debts, struggling over the last five years to maintain the properties he had inherited without the funds to keep them running properly.

'Three months is no time at all,' Beth whispered.

'It is plenty of time to remind Mr Ashburton of his promise to your father and get engaged. Once our creditors know you are engaged to one of the wealthiest men in England they will give us a little more time. And when you are married…' She gave a little satisfied nod to finish the sentence.

Then Mr Ashburton would solve their money problems once and for all.

'Then Annabelle will be able to stay at Birling View.'

'She will.'

Elizabeth nodded. It was important her sister got to keep her home. Annabelle had never left Sussex, never ventured further than a few miles away from the house on the cliffs, and Beth wanted more than anything else to allow her sister the security of staying somewhere she knew.

'You owe that to her, Elizabeth,' her mother said sharply.

'I know.'

Lady Hummingford sat down, her demeanour softening a little now she had obtained Beth's acquiescence.

'You need to give this your whole attention, Elizabeth. You are a pretty enough girl, and heaven knows I strived to make you have all the accomplishments the daughter of an earl should.'

'I know, Mama.'

'Mr Ashburton isn't opposed to the marriage, he just needs to see you will make him a good wife. Which means behaving as he would expect someone of your rank and the wife of a viscount to behave.'

'Yes, Mama.'

Lady Hummingford fell silent and tapped her long, elegant fingers on the tablecloth for a moment.

'We need to get him out of London, away from distractions. He's a country man, and he needs to see you will make an excellent country wife. A wife who is capable of running a large household and a country estate.'

'It's the middle of the season, surely he won't want to leave London.'

'*You* have to make him want to leave. We'll have a small house party, say we are taking advantage of the unseasonably warm weather and invite a select few to the coast for three or four days.' Lady Hummingford took Beth's hand but the gesture wasn't particularly warm. She squeezed it so hard Beth winced. 'He will propose in that time. You will make sure of it.'

'Yes, Mama.' Something inside her felt as though it were shrivelling but Beth decided not to examine the feeling too closely. Everyone had duties, responsibilities for other people. She hadn't been called to war or asked to sacrifice her freedom or her life. All she had to do was marry a man who everyone told her was good and kind.

'We shall call on him today and issue the invitation.'

That was evidently the end of the discussion as her

mother stood and swept out of the room, probably already making a mental list of everything that would have to be done to make the party a success.

Slumping back in her chair, Beth closed her eyes. Even though she wished it weren't the case, her mother was right. She needed to step up and take responsibility or her family would face ruin. It might not be fair that all their hopes rested on her, but it was the way things were.

For a moment she allowed herself to picture Joshua Ashburton's smiling face and examined the spark of warmth she felt whenever she thought of him. She *was* attracted to him, she enjoyed his company more than that of any man she had ever known and she would miss the excitement and anticipation she felt whenever she knew she would see him.

Resolutely she made herself push thoughts of him aside. He was not her future. He was not her duty, and her mother was right. It was time to start focussing on the man who could save their whole family from destitution.

'Mr Ashburton,' Lady Hummingford said as she stepped towards him, all smiles and warmth.

'The wrong Mr Ashburton,' Josh said quickly. 'My brother is out unfortunately.'

Lay Hummingford didn't lose her smile but it stiffened somewhat and he could sense the frustration held coiled inside her.

'He's gone for a ride.'

'Do you know when he will be back?'

'No.' Josh didn't trust himself to look at Lady Elizabeth with her mother's eyes boring into him so instead he gave a half-smile and gestured for the two women to have a seat. 'I'm happy to pass on a message.' He mirrored Lady Hummingford's slightly brusque tone.

'It is a matter of some importance. I think it best we speak to Mr Ashburton ourselves.'

Josh shrugged. He felt irritable this afternoon and less forgiving of Lady Hummingford's snobbery towards him. It was probably due to the lack of sleep. Even after collapsing into bed as the sky was beginning to lighten, he had tossed and turned, his body and mind on edge from all the drama of the night before.

'Perhaps you know where your brother has ridden to?' Lady Elizabeth's voice was quiet and lacked her normal vitality and finally Josh allowed himself to look in her direction. She seemed smaller than usual, as if she had withdrawn into herself, and she wouldn't meet his eye.

Curious, he thought. Something had happened to sap the spark from her and he wasn't sure it was just exhaustion from their endeavours at the opera house.

He felt a sudden compulsion to know what had caused such a change in her demeanour.

'I'm sure we can find him,' he said, forcing a smile. 'I know the two or three usual routes my brother takes.'

'I wouldn't want to be an inconvenience.' Lady Hummingford seemed torn between wanting to track down Leonard and not appearing overly keen.

'Not at all. I've wanted to spend a little time with Lady Elizabeth—my brother has hinted we may be family one day soon.'

Lady Hummingford preened a little at the comment

as he'd known she would. Josh was aware it was under-hand, playing on her hopes in this way just to get a few moments alone with Lady Elizabeth, but he couldn't bring himself to feel too much remorse.

'Well, if you're sure, Mr Ashburton. It really would be kind of you.'

'Wonderful. It's a pleasant day for a stroll.'

Despite the warm temperatures he paused in the hall to put on his jacket, silently cursing these English aristocrats who thought it scandalous to walk around without at least three layers even on the hottest of days. In India he would often be found just in his shirtsleeves, rolled to the elbow, and his shirt open at the neck. He longed for that freedom again but dutifully reached for the heavy hat once he'd donned his jacket.

'Will you walk with me, Lady Elizabeth?' He flashed her the most innocent of smiles.

'Of course, she will,' Lady Hummingford said. His comment a few minutes earlier must have lodged some-where in the Countess's brain as she'd realised he was as good a route into his brother's favour as any. 'You young people walk ahead, I'll follow.'

Josh bowed his head, then offered his arm to Lady Elizabeth. She hesitated just a second, but he knew she could hardly refuse him with her mother standing right there. The Countess would demand an explanation and neither of them wanted that.

'Are you well rested, Lady Elizabeth?'

'I slept poorly,' she said abruptly, not taking her eyes off the pavement in front of them.

'Is something the matter?'

'No.'

'Good. Why do you need to see my brother with such urgency?'

Lady Elizabeth exhaled loudly and started chewing on her bottom lip. He thought she was going to ignore his question for a moment until she turned to look at him, her expression deadly serious.

'I can't do this,' she said, an almost pleading look in her eyes.

'You can't do what?'

'This.' She waved her hand vaguely between them. 'Talk to you. Be with you. Be anywhere near you.'

Josh raised his eyebrows. Yesterday she had clutched his hand whilst fleeing the fire and today she could barely look at him.

'I'm confused.'

'I need to marry your brother, Mr Ashburton.' She shook her head. 'I *will* marry your brother. In a matter of a few months. I have to focus on that and not allow myself to be distracted by...'

'Me?'

She nodded, her expression forlorn.

'Has something happened?'

'My mother reminded me of my responsibilities and I realised just how important this marriage is. I *need* to marry your brother.'

It wasn't anything she hadn't said before but Josh felt a stab of something that felt suspiciously like jealousy. He wasn't a jealous man and the last person he wanted to be envious of was his brother.

Lady Elizabeth glanced up at him and he realised she was on the edge of tears. He had the urge to stop and sweep her into his arms, his fingers twitching before he reminded himself of Lady Hummingford walking just a few paces behind them. She couldn't hear what they were discussing in hushed tones but she could see every movement, every gesture. In the end he lifted his hand to adjust his collar, allowing his fingers to brush against Lady Elizabeth's arm on the way. He saw her respond to the brief touch, saw the flush of heat on her cheeks, and felt his hand twitch as if contemplating less subtle contact. Next to him she pressed against him, her hand seeming to burn into his skin where it rested in the crook of his elbow. Josh had never known such an innocent touch could be so agonising.

'You've needed to marry my brother the whole time we've been acquainted—what's changed now?'

'I have to focus on my future, not what I wa...' She trailed off halfway through the word.

'Not what you want?'

Finally she looked at him, her eyes large and filled with angst.

'I think about you all the time,' she said so quietly he wasn't sure if he'd imagined the words. 'Ever since that first night in your brother's garden.'

'I think of you too.'

'But I can't. I shouldn't. I won't, not any more.'

He saw the turmoil inside her and knew he should do anything he could to calm it. Still there was something stubborn that didn't want to let this woman he barely knew go.

'Sometimes our desires won't be ignored.'

'Then I can never allow myself to be in a situation where I could make a mistake again.'

'The kiss we shared wasn't a mistake.'

'It was not…' she hesitated as if she couldn't bring herself to lie about it '…not an earth-shattering mistake, but a mistake all the same.' She looked at him again, her expression more resolute now. 'I need you to promise you will not stand in the way of me marrying your brother.'

'I would never do that.'

'Thank you.'

They were entering Hyde Park, treading the same ground they had walked the morning of Lady Elizabeth's attack, and Josh knew the moment she set eyes on the path that led to the spot she'd been ambushed. Her grip on his arm tightened a little and her step quickened.

Luckily a distraction came in the form of his brother on horseback a few hundred yards away.

'Leo,' he called, raising his voice to almost a shout. No doubt eyebrows would be raised at his ungentlemanly behaviour but right now he couldn't bring himself to care. He understood everything Lady Elizabeth was saying, agreed with it to an extent, but that didn't mean he had to like it.

Leo frowned as he looked around, the frown relaxing a fraction when he caught sight of his brother. Josh knew Leo would not tolerate being called from such a distance by anyone else, he would find it rude, but, a stickler for the rules of society, he seemed to have a blind spot when it came to Josh. Perhaps it was the desire to make up for twenty-five years of lost time or just the fact that their reunion was going to be so short-lived he didn't want to spoil it with unnecessary quarrels, but Josh knew Leo allowed him liberties he would not allow anyone else in his life.

'Lady Elizabeth, Lady Hummingford,' Leo greeted them from his horse. Josh thought he might dismount but his brother stayed firmly in position in the saddle.

'Are you having a pleasant ride, Mr Ashburton?' Lady Elizabeth had to shield her eyes from the sun to look up at him.

'Quite pleasant, thank you.'

Lady Hummingford moved towards her daughter and jabbed her firmly in the ribs.

'We are arranging a house party, Mr Ashburton,' Lady Elizabeth said dutifully. 'A little getaway from the heat of London to the cool of the Sussex coast. I am eager for you to come.'

'That is kind of you, although I'm not sure I can leave London right now. My brother—'

'Is invited too, of course,' Lady Hummingford said quickly. 'Elizabeth has told me of the limited time you have together. We hope Birling View would be a lovely experience of country life for you too, Mr Ashburton.'

'What do you think, Josh?'

Josh shrugged. Being cooped up in a country house with Lady Elizabeth whilst she tried to prove she would make the perfect wife for a future viscount wasn't his idea of an emotionally satisfying week, but he wasn't going to voice that opinion to the present company.

'Wonderful,' Lady Hummingford exclaimed, drawing a quickly suppressed smile from Leo. Josh had to smother his own. Neither of them had ever had an interfering female relative and it was fascinating to watch one at work. 'We won't keep you from your ride, Mr Ashburton. I will send over the invitations in a few days when the details are finalised.'

'I have an invitation of my own, Lady Elizabeth,' Leo said, his expression serious. 'Miss Culpepper is eager to get to know you better and I promised I would facilitate. She has invited us to take tea with her tomorrow afternoon.'

'I would be delighted to accompany you,' Lady Elizabeth said dutifully.

'Good.'

With a short farewell Lady Hummingford swept Lady Elizabeth away as if worried the two men might change their minds about the house party if they dallied any longer.

Once they were out of sight Leo dismounted and took his horse by the reins.

'What a peculiar woman,' he said, looking after her. 'The daughter seems normal enough, but Lady Hummingford is rather insistent.'

'Do you know what you're getting into?' Josh studied his brother. He couldn't imagine Leo would walk into this marriage without knowing the deepest secrets of the Countess and her daughter—he was so thorough in everything he did. But then again Josh wasn't sure what the debt that Leo owed the late Earl was, and how much he was happy to overlook.

'What do you mean?'

Josh hesitated. He knew how much this marriage meant to Lady Elizabeth and he had to be sure he was voicing his doubts for the right reason. Desire for his brother's future wife was not a good enough reason to potentially make his brother think again, but as he contemplated he knew he had a duty to his brother. Marriage was for life, not a decision to be rushed, and Leo deserved Josh's honesty about his misgivings.

'They're almost destitute.'

'I know.'

'Right on the brink. I have the impression they could lose everything in the next few months if the marriage isn't settled soon.'

Leo's eyebrows rose a fraction, but he didn't look overly surprised.

'That bad? I knew they were struggling with the up-keep of that country house of theirs and had sold their London home.'

'I get the impression that if the marriage to you falls through they will be ruined.'

Josh watched as his brother nodded thoughtfully.

'It would explain Lady Hummingford's desperation.' Leo began to lead his horse down the path and Josh realised he didn't mean to continue on with the ride.

'Their predicament doesn't have to impact on your decision whether to marry her,' Josh said, knowing he sounded completely heartless.

'I know. Still, I need to marry someone. I suppose if an ancient family is saved from destitution in the process at least something good is coming out of it.'

'What was the debt you owed the old Earl?'

For a long moment Josh didn't think his brother was going to answer. There was a faraway look in his eyes and a sadness that emanated from him.

'He helped someone I cared about, when I couldn't. He stepped up and did the right thing even though it put him at risk.' It was an answer, but still a cryptic one. 'When I found out what he'd done I wanted to repay his kindness, so I agreed to consider marrying his daughter when she came of age.'

'There would be other ways to repay the debt,' Josh said quietly, wondering even as he said the words why he was protesting so much.

'Money? I've tried that. When the old Earl first passed away I offered to settle a sum of money upon the family, in lieu of the marriage. Lady Hummingford declined. A few months ago, when she wrote to inform me they would be coming to London for the season and she hoped to settle on an arrangement, she hinted again that only marriage would do. I suppose their debts are too great for me to pay up outright, they want the weight of my name and the family fortune I will inherit to hold off their creditors.' Leo looked at him for a long moment. 'Is there a reason you're opposed to the match?'

'I don't remember Mother and Father well, but I did have the privilege of growing up with two people who cared very deeply for one another.'

'Your guardian?'

'Yes. He and his wife loved one another. They've been married for almost forty years and have stayed strong and loyal throughout all that time. I think it is important to care for the woman you marry and I get the impression you wouldn't much notice if it were Lady Elizabeth or one of a hundred other debutantes walking down the aisle.'

Leo ran his hand through his hair and patted his horse distractedly on the neck as he considered Josh's words.

'You're not wrong. I find myself unable to feel anything for someone I barely know and my enthusiasm for the task of getting to know her is limited, but I'm not sure I agree that affection is important for marriage.' He gave a sad little smile. 'In fact, I think love can be destructive. Better to have a union where the focus is on duty rather than love.'

'Do you truly believe that?'

'Yes.' He sounded so definite, so convinced of his own point of view that Josh fell silent. He wasn't privy to all the major events in his brother's life. The letters he'd received had told him of graduating university, taking over the running of the estates for Lord Abbingdon, trips to the continent and interesting insights into rural English life, but they hadn't been very rich on personal details. This fitted with the staid and serious personality of the man walking next to him, but Josh did wonder if Leo was hiding behind that persona just a little. Just as he wondered if someone, a woman, a lover, had helped shape the unromantic stance Leo was taking. If perhaps his serious older brother had once had his heart broken.

Leo clapped him lightly on the shoulders. 'Do not worry, let us see what happens in Sussex. Nothing is settled yet.'

Chapter Eight

'Brace yourself,' Joshua Ashburton murmured in her ear as they ascended the steps to Miss Culpepper's neat town house.

Beth was flanked on each side by an Ashburton brother, feeling decidedly small between the two towering men.

'Josh,' Leo said admonishingly and then cleared his throat. 'Although I do have to warn you, Lady Elizabeth, Miss Culpepper can sometimes be a little…' he searched for the right word '…abrupt.'

Abrupt she could deal with. She might have lived a sheltered life in Sussex, but she had still socialised and she was well aware of Miss Culpepper's type. Single spinsters of a certain age with tongues that spat words to sting like a flick of a whip. Beth had encountered enough in her time to know that the best way to deal with women like that was to be polite, unfalteringly cheerful, but firm. It was important not to let yourself be bullied.

'You don't have to come in,' Leonard Ashburton said across her head to his brother.

'I wouldn't miss this for the world.'

She caught the look between the two men and she wondered, not for the first time, why Joshua Ashburton was there.

As Leonard Ashburton stepped up to Miss Culpepper's door she leaned over and whispered quietly, 'Why *are* you here?'

'Miss Culpepper will not be pleased to see me,' he said grimly. 'But I had this strange compulsion, this need to come and meet the woman who separated me from Leo when we were mourning our parents.' He shrugged. 'You should thank me. I'm sure most of her spite will come in my direction and not yours.'

The door opened and an elderly butler ushered them inside, showing them through the neat but plain hallway into a drawing room.

Miss Culpepper sat in an upright chair next to the fireplace. She acknowledged them when they entered but did not rise. Beth found herself watching the interaction between Miss Culpepper and Leonard Ashburton. She had raised him, looked after him from the age of eight, but she didn't move to embrace him.

'Have a seat. Mr Watkins, will you see that tea is prepared? I will ring the bell for the maid to bring it in when we are ready.'

The butler silently glided from the room and closed the door behind him. Beth sat, feeling the tension in the room already as Miss Culpepper glared openly at Joshua Ashburton.

'I didn't realise you were bringing your brother, Leonard.'

'I wanted to meet you. We are family, after all.'

'Hmm. I understand you will soon be leaving again for India. There is hardly any point in trying to forge relationships.'

It was the first time Beth had ever seen Joshua Ashburton at a loss for words. She wanted to reach out and take his hand, to squeeze it and remind him he wasn't the little boy who had been rejected, that he was a successful and well-loved man. He had spoken warmly about his guardian and she didn't doubt, even though Joshua had been the one unwanted by any of his own family, he'd had the more loving upbringing.

'Lady Elizabeth, I hear my great-nephew is considering you for his future wife.'

'We are considering each other, Aunt,' Leonard Ashburton corrected her quietly but firmly.

'Strange arrangement. What do you think you would bring to the marriage?'

Beth blinked. She'd expected an interrogation, but had thought there would be at least a little bit of small talk first. Instead Miss Culpepper had jumped right in with the questions she wanted Beth to answer.

'She is the daughter of an earl,' Joshua Ashburton said, leaning back in his chair and crossing one foot over the other. 'Even I know an earl is higher in the hierarchy than a viscount.'

Miss Culpepper flashed him a look filled with icy disgust.

'Indeed. Although all of society knows Lady Elizabeth needs this match more than Leonard. The dire situation of your family's finances is often gossiped about.'

Feeling her stomach clench, Beth glanced at Josh

and could see he was about to jump to her defence, so she spoke quickly.

'My family may be struggling now, Miss Culpepper, but we did not through my formative years. I had the finest education, the best opportunities. My mother ensured I excelled in all the skills a well-bred young lady should, but also saw I was versed in the practical side of a marriage. I can run a large household, throw sumptuous dinner parties, make small talk with the peers of the realm. I would be an asset to your great-nephew. Other women might come with more money, but they wouldn't have the same refinement.'

Miss Culpepper's lips tightened but Beth saw the minute nod of acknowledgement. The old lady could appreciate the truth of what Beth was saying.

She felt a little nauseous. It was the first time she had tried to sell her skills, to show why she would be the right choice of wife for Leonard Ashburton, and none of it felt right. This was what she had been preparing for her whole life; every tutor, every dinner party they'd thrown, every moment had been leading up to this.

'Did you grow up here, Mr Ashburton?' She turned to Leonard Ashburton, asking the question quickly to try to avoid any further probing from Miss Culpepper.

'I spent some of my childhood here and some in the countryside.'

'Lord Abbingdon has a number of estates and when he heard I agreed to raise Leonard he allowed us use of one of the more moderate-sized country houses in Kent,' Miss Culpepper said briskly.

'You are not related to Lord Abbingdon?' For some

reason Beth had thought Miss Culpepper and Lord Abbingdon must be brother and sister.

'No. Lord Abbingdon is from Leonard's father's side of the family, I am from his mother's.'

'*Our* mother's,' Josh corrected her quietly. 'She was my mother too.'

Miss Culpepper didn't say anything to this, instead stood abruptly and went to pull the bell cord situated in the corner of the room. Ten seconds later a maid hurried in with a tray piled high with cups and a large pot of tea.

They all sat in silence as Miss Culpepper poured the tea. Beth knew if her mother were here she would be urging Beth to make conversation, to distract from the awkwardness in the room. It was her chance to show her skills at smoothing things over, but she found she had no desire to. Joshua Ashburton might be a successful man in his early thirties, he might have people who loved him, a business of his own and a way of seeing the world that meant opportunities were endless, but he was still being held back by the knowledge that this woman had looked at him at the age of six and decided he was not worthy of her care.

Leonard Ashburton was being his customary silent self, observing the interactions, but even though he was the figure that connected them he still seemed to be on the outside of it all.

'Here is your tea, Lady Elizabeth. I assume you don't take sugar. You wouldn't be very attractive if you grew fat.'

Next to her she caught a glimpse of the movement of Joshua Ashburton's shoulders shaking as he tried to hold in a laugh. It must have been too much effort because within seconds he let out a shout of laughter that startled Miss Culpepper into dropping the delicate silver spoon into the teacup she was holding with a rattle. Tea splashed onto the saucer.

'Oh, I'm sorry. Did I startle you?' Joshua Ashburton leapt forward with exaggerated concern.

'You did.'

'I couldn't help myself. I think you must be one of the rudest women I've ever met, Great-Aunt Culpepper.'

'Don't call me that.'

'You might have excluded me from the family as a child, but you still are my great-aunt.' He seemed much more relaxed now he was actually saying what he was thinking rather than trying to hold it inside.

'Josh,' Leo said in a warning tone, but Beth got the impression he wasn't going to step in, as if he realised his brother needed to get the trauma of rejection off his chest.

'Lady Elizabeth, would you care for a spoon of sugar?' he asked, barely taking a breath. 'I for one think you would look most charming even if you were plump.'

'I apologise for Mr Ashburton's behaviour, Lady Elizabeth,' Miss Culpepper said, standing and towering over them all. 'Leonard, you should not have brought him.'

'I am not his keeper,' Leonard Ashburton said simply, and Beth found she had more respect for him in that moment than she ever had before.

'Enough. I've had enough. Lady Elizabeth, despite your destitute status I suppose you will do. Leonard, hurry up and stop dawdling with your decision. And, *you*—' she turned back to her other great-nephew '—I doubt we will ever see each other again so I will save my words.'

She left the room without a backwards glance. Beth and the two Ashburton brothers remained silent for a few seconds as if waiting to see if she would reappear before letting out the breaths they had been holding.

'Good Lord, Leo, she's a dragon. How on earth did you survive an upbringing by her?'

'Shall we leave?' Leonard Ashburton ignored his brother's question, instead standing and motioning for Beth and Josh to precede him from the room.

Beth walked out first, hearing Leonard Ashburton lean in and murmur to his brother when he thought she was out of earshot, 'I'm sorry, Josh. I know you wanted more from that encounter. I think she was so abrupt because she feels guilty for what she did all those years ago.'

Joshua Ashburton shrugged, but even from her position in the hall Beth could see the pain he was trying to hide in his eyes.

'I apologise, Lady Elizabeth, that was not how I wished the afternoon to go,' he said once they were outside. 'I should have arranged for a separate meeting for you and Miss Culpepper, rather than combine it with taking Josh to see her.'

'Lady Elizabeth got the dragon's seal of approval,' Josh said cheerfully, 'so it wasn't an entirely wasted afternoon.'

'Hmm. Josh, would you be so kind as to see Lady Elizabeth home? I should go and smooth things over with our great-aunt.'

'It would be my pleasure.'

They watched Leonard Ashburton make his way back inside the house before Josh offered her his hand to help her into the waiting carriage. Beth settled against the plush seats as he took his place opposite her, their knees almost touching.

'I'm sorry,' he said quietly after the carriage was moving. 'You shouldn't have had to see that.'

'You don't need to apologise.'

'I do. I should have stayed away, let you meet Miss Culpepper without my dislike of the woman getting in the way.'

'You needed to confront her, and I doubt she would have agreed to meet you otherwise.'

He was silent for a moment. 'I did need to confront her. What does that say about me?'

Beth leaned forward and placed her hand over the top of his, feeling the warmth of his skin even through her gloves. It was an intimate gesture, one of friends or lovers, but it felt right to try to comfort this man who had come to mean so much to her.

'Of course you're going to have questions for the woman who could have changed the course of your life.'

'I don't understand why I'm still so angry. It turned out well for me. I got a loving family, a life of adventure, and soon I'll be in charge of one of the most successful businesses in India. I should be thanking her for setting me free.'

'It did turn out well,' Beth said slowly, 'but I think you're angry for two reasons. The first is she separated you from your brother when you needed him the most. And the second is she did it all without *knowing* it would turn out well. It was only luck that Mr Usbourne stepped up and took you in—when Miss Culpepper refused you she didn't know what life she was condemning you to.'

'You have a logical head on you, Lady Elizabeth.' As he looked at her she could see some of the pent-up anger seeping from his body. His shoulders began to relax, his jaw unclench, his posture soften.

The journey was short and already the carriage was slowing to a stop in front of her town house. She shifted in her seat to prepare herself to step down, but Joshua Ashburton gripped her hands and stilled her.

Beth looked up, her eyes meeting with his, and for a moment it felt as though their thoughts were as one. She felt every hurt and every hope of the man sitting opposite her. She knew he wanted to kiss her, wanted to take her into his arms and forget the world outside the carriage window, but she also knew he would respect her request to not jeopardise her chances of marrying his brother. For a moment she cursed herself for making the request and wondered how foolish she would be if she leaned across the space between them and kissed him.

'I will see you in Sussex, Lady Elizabeth,' he said softly.

With a great effort she nodded and tore her gaze away from his. As she stepped out of the carriage she made the mistake of glancing back, and felt the sudden realisation that it was something much deeper than pure desire that filled her heart. Quickly she pushed the thought aside, but she knew it had lodged somewhere deep down as she felt her heart squeeze at the thought of this man leaving her life for ever in a few short weeks.

It took a gargantuan effort to compose herself enough to enter the house, knowing her mother would be waiting just inside the door for a detailed account of exactly what had passed. Beth didn't know if she could recount it all without letting slip her feelings for the wrong Ashburton brother.

Chapter Nine

The salty breeze swept Beth's hair from her face and whipped it around her neck. When she'd left the house she'd been perfectly groomed but the weather was conspiring to make her look less than poised and perfect, although Beth couldn't bring herself to care. It was one of those beautifully warm days where in sheltered spots it felt as she imagined tropical climes to be, but when the wind blew you were reminded you were still in England, not nearer the equator.

Gently pulling on the reins, she turned her horse's head and tapped lightly with her feet to urge her into a trot. They moved parallel to the cliff edge, climbing the slope until they had a fantastic view of the chalky cliffs and the blue-grey sea beyond. This was where Beth felt at her happiest. She loved the sea, loved watching the crashing waves in winter and the lapping tides in summer. She loved how the clouds above changed the colour of the sea below and the way the weather was more dramatic at the coast.

'Good morning,' a voice called out from behind her.

Beth almost fell from her saddle. She would have sworn she was alone on the clifftop.

'Mr Ashburton.' Mr Joshua Ashburton, the man she hadn't been able to banish from her mind no matter how hard she tried.

'I'm sorry to startle you. I was keen to catch a glimpse of these famous cliffs.'

'When did you arrive?' Beth knew she was being blunt, rude even, but his sudden appearance had unsettled her.

'Half an hour ago.' He gave a little smile as he saw her peer around him. 'I'm alone.'

'Your brother…?'

'Is freshening up. Something he tells me every gentleman should do after travelling on horseback for any period of time.' He shrugged and Beth felt drawn to his carefree attitude. 'I didn't think the sea would mind my ruffled appearance.'

He looked anything but ruffled. Even the wind suited him, tousling his hair and whipping at his clothes.

'My mother is going to be livid,' Beth murmured as she glanced towards home. She couldn't see Birling View from here but already she could imagine her mother's ire at Beth being out when their guest of honour arrived. 'You weren't meant to be here until this afternoon.'

'Blame me. Leo calculated the time it would take in a carriage but this morning I persuaded him to complete our journey on horseback.' He turned his horse so he was alongside her and for a long moment looked out at the sea. 'I can see why you don't want to leave.'

Beth shot him a sharp look. She'd never said in so

many words she didn't want to leave Sussex and she wondered if she were that transparent that he could tell her emotions just from inference and glances.

'Who would?' His eyes were fixed on the horizon and there was a wistful expression on his face.

'I should return home. My mother...' Beth shuddered. Her mother would be pacing the halls, waiting to say how disappointed she was in Beth's behaviour yet again.

'She will be angry if you return half an hour late or forty minutes. An extra few minutes won't change things.'

'You're inciting me to defy my mother, Mr Ashburton.'

'We all need a little danger in our lives.' He turned back to the sea and took a deep breath. 'Five minutes. Ride with me to the top of the cliffs.'

She shouldn't do it. For the past two weeks, ever since they'd left London to prepare for the house party, she had told herself she would spend the week avoiding Joshua Ashburton. He brought something out in her that wasn't sensible, wasn't rational. She glanced over at him, catching the way he was looking at her, and felt her skin begin to tingle and her heart start to pound just that little bit faster.

Willow, her beautiful mare, tossed her head and pulled in the direction of the clifftop.

'Traitor,' Beth murmured, but allowed the horse to fall into step alongside Mr Ashburton's. 'How was your journey?'

'Uneventful. Now tell me, who is your mother hiding in that lovely old house of yours?'

Beth felt herself stiffen in the saddle and had to force herself to let go of the breath she was holding.

'Hiding? What makes you think she's hiding someone?'

'When we arrived she was very keen to usher us inside even though it is a glorious day. She kept looking at the garden and I fancied I saw someone in amongst the flower beds. Someone it seemed your mother didn't want us to see.'

'Nonsense.' Beth knew her voice gave her away. She wasn't sure why her mother was quite so keen to hide Annabelle from the world. When they had returned to Sussex from London in preparation for the house party her mother had initially planned to send Annabelle away whilst they had guests but Beth had coaxed and cajoled her mother into letting her sister stay. Annabelle hadn't been away from Birling View ever, and, even though the proposed destination was only the farm at the edge of the estate, Beth didn't think it fair her sister be discarded like that.

'I thought it might have been your sister, but then couldn't work out why your mother would be so keen for her not to meet us.'

Joshua Ashburton was an astute man. Even though Annabelle meant the world to her, Beth had steered clear of mentioning her too much in his company, but still the man's interest had been piqued by this younger sister who must seem elusive.

'It may have been Annabelle. She does enjoy the gardens.'

'I suppose we will meet her at dinner tonight.'

'No.' Beth avoided eye contact and instead spurred

Willow on to the very top of the cliff. The hills here
undulated up and down with many points on the cliff
where it felt as though you were at the highest point,
but Beachy Head really was the top.

'Tomorrow, then, perhaps at breakfast?'

'No.'

'Ah, I understand. Some people prefer to eat alone.
Perhaps she will join us for a walk along the cliffs.'

'Why do you care?' Beth rounded on him, her voice
rising, carried on the wind and echoing off the hills.

Mr Ashburton regarded her for a long moment, his
expression for once serious.

'Something here isn't right,' he said eventually. 'It
has been niggling at me for two weeks. Here you are,
two and twenty.' He waited for her to give a short nod
of confirmation before continuing. 'Doing everything
in your power to save the family. Yet your sister, who
is a mere year younger, is hidden away here in Sussex,
not out husband hunting with you.'

'You know nothing about me, about my sister, about
my family.'

'That's not true,' he said quietly, and Beth was forced
to look at him by the intensity in his voice. 'I may not
have known you long, Lady Elizabeth, but do not pre-
tend we do not have a connection. I may not know you
by the standards of society, but I understand you.'

Beth felt the piercing of her heart. It was what she
imagined everyone wished for—someone to understand
them. Even Annabelle, who she was as close as sisters
could be to, didn't *understand* her. His eyes were burning into her, hot and intense, and it made her want to
squirm in the saddle.

'*Something* is wrong here.'

Shaking her head, she felt the tears threatening to spill.

'Isn't there something wrong in every family?' she said quietly.

'Of course. Look at me and Leo: he was wanted, I was not.'

'Yet you are peculiarly well adjusted.'

He shrugged. 'We're not talking about me.'

'I need to get back home, Mr Ashburton. May I suggest we don't arrive together?'

'Josh,' he said, holding her eye. 'My name is Josh.'

'I can't call you Josh.'

'That's your decision, but you can think of me as Josh even if you can't use my name.'

'Josh,' she murmured, knowing she wouldn't be able to think of him as Mr Ashburton any more. That would be reserved for his brother.

Reminded once again of her duty, she pulled on Willow's reins and without another word pushed her into a trot. She got as far as the bottom of the first hill before she lost the battle with herself not to look around and glanced back over her shoulder to see Josh still watching her.

'Mother is furious.' Annabelle's face peeked out of the darkness as Beth crept along the upper landing towards the bedroom she shared with Annabelle.

Quickly she slid into the room and embraced her sister, making sure the door was closed firmly behind her.

'With me?'

'She's furious with everyone. With the Ashburtons

for arriving early, with you not being here to greet them when they arrived, with me for having the audacity to walk in the gardens when we might have guests arriving.'

Beth paused in her pacing, regarding her sister. It must hurt, this need of their mother's to keep Annabelle hidden away, but the bitterness that should be there wasn't always present.

'You could join us, you know, for the party.'

Annabelle scoffed. 'And incur Mother's eternal wrath? No, thank you.'

'She wouldn't be able to do anything, not if you came down when all the guests were present.'

Annabelle looked at her with a mixture of sadness and pity and, as often happened, Beth felt like the younger sister. 'I don't want to come down, Beth. I don't need to.'

Nodding, Beth knew she couldn't push the matter. It was Annabelle's choice, although she had been conditioned to feel ashamed of herself, of her appearance. Self-consciously Annabelle touched the deep scar on her face, letting her fingertips linger on the puckered skin.

'The Misters Ashburton are very handsome,' Annabelle said, moving behind Beth as she sat in front of the mirror to straighten her windswept hair. Expertly Annabelle pulled the pins loose as Beth began to run a brush through the tangled strands. They had never had a lady's maid of their own, funds being too tight ever since they had reached adulthood, so instead had learned to dress each other's hair and look after their own clothes.

'They are.'

'*Very* similar in appearance, but you say they are not twins.'

'No. Two or three years separate them in age, I believe.'

'Of course, they are easy to tell apart by their expressions and the way they carry themselves.'

'You got close enough to see their expressions?' Beth pulled at a particularly large knot with the brush, wincing as it tugged at her scalp.

'I know every passageway and every nook in this house. I was able to observe them once I had been summoned in from the garden.' Annabelle had not left the estate, not since the accident that had scarred her face. It meant she knew the house better than the servants, and the gardens were her own personal paradise.

'Which one is the taller of the two, the one with the quick smile and the kind eyes?'

'Josh... Joshua Ashburton, the younger brother.' Beth didn't meet her sister's eye but knew she would have picked up on the high-pitched note in her voice. Normally she told Annabelle everything, confided all her secrets, her hopes and fears. They'd had long discussions about the trip to London and Beth's impending marriage before she'd left Sussex, but, despite her sister pressing her since her return, she hadn't told her much about the Ashburtons out of fear of letting something of what had happened with Josh slip.

Annabelle wouldn't disapprove. It was more the opposite reaction she was afraid of: that her sister would encourage her to ruin the chance of saving the family for an ill-advised romance. Beth scoffed, the sound out of her mouth before she could stop it. *Now* she was dreaming. Josh Ashburton hadn't offered her romance, just one kiss, and the information that he was leaving the country for good in a few short weeks.

'So the one you're meant to marry is the serious man, the one who carries himself as if he has a broom wedged down the back of his shirt?'

A smile cracked on Beth's lips. Annabelle always had been good at getting to the essence of people quickly.

'Yes. Leonard Ashburton. He's very…sober in his manner.'

'It's a shame it's not his brother.' Annabelle's words were said lightly, without any hidden meaning behind them, and Beth had to stop herself from reacting. Instead she focussed on jabbing the pins into her hair, handing the spares to Annabelle to secure the back. 'Mother said to tell you to wear the yellow dress.' Annabelle screwed up her nose. 'I did say it was far too itchy to wear all afternoon, but she wasn't interested in my opinion.'

They both turned to the wardrobe, Beth grimacing as she caught sight of the yellow dress. It had been a gift, passed down from a friend of her mother's. It was beautiful, albeit not of the most current fashion. The top was a lovely pale yellow silk, edged with a delicate trim of lace. A gold ribbon pulled in a high waist and from that the heavy silk skirts flowed. It was designed to be worn with at least two petticoats and the material was not the most breathable for the summer months it was meant for. She couldn't deny it looked spectacular on, but for some unfathomable reason it was almost unbearably itchy and Beth found she couldn't sit still when she wore it, often fantasising about ripping the material from her body and throwing it from the cliffs.

'She won't be happy if you don't wear it.'

'She knows how uncomfortable it is.' Beth silently wondered if it was her mother's way of punishing her for not being present when Mr Ashburton arrived.

'You could defy her.'

Biting her lip, Beth crossed to the wardrobe and ran her hand along the line of dresses hung in the small space. It wasn't an extensive collection: she had three dresses for day-to-day wear, the yellow dress her mother liked so much, two evening dresses bought specially for her time in London and a thin, floaty white dress she had worn to the local balls as a debutante.

Deciding today was going to be torture enough, she selected her smartest day dress, made of dark blue cotton with a lighter blue sash around the middle. She had always thought it made her look elegant but understated, and it didn't make her want to rip her skin off every time she wore it.

'Good choice,' Annabelle murmured as she helped Beth fasten the dress at the back.

'Are you sure you won't come with me? We could walk into the drawing room together.'

Annabelle shook her head and Beth knew she shouldn't push her sister any further.

'Promise to tell me all about it later.'

'I promise.'

Chapter Ten

Josh closed his eyes, let his head rest back on the bench and enjoyed the warmth of the sun on his face. Even in what his brother had hailed as the hottest May in memory, it wasn't anything like the heat of an Indian summer. In that heat sometimes you felt as if you couldn't breathe, the humidity meant the sweat rolled from your skin and the sun would burn you within minutes. This felt like a pleasant spring day in comparison.

He was sitting outside the drawing room, on an ornate stone bench that someone had positioned with loving care to look over the gardens and to the cliffs beyond. The gardens were a curious design, now overgrown in many places and left to run wild, the sea air culling many of the plants not designed for a coastal garden. Nevertheless, it was charming in its own unique way with patches of colour in amongst the winding paths.

'Ah, there you are,' Leo said as he stepped out of the drawing room.

'Have you finished your letters?'

His brother grimaced and shook his head. 'Almost. The writing desk is very low in my bedroom so I thought I would take a little break and stretch my legs before the other guests arrive.'

'Not keen on socialising?'

'Remind me again why we agreed to come all the way down here for four days?'

Josh laughed. Only an Englishman would think eighty miles was a long way to travel.

'For your intended. To woo her, I suppose.'

'That's not exactly my way.'

Leo sat down on the bench next to him and turned his own face up to the sun just as Josh had a few minutes earlier.

'It's good for you to be away from the demands of Lord Abbingdon for a couple of days, at the very least.'

Just as Leo was about to reply Josh saw a flash of movement behind them and Lady Elizabeth stepped out of the drawing room.

'Oh.' She didn't look particularly pleased to see them, although she covered her initial reaction with a smile that didn't reach her eyes. 'Good afternoon, Mr Ashburton and Mr Ashburton.' She gave a pretty little curtsy and then glanced around the garden as if trying to work out an escape route.

'We were just admiring your garden and enjoying the sunshine,' Josh said.

Leo remained silent.

'Would you like to take a stroll around the garden, Mr Ashburton?' Lady Elizabeth addressed herself squarely to Leo.

'No. I have letters to write.' Even to Josh's ears Leo

sounded blunt and he saw Lady Elizabeth blink in surprise. 'Take Josh.'

Leo stood, bowed and walked quickly back inside
the house, leaving Lady Elizabeth standing awkwardly
staring after him.

'Was it something I did?'

'He really does have letters to write.'

'How are we meant to determine if we suit if we
never spend any time together?'

Josh didn't answer; there wasn't anything he could
say. Instead he offered Lady Elizabeth his arm and
waited whilst she contemplated whether to take it or not.

He leaned in. 'I promise not to kiss you.'

'Stop it.'

'Fine. I promise I will kiss you.'

'I'm not going for a walk with you if you behave
like this.'

'Ah, but what if Leo is watching from his window
and realises we're not strolling companionably around
the gardens?'

Letting out a little snort of frustration, Lady Elizabeth took his arm and began a fast march away from
the house. Josh had to suppress a smile as he length-
ened his stride to keep up.

'Here are the roses,' she said, pointing to a sad-look-
ing bed of thorny tangles with not a single bud in sight.
'Here is the fernery. And here is the summer border.'
A few droopy plants with sparse flowers hung limply
in the summer border.

'Impressive,' he murmured.

'Do you have any idea how difficult it is to grow *anything* this close to the sea?' Lady Elizabeth exploded,

her voice carrying on the breeze much further than he thought she would want it to.

'Either you planted these sorry specimens yourself and nurtured them to their current state or your anger at me is about something else.'

'Of course it is about something else. The garden is just the garden, it hardly looked any better when we had two full-time gardeners rather than me and Annabelle in our old boots trudging about with watering cans.' It was an image that was strangely appealing to Josh. He pictured Lady Elizabeth in a flimsy dress, the material blown by the wind revealing far more than it should, watering can in hand and heavy boots on her feet.

'Enchanting,' he murmured. 'What part of my behaviour exactly has offended you?'

'All of it.'

'That's not true, Lady Elizabeth.'

As she clenched her teeth he could see the little muscles just under her earlobes bulging and relaxing in little pulses.

'Why do I like you so much when you're so difficult to be around?' she blurted out eventually.

He smiled even though he knew it would infuriate her more.

'Perhaps you find me so difficult to be around because you like me so much.'

She glared at him as if everything were his fault, her fingers distractedly toying with the flower stems to her left. As if deciding something, she spun on her heel and began to stalk along the path at great speed, only stopping when she was halfway along to turn back and look at him questioningly.

'Aren't you coming?'

'I didn't realise the tour was continuing.' He followed, walking even faster to keep up with her as she weaved in and out of the forlorn flower beds. There was a little summer house at the edge of the garden, obscured from sight of the house by a few scraggy trees that had grown all in one direction, their leaves all on the side away from the cliffs as if they were desperately trying to escape the wind that whipped over the precipice and hit them with full force much of the year.

The summer house was octagonal, made of wood and painted white although it looked as though the last coat of paint had been more than a decade ago. It was peeling badly with the bare wood showing through in places and even a few tell-tale cracks and bows. Inside there was a simple wooden bench that ran around the periphery and allowed the occupants to enjoy unrivalled views of the sea.

As Josh stepped up into the summer house Lady Elizabeth took a deep breath in and then reached out and gripped him by the lapels of his jacket. Before he could guess what was happening she was kissing him, long and hard. At first he was too stunned to react but soon his mind caught up with his body and he shifted slightly, pulling her in closer to him. As he moved he felt Lady Elizabeth let out a small sigh and the intensity of the kiss changed. It had been firm and insistent at first, as if she was trying to prove something, but now she abandoned herself to the kiss it was as if their bodies had become one.

Josh trailed his fingers down her back, feeling the curve of her spine and the tantalising hollow just above her buttocks. He'd never wanted a woman as he wanted Lady Elizabeth and, even though he'd spent the last two weeks repeating to himself why any sort of dalliance with her was a bad idea, all he wanted to do was tumble her to the ground and spend the next few hours exploring every inch of her body.

He felt her grip on his lapels intensify and her body brush against his as she moved closer and then, with a low moan, she pulled herself away.

'What…' he asked, his hand still lingering on her back '…was that?'

Lady Elizabeth didn't answer him, instead shaking her head and frowning.

'Not that I'm complaining, but I thought we'd agreed not to do that again.'

She stepped away, turning her back to him and walking to the edge of the summer house. For a moment he thought she was going to leave without another word, but eventually she turned back to face him.

'I thought I could prove to myself a kiss didn't mean anything. That I didn't really feel anything for you.'

'And what were the results?'

Pressing her lips together, she didn't answer.

Josh wanted nothing more than to gather her in his arms and kiss her until the frown on her brow disappeared and she thought of nothing but him, but he knew he couldn't. Two months and he would be returning to India. He didn't want a wife; he wasn't made for marriage; the business was his priority. Lady Elizabeth needed to marry someone rich, and although he would be taking over his guardian's business all the funds had to be reinvested to make it a success. Two very good reasons to keep his hands off her even before they came to the complication of Leo.

With great effort he took a step back and sat down on one of the wooden benches. What he wanted was to have Lady Elizabeth as his lover. To enjoy her for the few weeks he was in England, to spend lazy mornings in bed appreciating her beauty and her body and long nights talking until the sun rose. *That* was impossible. She was the daughter of an earl. The innocent daughter of an earl, and even he knew you did not even fantasise about a lady in that way.

'There is another path,' he said softly, forcing the words out. 'I like you; you like me.'

'I will not be your mistress.'

'I wouldn't ask that of you.'

'Then what?'

'We could be friends.'

'Friends?'

'It is better than trying to avoid one another for the next few weeks. We get to spend time together, enjoy one another's company.'

'What about...?' She couldn't finish her question.

'The attraction?' He shrugged. 'We ignore it. I'm sure you've overcome greater challenges in your life, Lady Elizabeth.'

It felt like an eternity as she considered his proposal but eventually she nodded, coming to sit on the bench a respectable distance from him. Josh stopped himself from reaching out and taking her hand, settling on his friendliest smile instead.

'Beth,' she said. 'When we are alone, I would like you to call me Beth.'

'Beth. It suits you.'

'Thank you, Josh.' His name sounded like velvet coming from her lips, smooth and soft and seductive.

'I think I need to go,' she said, studying his face for a moment. 'There will be guests arriving soon and my mother is already irate I missed your arrival. I'd better not miss any more.'

'Better not.'

For another few seconds she didn't move, and then, with a swish of skirts, she sped from the summer house without glancing back.

Josh closed his eyes and leaned his head back on the peeling paint.

'You're a fool, Joshua Ashburton,' he muttered to himself. It was a foolish idea, trying to be friends with a woman he couldn't stop fantasising about. A woman he had now kissed twice. He knew if she kissed him again he wouldn't be able to push her away, however much he should.

Chapter Eleven

'You look flushed, Elizabeth. I hope you haven't been spending too much time in the sun. It is unbecoming for a young lady of good birth to have freckles.'

Beth hadn't even noticed her mother standing by the wide glass doors in the drawing room, looking out over the garden. Lady Hummingford was as still as a statue, only her eyes moving as she looked through the glass. Even so, normally she would have noticed her, but she was so completely distracted by Josh she hadn't noticed anyone was in the room.

'No, Mother.'

'I don't want you going off riding for hours on end whilst we have guests.'

'I won't. Although I do believe Mr Ashburton is fond of riding. I thought I might suggest a ride and picnic one day.'

At the positive suggestion her mother softened a little and stepped away from the window.

'Good girl. Perhaps tomorrow. I worry later in the week there may be a storm. Surely this humidity can't last much longer.'

'I will speak to Mr Ashburton.'

'It will be better just the two of you, of course, but if he is unsure we can arrange a little trip out for all the guests.'

'Yes, Mother.'

The door to the drawing room opened behind them and Lillian, their hard-working maid, stepped into the room. She was one of three servants they still had after having to dismiss the rest over a year ago. Lillian did most of the cleaning and general looking after the house. Mrs Turner was both cook and housekeeper now and saw everything ran smoothly. Ben was a young lad who saw to any heavy work as well as looking after the horses. In her father's time they'd had a butler and a dozen servants, but now it was a stretch to afford just these three.

For the duration of the house party her mother had instructed Mrs Turner to hire some local boys from the village as footmen and a maid to help her in the kitchen, but Beth knew it was an expense that could break them if she didn't secure a proposal soon.

'A carriage is approaching, my lady,' Lillian said, straightening the cushions as she spoke.

'Thank you. Come, Elizabeth, we should greet our guests. Hopefully everyone will arrive in good time.'

The next hour was spent smiling and chatting to the select few guests her mother had strategically invited to the house party. Beth knew a lot of thought had gone into the guest list to make it an interesting mix of people to keep Mr Ashburton amused and the party a success. Her mother had made certain there were no other attractive eligible young ladies to make his eye wander and to make it easier to push her and Mr Ashburton together as much as possible.

The Potterton sisters from the village had made the list, two spinsters in their mid-twenties, accompanied by a mother who was cheerful and friendly but despaired of what to do with her daughters. Mr Williams and Mr Ralph, two young gentlemen Lady Hummingford knew from her friendship with their mothers. They were pleasant enough gentlemen, high in spirits, and Beth had met them on a few previous occasions so felt comfortable in their company. Lastly were Lord and Lady Melbon, the viscount and his wife from the neighbouring estate. They would not be staying, of course, but would come for the various dinner parties and excursions out. Lady Melbon was a difficult woman to get to know, quiet and withdrawn, but her husband made up for it with his loud anecdotes and opinion on everything.

Once everyone had arrived and been shown to their rooms, with the exception of the Melbons, Lady Hummingford had arranged for some light refreshments to be served. It was such glorious weather Beth suggested they carry a couple of tables and chairs outside and have the tea and cake on the lawn, shaded by the silver birch trees that grew along one side.

She was just supervising the moving of the tables by the two young new footmen when she felt a presence behind her.

'Is now really the time to be having a spring clean?' Josh asked, his eyes flitting backwards and forwards over the proceedings. The two young men were willing enough but clumsy and new to taking orders and had to be told where to put everything at least twice, which made for a farcical show.

'I thought we might have tea and cake on the lawn, but we don't have any garden furniture.'

'Ah. I see. Under the shade of the trees?'

'Exactly.' Beth sighed as one of the footmen put a table down in full sun.

'How many seats do you need?'

Beth counted up the guests in her head.

'Eleven.'

Without another word Josh had hoisted a table into the air, picking it up and carrying it as if it were no heavier than a packet of letters. Beth watched in surprise for a moment before hurrying after him.

'Put it down, you can't do that.'

He grinned at her, ignoring the instruction and transporting the table to the spot in the shade she had indicated. Quickly he organised the two young temporary footmen to reposition the second table and then sent them to fetch the chairs.

'Sometimes it is easiest just to do something yourself,' he said, smiling at her in a way that made her heart flip in her chest.

Friends, she repeated to herself silently. *Just friends.*

Once the chairs were positioned, he surveyed the scene and then selected a chair. If Beth sat next to him, they would be the only ones on that side of the table. He gestured to the empty chair and watched her as she hesitated.

'What if I promise to be on my best behaviour?'

'I'm not sure your best behaviour is anything to boast about, Mr Ashburton. I know you, remember.'

'We're alone, Beth—you said you would call me Josh.'

She inclined her head, watching the house for any sign of movement. Her mother should be out here by now; if it were any other gentleman she wouldn't leave Beth unchaperoned for so long, but, given her previous difficulties in identifying Leonard Ashburton, it wouldn't surprise Beth if her mother thought she were sitting outside with Leonard and not Josh.

'So how do I compare?' Josh asked, closing his eyes and stretching out his legs. If he leaned his head back his face was in the sun and he looked like a cat basking in its warmth, a satisfied look on his face.

'Compare to what?'

'To the other men you've kissed.'

'I'm insulted. You forget I'm a gently bred young lady. One does not go around kissing strange men.'

'Except me.'

'A terrible lapse in judgement.'

'Of course...' he paused for a moment then continued, still with his eyes closed and his head back '...but you still haven't answered my question.'

Beth fiddled with a stray strand of cotton from her dress, trying to resist the urge to tug on it, knowing it might result in hours of mending with a needle, which she hated with a passion.

'How do I compare?' she asked, throwing the question back at him.

'Hmm.' He took half a minute to consider.

'Now you're being ridiculous. There can't be *that* many kisses to compare it to.'

'I am thirty-one years old.' He sat up and leaned forward so their knees were almost touching.

'Is this what friends do?' Beth had never had a friend like Josh before. Even female friends were in short supply when you hardly ever left the estate. She had Annabelle, and a few young women from the local area who she talked to at the dances and dinner parties, but no one she would class as a close friend.

'I wouldn't know. I've never kissed a friend before.'

'I don't mean that. I know *that's* not what friends do.'

He grinned at her and looked as if he was about to say something more when a group of guests came out of the doors from the drawing room. Leonard Ashburton was at the front, his expression serious as usual. He nodded in greeting to Beth and bestowed a shoulder squeeze on his brother.

Beth watched in interest as he chose his chair, noting without much emotion that he left the one next to her empty and sat himself in the one beside his brother instead. It should hurt her, this indifference he seemed to have towards her, but she had to admit she felt much the same about him. If he weren't incredibly wealthy and didn't have the means to save her family from destitution she wouldn't even consider him as a future husband.

She closed her eyes as she felt the self-disgust almost overwhelm her. It all felt so shallow, so dirty, choosing who she would marry purely based on how much they were worth.

Silently she reminded herself she was doing it for Annabelle. For her sister, whose future she'd ruined when they were no more than little girls, who would never get out into the world and marry or have a family.

The other guests made their way over to the chairs leisurely, enjoying the afternoon sunshine. When everyone was seated Lady Hummingford stood, waiting until all eyes were on her before she spoke.

'Elizabeth and I are so pleased you could all join us for this intimate little party. We have glorious weather and a beautiful setting. Of course, we will organise a few excursions and games, but we want you to have time to relax, to enjoy being away from the hustle and bustle of London.'

There was a murmur of agreement around the table and Mr Ralph nodded vigorously.

The two new footmen appeared on cue carrying a tray of cups and pots of tea as well as tall glasses of cold lemonade. Beth reached for one at the same time as Josh, their hands brushing. She pulled back quickly, too quickly, and as she recovered her composure she felt Leonard Ashburton's eyes on her. His head was tilted ever so slightly to the left and he regarded her with a coolness that made her want to squirm in her seat.

Josh didn't even seem to notice their hands had touched and was drinking from the glass of lemonade, looking as though he didn't have a care in the world.

'I'd like to see some of the coastline whilst I'm here,' Josh said, addressing his remark to the general group but Beth knew it was directed at her. She allowed herself a moment to imagine riding out with him for a long day of exploring the little coves and high white cliffs of her home.

'Good idea,' Leonard Ashburton said. 'Perhaps we could go for a trip tomorrow.'

He looked at her expectantly and Beth had to force herself to speak.

'Yes. Perhaps we could take a picnic, ride over to Seaford and back.' It was hardly the intimate picnic her mother would want her to arrange with Leonard Ashburton, but it was a trip out together all the same.

'Wonderful,' Josh said. 'Now, tell me you've got some lawn games to play. Bowls perhaps? Or shuttlecock? Do you remember how I always used to thrash you at shuttlecock, Leo?'

'My recollection is a little different.' It was the first time she'd seen Leonard Ashburton smile. He looked different when he smiled. Still nowhere near as handsome as his younger brother, but friendlier, kinder.

'Ah, I see you're afflicted with the poor memory of the old, dear brother. I always was the more talented, the more coordinated at shuttlecock.'

'You used to drop it on the second hit every single time.'

'Nonsense.'

'I have a way to settle this argument,' Beth said, standing up in between the two men. 'I have two rackets and a shuttlecock. Would you care to prove who is the more accomplished at the game?'

The garden equipment was all kept in a dilapidated shed hidden in a little copse of trees to the side of the house. It had never been her favourite place to go as it was perpetually covered with cobwebs and dark and dirty. She would, however, be willing to brave it to see the Ashburton brothers compete at the childhood game.

'I'll give you a hand,' Josh said, jumping to his feet and gesturing for her to lead the way.

'It's just in here.' They walked side by side around the house, stopping when they were right in front of the shed.

'It's locked.'

Sure enough a hefty padlock hung from the door. Beth reached out and touched it, frowning. There never used to be a padlock on the door, although she hadn't ventured into the shed for years. She and Annabelle had played shuttlecock and bowls as children, but as the years had passed the games in the shed had been almost forgotten.

'I suppose someone must have the key.'

Josh took a step back and looked at the shed, grinning as he took a step to the right. 'No need to go searching. The window has been left ajar. I'm sure we can get inside and find what we need.'

Beth looked up at the high window with a frown. It was the type of window that was hinged at the top, allowing it to swing out and rest on a metal prop. It was half open now and likely had been for years.

'You'll never get up there.' It was high, above shoulder height even for Josh. The window was big enough to squeeze through if you could get up there, but would leave you with your clothes ruffled and dirty.

'You will. If I lift you.'

'I'm not going through the window.'

'It'll be the work of a few minutes.'

'Why wouldn't I just go and find the key?'

'Do you know where it is?'

She had absolutely no idea. There were hundreds of

places a key like this could be kept and she doubted any of the servants would know. By the grimy state of the padlock it had been put on years before, probably when they'd still had a gardener. The old man might even have taken the key with him when he'd left.

'Perhaps we could play something else.'

'Are you scared, Lady Elizabeth?'

'Stop it. We're not children and I will not respond to your jibing.'

He smiled, flashing her his white teeth, and she felt some of his good humour flow her way.

'Just try. I'll boost you up and you can slip inside and pass out the shuttlecock and rackets.'

'Then how do I get out?'

'A good shed always has something to climb on. Just pull it to under the window and climb up. I'll be out here to help you out.'

Beth knew she shouldn't. As a child she'd loved to climb, scaling the trees on the estate and propping herself up in their high branches. There was a freedom to being up in the air and she'd enjoyed the unparalleled view from her position above the ground. Still, she wasn't eight any more and it was completely undignified for a well-bred young lady to be climbing through the window of a dirty shed.

Glancing over her shoulder, she considered. No one else was coming and they were hidden from the view of the rest of the guests by the side of the house. If she was quick she could be in and out of the shed in two minutes.

She stepped closer to Josh, waiting for him to make a cup out of his hands for her to put her foot on. He boosted her without any effort at all, lifting her so her torso was level with the window.

'What if I get stuck inside?'

'You'll have a peaceful few days.' He laughed at her expression before continuing. 'Then I promise to rescue you.'

'There will be spiders in there.'

'Probably one or two. But remember they're more scared of you than you are of them.'

Beth doubted it. She *hated* spiders.

Gripping hold of the narrow ledge below the window, Beth manoeuvred herself through the gap, only realising when she was halfway through and completely committed that she was heading into the shed head first. Squirming, she managed to somehow turn herself round so she was able to grip onto the window on the inside and lower herself down.

When her feet hit the floor she took a moment to catch her breath, panting hard from the exertion. It was dark in the shed, with only the light from the single window above her and a little where it came through near the hinges of the locked door. She looked around, wrinkling her nose at the number of cobwebs, trying to make herself smaller so she didn't touch anything. She loathed spiders, hated the way they moved and especially hated the ones with hairy black legs.

'See what we need?' Josh shouted in, his face appearing at the window. He must have pulled himself up from the ground and Beth was momentarily distracted by the thought of how it had felt to be held in those strong arms of his.

'There's so much junk in here.' She looked around,

unsure where to start. Vaguely she recollected the garden games equipment being stored in the back right corner of the shed and started to rummage through things, checking carefully for any signs of spiders first. 'Here.' She gripped the handle of one of the shuttlecock rackets in triumph, pulling it out. In her excitement she forgot to look at it before she began brandishing it, waving it around in front of her face.

As if time had slowed she saw the huge black spider sitting on the strings as the racket passed her face. Her arm jerked and immediately she knew that instinctive reaction had been the wrong thing to do. The spider flew through the air, dislodged from the racket, hitting her squarely in the chest. Beth screamed, feeling the fat legs begin to writhe against her. Frantically she tried to brush it off but only succeeded in knocking the arachnid down the front of her dress.

'Get it out. Get it out,' she cried, starting to rip at the material of her dress.

All of a sudden she felt a presence beside her as Josh levered himself through the window and landed with a thump on the floor of the shed. Unceremoniously he pulled out the front of her dress and peered down into her cleavage. Beth knew she should feel self-conscious although nothing but the thought of the spider crawling over her skin was being allowed in her mind. She saw him grimace, then spin her round and begin to unfasten the sash that held the dress tight, and within a few seconds he tugged at the material and pulled it down, lifting her out of it as it fell around her ankles. Watching in horror, she saw him pick up the dress and shake it gently, and she shuddered as the fat black spider fell out of the material and skittered away into the shadows.

Her skin felt itchy with every nerve ending on edge and Beth had to give in to the impulse to smooth the cotton of her chemise and petticoats to check there were no other spiders hiding inside.

'Thank you,' she said, shivering from the memory of what had just happened. She crossed her arms in front of her body, hugging her sides. 'I really don't like spiders.'

'I'm sorry, I didn't realise. I know you said, but I didn't realise they made you that scared.' He reached out and placed a hand on her bare arm, his hand warm on her skin. 'I would never have suggested you come in here if I'd known.'

'How did you get in?'

'I pulled over a flowerpot.' He grimaced. 'I think I broke it when I pushed myself up from it.'

Carefully he began checking her dress over again, looking in all the folds of material.

'Nothing in there.'

'Thank you.' For a moment Beth forgot where she was as Josh stepped in closer to her. Although she was still clad in her chemise and petticoats she felt practically naked under his gaze and her whole body shuddered with anticipation as he raised a hand and trailed his fingertips across her shoulder. Letting her head fall back, she closed her eyes and revelled in his touch, almost crying out when she felt his lips brush against the skin on her neck.

'I'm sorry,' he murmured quietly. 'I couldn't stop myself.'

Beth almost cried out as he stepped away, wanting to

beg him to take her in his arms but knowing she had to maintain whatever little dignity she had left.

Taking the dress from his hands, Beth began pulling it over her head, trying not to mess up her hair any more than it already was. She felt Josh move behind her, helping her straighten it, pulling it down and then his fingers deftly fastening it. He seemed to know exactly what to do and she wondered how many women he'd helped to dress.

Once the sash was tied Beth spun around, not realising Josh was still standing so close. They were body to body and if she tilted her head her lips would only be a couple of inches from his. It was a dangerous position to be in, especially when she was so aware of every part of him.

'Perfect,' he murmured, reaching out to tuck a stray strand of hair behind her ear. She wasn't sure if she imagined the trailing of his fingertips on her neck for just a second, but her body reacted all the same. 'No one will ever know.'

Beth tensed all her muscles for a second and then forced herself to take a step back.

'How do we get out of here?'

'Same way we got in. I'll boost you up—just be careful of the flowerpot when you're dropping down on the other side. I'm sure I can move something to help me climb through the window.' He eyed her, adding quickly, 'Although I won't move anything until you're outside.'

Beth was careful not to brush against any spiders' webs as she manoeuvred herself into position underneath the window. It was easier going out, having practised how to spin round at the top on the way in, and within a few seconds her feet were back on the grass. She shivered in the sunlight, knowing she would never forget the feel of the spider dropping into her dress. Closing her eyes, she forced herself to stop thinking about it, instead touching her neck where the skin still tingled from his touch.

'Is there a problem?' Leonard Ashburton's clipped voice came from behind her. She turned slowly, making sure her expression was neutral before she faced him.

He could only just have rounded the corner of the house and stepped into view of the shed, but her heart began to hammer in her chest all the same.

'The door of the shed was locked,' she said, smiling serenely, 'and I have no idea where the key is.'

Leonard Ashburton frowned as his brother's head appeared in the window. The shuttlecock and rackets clattered to the ground as he dropped them before swinging himself out. Beth thought he looked like a cat, landing lightly on his feet.

'So my brother thought he'd climb in to get them?'

Beth nodded, holding her breath, wondering if she could be lucky enough for Leonard Ashburton to believe it had just been Josh in the shed.

'I *really* want to thrash you at shuttlecock,' Josh said, handing one of the rackets to his brother and starting to walk away. Leonard Ashburton frowned, leaning in closer to Beth, his hand coming up to pick something out of her hair. He held it out between them and inspected it.

Beth felt a churning in her stomach as she realised it was a big ball of dust. Leonard Ashburton didn't say anything, just regarded her for a few seconds longer, then spun and followed his brother back to the lawn where the other guests were assembled.

Chapter Twelve

Josh leaned back in the comfortable armchair, sipping the fine brandy and closing his eyes. It had been a tiring day, with the ride to complete their journey to Birling View in the morning and spending the rest of the day socialising. He still felt as though he were playing a part when amongst these people Leo called his peers, as if he were just pretending to be a gentleman.

'You look pensive,' Leo said, pulling at the cravat at his neck to loosen it. They were the only two still in the dimly lit library, the rest of the guests having retired to bed at various points in the evening. Josh had never needed much sleep, always late to bed and early to rise. He hated tossing and turning in the sheets and had found he only actually needed about five hours in bed to be fully rested. On his return to England he had found Leo was the same.

He'd been thinking about Beth, about all the moments he'd shared with her, but most particularly about the moment in the shed this afternoon when she'd stood in front of him in just her chemise and petticoats, her eyes rising up to meet his, and the feeling right in the centre of his chest—the feeling that he'd been hit by an arrow to the heart.

'If Lord Abbingdon wasn't making it a stipulation of his will, would you get married?' He tried to make the question light, but saw the way Leo's interest was piqued, the sharpness behind his eyes giving him away.

'No,' he said after some deliberation.

Josh nodded. It was what he thought. Despite their differences in personalities, their completely polar upbringings, he and Leo seemed to share the same view on many aspects of their lives.

'Why not?'

'What about you? Will you marry?' Leo asked rather than giving an answer.

'I doubt it.' He thought of Beth's warm smile, the way she moved, the way her body felt in his arms.

'Why not?'

Josh began speaking, began giving the answer he always did when someone asked him why he wasn't married, why he wasn't searching for a wife, but then he paused. If he couldn't tell the truth to his brother, then who could he ever be truthful with?

'I always tell people that it is because my life is not compatible with marriage, that I couldn't ask a woman to give up the comforts of home and join me in the foothills of India.' He shook his head and took another sip of brandy. 'Of course, that's nonsense. Rose, my guardian's wife, has led a very happy life in India and has never once regretted leaving England with her husband. And there are the women who already live there, of course, the daughters and sisters of other landowners.'

Leo watched him silently, giving him space to continue.

'I think it was losing our parents at such a young age…' He trailed off.

'You don't want to let anyone too close in case you lose them too.'

He heard the emotion in Leo's voice and felt a little comfort that he wasn't the only one who felt this way.

'You feel the same?'

Nodding, Leo swirled the liquid in his glass around as if needing a distraction from the intensity of his thoughts.

The candle that sat between them had burned low and was flickering now and Josh welcomed the interlude of standing to fetch another from on top of the mantelpiece.

'I would never presume to tell you what to do,' Leo said slowly, 'but I can see you happily married, perhaps with children. You're good with people, sociable.'

Josh sat back in his chair, the fresh candle giving out a slightly brighter light.

'I always tell myself I need to focus on the business, not get distracted.'

'No one could question your dedication, Josh. All these years you've worked, getting to know every aspect of the company you will soon run. It is admirable and I doubt a wife would take away anything from your ability to make the business thrive.'

Thinking of how distracted he felt every time Beth entered a room, Josh grimaced. If she were his wife he would find it hard to leave his bed in the morning, tempted to always stay for one more kiss, one more touch.

'I don't intend to let my nuptials distract me from

looking after the estates and growing the inheritance my children will one day receive.'

Josh was about to murmur something non-committal when a clatter at the veranda door made both men stand up suddenly, setting their glasses down on the table. Josh moved first, darting through the veranda door, his eyes taking a moment to adjust from the candlelit room to the complete darkness of the garden, but nevertheless he saw the movement to his left and reached out and grabbed the person skulking in the shadows.

As soon as his hands touched the person's wrist he knew it was a woman. The bones were too delicate, the arm too small, to be a man's. He relaxed his fingers, but the mistake had already been made and the woman in his grasp let out a loud scream.

Josh took two steps back, holding his hands out to try to show he wasn't a threat.

'I'm sorry,' he said, peering into the shadows, trying to make out which of the female guests had been walking in the dark of the night. 'I thought you were an intruder.'

Behind him he felt Leo's presence and he watched in amazement as Leo reached past him and held out his hand.

'Come, my brother meant you no harm.'

A delicate, pale hand inched forward hesitantly and eventually rested in Leo's, allowing him to pull the woman out into the moonlight.

Her head was bent, her free hand up trying to cover one side of her face. It wasn't any of the female guests, nor any of the maids he'd seen hurrying backwards and forwards throughout the day.

As she took a step she stumbled, her free hand flying from her face, shooting out to steady herself. Josh forced himself not to react as the scars became visible on the pale skin. Three deep, crisscrossing red tracks on her left cheek that pulled and puckered the skin, visible even in the moonlight.

The woman's eyes shot up, fear filling them as her gaze met his. Josh gave a gentle smile.

'I'm sorry for startling you,' he said again.

'Annabelle.' Beth's concerned voice made the three of them on the veranda freeze.

So this was Beth's mysterious sister.

'What happened?' Beth covered the rest of the distance to her sister quickly, almost running to be by her side. She wrapped an arm around Annabelle's shoulder and then looked accusingly at Josh.

'She's shaking.'

'It's fine,' Annabelle said, finally finding her voice. 'I'm fine.'

'You're not, you're trembling. What happened?'

'We were in the library and I heard a noise at the door. I thought it was an intruder,' Josh explained.

'I didn't realise there was anyone still up. I was just taking a stroll around the gardens and I thought I would go back in through the library door. I'd already started to turn the handle when I saw a flicker of the candle and realised the room was occupied.'

Josh frowned, wondering why she'd run rather than coming in through the library.

'It was nothing, Beth, a silly mistake.'

Beth nodded, giving her sister a squeeze. 'I was so worried when I heard you scream.'

'It is nice to meet you, Lady Annabelle,' Josh said.

Beth hesitated for a second and then must have realised she couldn't just hurry her sister away in that protective way of hers. 'Annabelle, this is Mr Joshua Ashburton and Mr Leonard Ashburton, gentlemen, this is my dear sister, Lady Annabelle.'

Annabelle dipped into a formal little curtsy, her hand dancing from her waist to her collarbone and back again. Josh could see all she wanted to do was hide her scars behind her fingers but was conscious of drawing even more attention to them if she did so.

'Lady Annabelle.' Leonard Ashburton inclined his head, and then gestured for the ladies to step inside ahead of him.

In the library Josh could see Beth and her sister were torn between being polite and rushing off upstairs to their private sanctuary.

'Brandy?' he offered, crossing to the decanter and reaching for two more glasses from the tray.

'We shouldn't...' Beth began, but Annabelle nodded, holding her hand out for a glass.

Beth shrugged and took a glass of her own, sinking down into the armchair Josh had been sitting in moments before.

'Do you often take a walk so late at night, Lady Annabelle?' Leonard Ashburton was regarding her seriously. Josh saw his brother's eyes were not focussed on the scars, but Lady Annabelle looked self-conscious all the same.

'No. Yes. I enjoy the garden by moonlight—it is peaceful.' She was softly spoken, her words directed more at her shoes than the rest of the room.

'We didn't see you today on the lawn.'

Josh glanced sharply at his brother. He could see Beth looking uncomfortable and wanted to tell Leo not to push the fragile young woman, but it would seem he needn't have worried.

'I don't socialise much,' she said, lifting her head and looking Leo in the eye.

'Ah.'

There was a silence as everyone took a mouthful of brandy, and then at exactly the same time Leo and Lady Annabelle both spoke.

'I think it is time for me to retire,' Leo said.

'Please excuse me, it is late and I find myself suddenly weary,' Lady Annabelle murmured.

They both looked at one another for a few seconds and then Lady Annabelle inclined her head and glided from the room. Leo waited for a few seconds and then placed his glass on the tray before bidding Josh and Beth goodnight.

'I should go too,' Beth said as Leo disappeared through the door.

'Sit with me for a moment.'

'I can't.'

'Of course you can. Just a minute. If you sit there and I sit over here by the fireplace we have a good eight feet of space between us, even your mother couldn't object to that.'

'You don't know my mother,' Beth murmured, but she sat all the same.

'You appeared very quickly on the veranda.'

Beth sighed. 'I woke and found Annabelle gone. I

was worried where she might be so thought I would have a look around for her.'

'Is she allowed…?' Josh began, but found he couldn't find the right words to complete the question. He didn't want to sound as if he was questioning Beth's love for her sister—that was apparent by the way they interacted—but he did wonder if the younger woman's exclusion from society was her own choice or her mother's.

'I'm not her keeper,' Beth said sharply. 'I would love nothing more than for Annabelle to attend the balls and dinner parties with me.' She laughed but it was mirthless and bitter. 'You don't know how many times I've begged her to.'

'It's her choice to keep hidden away.'

'Hers and Mother's.'

Josh fell silent, waiting for Beth to elaborate, but instead she stared morosely into the glass in her hand. With a sigh she placed it on the little table beside her and stood.

'I'm restless. Would you join me for a stroll in the gardens? I promise we'll keep well away from the cliff edge.'

'Is that wise?' It felt as though their roles had been reversed. Until this point it had been him pushing Beth to be reckless on occasion and her cautious but willing to be persuaded.

'If we go out of the side door from the dining room, none of the bedrooms look out that way. I doubt anyone will be awake still anyway.'

'Very well.'

They moved silently through the house, Beth taking

a key from inside a cabinet in the dining room to unlock the door before stepping out into the darkness beyond.

For the first few minutes they walked without talking, both conscious they were still close to the house even if none of the bedroom windows faced in this direction. Only once they were a good distance from the house did Beth speak.

'It's my fault, you know.'

'What is?'

'Annabelle, her scars. They're my fault.'

Josh opened his mouth to protest, to tell her she must be mistaken, but quickly clamped it shut again. What did he know? They might very well be her fault, not that he could see the gentle woman beside him doing anything with malice.

'What happened?' he asked instead.

'It was when we were children. When I was five and Annabelle was four. Our nursemaid was sick and Mother was looking after us for the morning.'

Josh couldn't imagine Lady Hummingford as the most maternal towards two little girls, but he listened on intently.

'She needed to speak to Cook about the dinners for the week and Annabelle and I were being loud and playful. So she sent us to play in the drawing room whilst she finished with Cook. She told me to keep an eye on Annabelle, to look after her.' Beth paused, a smile on her face for a moment. 'Annabelle used to be so mischievous and *loved* to climb. We bickered all the way to the drawing room, I can't remember what about, and when we got there I was in a huff.'

Josh felt the tension in Beth's body as she told the

story, heard the building stress in her voice. He wondered if she had ever told it before and instinctively knew she hadn't. This was something very personal, very painful she was sharing with him.

'I don't even know what happened next. I had my doll with me and refused to let Annabelle share, instead turning my back to her. The next thing I knew she was halfway up the bookshelf, climbing like a monkey.' Beth shuddered and he laid a hand over hers as they walked, squeezing it gently.

'I shouted and Annabelle lost her grip, she came tumbling down but pulled half the contents of the bookshelf with her. Including a vase.' She swallowed, her voice strained as she continued. 'The vase smashed on her face and somehow she then managed to fall on top of it, pushing the shards even deeper in.'

Josh pictured Annabelle's scars. The way the skin puckered around them showed the wounds must have been deep and he felt for the scared little girl who must have been in such pain all those years ago.

'It took the doctor two hours to remove all the shards of ceramic. Annabelle had to be heavily medicated, of course, and wore bandages on her face for weeks. When the bandages came off Mother couldn't look at her and Annabelle wasn't the same afterwards. She lost some of her vitality, her spirit.'

Beth fell silent and Josh could see the tears glistening in her eyes. They'd walked a fair distance from the house now and were in a part of the garden that had been allowed to grow wild. The trees were taller here and the grass high on either side of the path. In the moonlight it looked as though they were in an enchanted forest with the pale beams of light streaming through the gaps between the leaves and illuminating sections of the ground below.

'It's tragic,' Josh said slowly. 'Absolutely awful. I feel for your sister, I can't imagine having the course of your life changed by one small accident.' He paused, stopping and waiting until Beth had turned to look at him. 'But you do realise that none of it was your fault.'

'Of course it was. I was meant to be looking after Annabelle and instead I was too busy playing with my doll.'

'You were five years old. If anyone is to blame it is your mother, she left two very young children to their own devices, but actually I'm not sure it is even fair to blame her. It was an accident, a horrible accident with awful consequences, but an accident all the same.'

Beth shook her head stubbornly.

'Do you blame your sister? Do you blame her for being so careless?'

'Of course not.' There was an edge of anger to Beth's voice.

'Then you can't blame yourself. You were five years old.'

For a moment he thought he was getting through to her, but then she shook her head.

'It is my fault,' she said stubbornly.

With those words everything about Beth fell into place. The insistence that she had to be the one to save her family from destitution, the over-the-top protectiveness of her sister, the internal struggle between doing what she wanted and what she thought was expected of her.

'You feel like you owe your sister a life,' he murmured quietly.

Beth looked as though she might protest, but then nodded. The tears that had been brimming in her eyes fell onto her cheeks and Josh felt a surge of affection for her. He wanted to show her none of it was her fault, that she could love her sister, care for her sister, but she didn't have to give up her whole life to make amends for something that was an accident and nothing more. Gently he reached out and wiped away the tears from her cheeks with the pad of his thumb, unapologetically letting his hand linger.

'I do owe her a life. If I'd looked after her better... if I'd stopped her from climbing the bookcase, she wouldn't have been injured, she wouldn't have the scars. She would be out there finding a husband of her own, having a family of her own, having a life of her own. Instead she is shut up here with no prospects and no future.'

'She could have all those things. Not every man is so shallow a few scars would prevent him from seeing the person underneath.'

Beth looked at him long and hard and then sighed. 'I do try to persuade her to leave the house. I begged her to join us for this house party, but people are cruel, Josh. As a child the few times she did come into contact with someone outside the immediate family they would at best stare and at worst make hurtful comments. Not always to her face, she is still the daughter of an earl after all, but she heard them all the same.'

'It can't be much of a life for her, cooped up here.'

'It's not. Some people would say she's lucky, that

she has a comfortable house and plenty of space outdoors, but it is a prison of sorts, even if it is partially of her own making.'

'And your mother?' Josh had never warmed to Lady Hummingford but that mild dislike was turning into outright disgust at how she was treating her daughters.

Beth grimaced, looking off into the distance as if trying to find the words to explain the situation diplomatically.

'She prefers Annabelle to stay here, to stay hidden.'

'Why?'

'I suppose she doesn't want her to get hurt.'

Josh thought that was a charitable view on Lady Hummingford's motivations but didn't challenge Beth. Instead he took her hand, feeling the warmth of her skin on his. Her fingers were long and delicate, the skin wonderfully soft. She seemed to still as he took her hand in his, the restless energy departing and being replaced with a deep calm.

'I know I haven't seen the years of interactions between you and your mother and your sister, and your father when he was still alive, so perhaps I am not in a position to comment on how Annabelle's life could have been different, but I do know you. You're punishing yourself, martyring yourself, to try to make up for the consequences of an accident when you were a small child.'

'I owe it to Annabelle to ensure the life she is comfortable with can continue.'

'No,' Josh said firmly. 'There is nothing wrong with wanting to protect your sister, to do something like marry a wealthy man for the stability of your family, but *this*, this is self-sacrifice for a debt that shouldn't be there.'

Beth looked into his eyes and for a moment he thought he had got through to her. He wanted her to see that she shouldn't feel she had to marry Leo for the sake of her sister. If she chose to, if she decided she wanted to put her family's happiness before her own, that was a different matter entirely, but he wanted her to see it was a conscious choice she had to make, not a foregone conclusion.

She pulled her hand from his and took a few steps away.

He watched her for a moment, not approaching straight away, giving her a minute to go over everything they had discussed. She looked beautiful, ethereal, in the moonlight. Her hair was loose down her back, reaching almost to her buttocks, straight and thick and golden. He had the urge to tangle his hands in it, to inhale the scent of roses he knew she used.

She could be a fairy or elf from the legends the way she looked in amongst the trees. Her light skin contrasted wonderfully with her dark dress and her pale blue eyes sparkled out of the darkness.

'I have to protect her,' Beth said quietly.

Josh nodded, knowing it wouldn't help to argue any more. Perhaps his words would work their way into her mind and, given time, she might see there was some truth there.

'Come.' He walked over to her and wrapped her in his arms, enveloping her entirely. At first she was tense and stiff against him but slowly she relaxed, her own arms looping around his back and her head turning so her cheek was rested against his chest.

Without thinking he dropped a kiss on the top of her hair, closing his eyes and allowing himself to enjoy being so close to her.

They stayed wrapped in one another's arms for a long time, Josh able to feel Beth's heartbeat through the layers that separated them.

'We should go back,' Josh said eventually. He had felt Beth start to shiver and knew they shouldn't stay out any longer despite his inclination to remain all night under the canopy of trees.

Beth nodded and silently they made their way back to the house. He kissed her hand lightly once they were back inside, seeing her hesitate and linger a second, before gaining control of herself and hurrying up the stairs to bed.

Chapter Thirteen

'What did they say about me?' Annabelle tried to sound nonchalant as Beth changed into her riding habit. Her sister had been hovering, as if eager to ask something but not quite sure how to say it.

Beth didn't look up, knowing her sister's world revolved around moments like these, moments where she wondered what other people thought of her, where she hoped not to be noticed but also craved the normality of someone looking at her and seeing just a normal young woman.

'Not much. Leonard Ashburton went to bed at the same time as you. And Josh...' she looked up quickly to see if Annabelle had spotted the familiar use of his name '... Joshua Ashburton was more puzzled as to why you weren't joining us for the festivities than your appearance.'

'He only has eyes for you.'

'You've got the wrong brother. Not that Leonard Ashburton has eyes for me. Much to Mother's disgust.'

'But Joshua Ashburton does.'

Beth looked up from fastening the front of her riding habit and caught Annabelle's knowing look in the mirror.

'I'm not blind, Beth. I might have been preoccupied with my own appearance but even I could see Joshua Ashburton is smitten with you.'

'He is not smitten.'

'Fine. He desires you.'

'He's the wrong brother.'

'Is he?'

'Yes.'

Annabelle shrugged. 'I saw the looks between you, the way your bodies were angled towards one another. There was a synergy there.' She paused, softening her voice. 'I doubt Leonard Ashburton has missed it, unless he is particularly unobservant.'

Beth felt the blood drain from her head and had to sit down abruptly on the edge of the bed.

'What do you mean?'

'Is there something between you and Joshua Ashburton?'

'No. Yes. No.' Beth sighed. 'I like him,' she said eventually. 'As a friend.'

'A friend?'

'Exactly. A friend.' She could feel her cheeks colouring under Annabelle's steady gaze.

'A friend you've kissed?'

'How did you know?'

'I know you, Beth. You've been different ever since coming back from London and I only had to spend ten seconds in that room with you and the Ashburton brothers to see why.'

'It should be Leonard.'

'You can't force an attraction where there isn't one.'

'Leonard's not interested in me. He'll probably marry me, I get the impression he is a man of his word, but I don't think he wants to know anything about me.'

Annabelle pulled a face. 'Hardly the recipe for a happy marriage. Can't you marry Joshua Ashburton instead?'

'No.' It felt like a knife to the heart to hear her sister suggest so casually what she wanted to be true. She wished it were Joshua Ashburton she was promised to in marriage, Joshua Ashburton she was contemplating spending the rest of her life with.

'Don't just dismiss the idea. You like him. He obviously likes you. It's not as though he's an unacceptable match. He's the brother of the future Viscount Abbingdon.'

For a moment Beth felt the tiniest spark of hope and then, with a shake of her head, she let it fizzle out and die.

'You're being ridiculous.'

'You're being ridiculous. Why force yourself to marry someone you do not care for when a man you do is standing right next to him?'

'You don't understand.'

Annabelle raised an eyebrow and Beth was reminded her little sister wasn't a child any longer.

'What don't I understand, Beth? That you are martyring yourself to keep this roof over my head? That you are willing to make yourself miserable for the rest of your life out of some misplaced guilt, some feeling that you owe me for this.' She jabbed forcefully at her scars.

'It's the only way to keep our home.'

Annabelle stepped forward and took her sister's hand and held it to her chest.

'Home isn't a building or a piece of land. It is where you feel happy, where there are people who love you.'

'You and Mother need somewhere to live.'

'But it doesn't have to be here.'

Beth blinked, not understanding.

'We could sell. Pay off the debts. There would be enough left over for a small cottage and a modest yearly income. We don't have to live in a big country estate, pretending everything is as it was when Father was alive.'

'This is our home, Annabelle.'

'Your home will be with your husband, with the family you will one day have.'

'This is your home, then.'

'I would rather you were happy than I got to stay at Birling View whilst knowing I was the reason for your misery.'

'Leonard Ashburton is a good man. So everyone keeps saying.'

'You sound like you're trying to convince yourself.'

'Josh hasn't offered me anything,' Beth said quietly. It was the truth. Despite their kisses, despite their shared attraction, Josh hadn't once even mentioned the future. He hadn't begged her not to marry his brother, hadn't even suggested a future with him was possible.

Frowning, Annabelle walked over to the mirror and stared at her reflection. Beth hesitated, knowing she should go down to the guests but not wanting to leave her sister in the middle of their discussion.

'Where are you going today?' The sudden change of subject threw Beth for a moment.

'For a ride to Seaford. We'll probably stop on the beach for a picnic.'

'All of the guests?'

'I'm not certain. Everyone is invited.'

'And Mother?'

'She has one of her headaches.'

With a resolute nod Annabelle crossed to the wardrobe and pulled her riding habit out.

'I'm coming.'

'What?'

'I'm coming. You keep saying there's no need for me to hide away. The Ashburtons already know about me—it will be odd if I stay hidden. So I'm coming.'

Beth bit her tongue to stop the protest. This was what she had wanted for so long, for Annabelle to socialise, to forget about her scars and step into the world. It didn't feel right though, as if she were doing it for the wrong reasons, but perhaps it was better than not doing it at all.

Silently Beth helped her sister into her riding habit, fastening it at the back and securing the high neck.

They left the bedroom arm in arm and descended the stairs together. Beth could feel her sister trembling despite the smile on her lips and knew what an effort this was taking on Annabelle's part.

'Are you sure?' Beth whispered just before they entered the ballroom.

In answer Annabelle stepped forward. Beth winced as everyone fell silent as her sister entered the room. She looked for Josh, knowing instinctively he would step up and make her sister feel welcome, but he wasn't there.

Five seconds passed, then ten.

'Lady Annabelle, will you be joining us?' To her surprise it was Leonard Ashburton who moved away from the group and greeted her sister first. He bowed over her hand and offered her his arm, drawing her apart from Beth. Annabelle hesitated but after a moment slipped her hand into the crook of his elbow and allowed him to lead her away.

'What happened?' Josh murmured in her ear. He'd just entered the room behind her and was watching his brother and Annabelle taking a turn about the room.

'Annabelle is coming with us.'

Josh remained silent, his eyes boring into her for a long moment before he spoke. 'Good.' He waited for his brother to complete the slow circuit of the room before slipping in to greet her himself.

'Lady Annabelle. I'm so glad you've decided to join us. Lady Elizabeth tells me it is a spectacular ride across the cliffs.'

'It is our favourite, over the Seven Sisters to Cuckmere and then across the river to Seaford Head.'

'What a beautiful riding habit,' Theodora Potterton said, placing a hand on Annabelle's arm.

'The colour suits you,' Henrietta Potterton added.

Beth felt some of the tension seeping from her shoulders as the conversation continued. It was a little forced, a little stilted, but no one was being cruel to Annabelle, no one was drawing attention to her scars. In fact, they were all too polite to even mention the fact that they hadn't known Annabelle existed.

As they walked out to the stable block Josh slipped into step beside her.

'You persuaded her to come.' His voice was warm and approving.

'No, she suggested it.'

'Why now?'

Feeling the heat rising in her cheeks, she quickened her pace, hoping Josh wouldn't notice.

'I don't know.'

She thought he would challenge her, but he just shrugged and pushed on ahead to the stables.

'Your sister is making quite the effort with Leo,' Josh observed, pulling his reins so his horse edged closer to Beth's.

They were at the back of the party. Annabelle and Leo had ridden on ahead, Mr Ralph and Mr Williams were in the middle with one of the Potterton sisters on either side, and Josh and Beth had allowed their horses to choose their own sedate pace for the hilly terrain and now trailed at least a hundred feet behind.

'I think she is concerned about my future.'

'Good.'

'Good?'

'Well, someone has to be.'

Beth looked at him sharply. '*I'm* very concerned about my future.'

'You're concerned with doing the right thing by other people. I have a feeling your sister is making sure it is the right choice for you.'

'Are you saying I shouldn't marry your brother?'

'No.'

'Then what are you saying?'

'*If* you decide to marry my brother it should be because you want to, not because it is what is expected of you.'

'Do you even know how the world works? No debutante has a choice in who she marries, not really. Perhaps one or two a season marry for love and a handful more get a modicum of choice between this or that suitor, but the rest do what they are told by their parents. Marriages are arranged. This isn't a peculiar situation.'

Josh watched her stiff posture, noting the white of her knuckles as she gripped the reins hard and the minuscule muscle in her jaw, which she clenched.

'Now, I don't want to talk of my future or my marriage any more. Please can we speak of something else? Anything else.'

Josh knew to back down. The last thing he wanted to do was add to her stress.

'Tell me about the smugglers.'

'Smugglers?'

'You must have them here. It's a prime spot for it, only a couple of days' ride from London and a sparsely populated area.'

They crested the top of a hill and below them the river Cuckmere wound its way towards the sea. It was another warm day, overcast but with some breaks in the cloud, and as they looked at the landscape below them the sun peeked out and made the river below glitter.

'See down there.' Beth pointed to the estuary, the wide mouth of the river seeming to welcome the sea. 'That's where they land, or so Father used to say. The river is tidal and at high tide small boats can actually row into the river and upstream to one of dozens of potential unloading points. It is what makes it so hard to catch them.'

'Fascinating. Have you ever seen them?'

'Father was always insistent we stay in the boundaries of the estate after dark, and we are a half an hour's ride away from the river.' She paused, her eyes alive with excitement. 'But I do remember one time when I was nine or ten. It was late, everyone was in bed, but I awoke to hear a commotion downstairs. I crept down to see the front door open and a man slumped against the frame, bleeding.'

'A smuggler?'

Beth nodded. 'A trap had been set for them and most of the gang caught, but this man had escaped after being run through with a sword. We could never work out how he managed to make it so far with such horrific injuries.'

'What happened?'

'The King's men were in pursuit and arrived a few minutes later and hauled the man away. I doubt he would have lasted the journey to the local gaol.' Nudging her horse forward, she waited for Josh to join her again. 'Father increased the number of strong young men he employed for a while and would set them to patrolling around the perimeter of the estate at night, but of course that wasn't sustainable.'

'You think it still goes on?'

'Of course. It is a perfect unloading point for smugglers, and although the Custom's Officers are aware of it there isn't a settlement for miles. It makes it hard to patrol, hard to monitor, so for the smugglers it is still a good choice.'

The hill here was so steep they couldn't ride straight to the bottom, instead having to snake backwards and forwards across the grass to weave their way down.

'We will have to make sure we do not dally too long in Seaford—as much as I would find it fascinating to meet a smuggler, I think they would be far less interested in meeting me.'

They stopped down by the river, gathering in a little group as they discussed which was the best way to cross.

'It's low tide so we could ride across. There is the chance of getting a little damp, but it is quite safe. I've done it hundreds of times,' Beth said, seeing Leonard Ashburton's dubious face.

'Or for those who would prefer to stay dry there is the bridge a mile or so upstream.' Lady Annabelle spoke quietly, as if she was reluctant to draw attention to herself.

'I vote for crossing the river here,' Josh said. The area where he lived in India had many little streams that didn't have bridges. It was often the choice between riding across or a two- or three-day diversion upstream.

'It is quite wide,' Leo said dubiously. 'If you get stuck in the mud it could be the end of the horse.'

'I would never risk Willow. It is quite safe,' Beth said firmly.

'Mr Ashburton, I am planning on riding up to the bridge if you would be so kind as to accompany me. Anyone else who would like to is welcome too,' Lady Annabelle said diplomatically. She might not have the benefit of experience in society but the natural diplomacy of being born into an aristocratic family and raised as such was showing through.

The Potterton sisters decided immediately to join Annabelle and Leo and after a moment's discussion Mr Ralph and Mr Williams turned their horses towards the bridge too.

'Be careful,' Leo said, directing his words to Josh rather than Beth.

'We'll see you on the beach in Seaford,' Beth said with a forced smile.

'Something wrong?' Josh spoke quietly, waiting until the others were out of earshot to enquire.

'He is meant to be getting to know me. That was *his* suggestion, not mine. It was his idea to spend six weeks getting to know me, seeing if we would suit.'

Sensibly Josh remained silent, allowing Beth to continue her outburst.

'He's spent a total of about ten minutes in my company since. I know I probably wouldn't be who he chose for a wife if he hadn't made my father that stupid promise, but either he should reject me or he should actually make a little effort to get to know me.'

'Can I tell you something?' Josh waited for Beth to nod before he continued. 'This six weeks isn't for Leo. He takes his promise to your father very seriously and will abide by it. He is taking a little longer for you, for you to decide if you want to marry a man you don't know and don't particularly care for.'

Beth bit her lip. 'Mother will be pleased.' She sounded totally and utterly miserable. 'So if I told him tomorrow I was sure I wanted to marry him...'

'He would announce your engagement.'

Beth nodded.

'Will you?'

Slowly she shook her head. 'Perhaps another week, just to be completely sure, isn't such a bad idea.'

'Come. Show me where we're going to cross the river.'

Beth led the way to the bank close to the beach. Josh could see she'd been right even before his horse stepped into the water. It was shallow, so shallow he could make out the bottom. Aside from a few splashes from the horses' hooves it was a dry crossing and they were on the opposite bank in no time at all.

'Race you to the top of the cliff,' Beth said, the frown from minutes earlier replaced by an impish grin. She'd already set off before she'd finished issuing the challenge and Josh had to urge his horse on in an attempt to catch up.

As they rode Beth's hair began to stream out behind her, whipped by the wind from the pins that held it up.

She won, only by a second, but it was a victory all the same and Josh quickly dismounted to pick her a solitary purple flower as her prize. As he passed it up to her their fingers brushed and Josh's eyes flicked up to meet Beth's. He saw the desire flare, saw the minuscule movement of her leg so it pressed against his hand. Without thinking of the consequences he placed his hand just above her knee, feeling the firm muscle underneath her riding habit. From there it would be so easy to walk his fingers up her thigh and... Quickly he dismissed the thought. They were out in public, out in the open, and the rest of the party could be along at any moment. Even so it was too difficult to pull his

hand away. He lingered, fighting the image in his mind
of him lifting Beth from the saddle and tumbling her
into the long grass. With great effort he pulled away
and watched as she wove the flower into her hair, the
purple contrasting beautifully with the honey blonde.
All the time her eyes were locked on his and he felt as
though he'd been mesmerised by a nymph or a god-
dess from the ancient Greek myths he'd loved when
he was a boy.

'It is only ten minutes to Seaford from here,' she
said, pointing across the cliff to where the terrain
rolled slowly down to the little seaside town. Her voice
contained a slight quiver, just enough to tell him she
was as on edge as he was, wanting everything they
couldn't have.

Chapter Fourteen

Beth lay back on the sand and closed her eyes. Her mother would be horrified if she could see her with her face turned up to the sun and no bonnet or parasol in sight, but for once Beth did not care. She felt happy here with the sound of the waves lapping at the beach, interspersed with the swish and plop of the stones Josh was skimming across the water.

'Six,' he murmured before bending next to her and picking up another stone.

'I've never been able to skim stones,' Beth said sleepily. She felt contented, as if she could lie here for days, not having to think about the real world. 'My father could, and I can remember him trying to teach Mother and Annabelle and me, but I just couldn't ever seem to make them skip across the water.'

'Come here,' Josh said, offering her his hand and pulling her to her feet. 'It's all in the wrist action.'

He demonstrated, choosing a flat pebble and showing her how to hold it in her hand and position her feet.

'You have to do a sharp flick of the wrist and end

up with your hand pointing in the direction you want your stone to go.'

Beth picked up a pebble of her own and weighed it in her hand. She positioned herself as he'd instructed and tried a few practice flicks before releasing the stone. It sank with a loud plop under the gentle waves without skipping even once across the water.

'Try again,' Josh prompted, watching critically as Beth flicked the pebble from her wrist.

Again it hit the water heavily and sank immediately.

'I told you. I practised and practised when I was a child and I just could never get it.'

Josh stepped in closer and suddenly Beth was acutely aware of the fact they were all alone on the beach. A few couples strolled arm in arm along the promenade a hundred feet away, but there was no one actually on the beach with them.

'Here. Position yourself a little more to the side.' He looped an arm around her waist and shifted her stance by a few inches. 'Then sway your hips just a fraction, twist and then flick your wrist.' He picked up a stone and placed it in her hand and then held her waist. Every conscious thought left Beth's mind and all she could think about was Josh's body close to her, his touch, his heartbeat in time with hers.

Gently he guided her through the movements and Beth released the pebble, gasping with delight as it skipped three times over the water.

'I did it.'

'You did it. Let's go again.'

Again he guided her body, his hand resting on the

back of hers and applying just the lightest of pressure
to show her when to flick and when to release.

'Four,' she counted, amazed at how much pleasure
this simple game was giving her.

'Do you want to try by yourself?'

It would mean Josh stepping away; it would mean
the end to the wonderful closeness of his body. Quickly
she shook her head, even though she knew their prox-
imity was foolish.

'One more,' she said, feeling him move an inch
closer. For a moment she closed her eyes and allowed
herself the pleasure of standing on the beach with this
man whose company she enjoyed so much.

'One more time,' he repeated, guiding her as if they
were coupled in a dance until the pebble skimmed over
the gentle waves.

'You're a good teacher,' Beth said, leaning her head
back a little so she could look up at him. He smiled
down at her. There was warmth in his eyes, but she also
sensed some of the desire she'd seen up on the clifftop
as he'd handed her the flower. Every time she looked
at him, every time she saw the desire flare and burn,
she wanted to forget that she was meant to be an im-
peccably behaved young lady and give herself to him
completely. His hand rested casually on her waist, his
fingers pressing through the riding habit as if searching for the skin below. Beth knew he was as conscious
of her as she was of him, but somehow he still seemed
to be able to maintain a normal conversation.

'Thank you. You're a good student.'

Beth laughed. 'My governess didn't always think so.'

'I can't believe you were mischievous?'

'We had a *very* dull governess when we were growing up. Our lessons were hours on end of her reading something from a book in a flat voice. Even a saint would have had to find some other way of amusing themselves.'

'What did you do?'

'We would play little tricks on her, nothing malicious, just things like changing around bits of furniture when she stepped out of the room or bringing small creatures into the schoolroom. Mainly to see if she noticed and to try to get a reaction from her.'

'Did you succeed?'

Beth grimaced. 'At the time we thought she was completely in her own world, seeming not to notice when her chair was moved from one side of the room to the other or the tables turned around, but, looking back, I think she just chose to ignore the behaviour.'

'Certainly one tactic,' Josh said with a smile.

'What about you? Did you go to school or were you educated at home by a tutor?'

'A little of both. I had a tutor until I was twelve and then spent a few years boarding at a very small school. It was for the children of the wealthy British and at one point only had eight pupils.'

She liked hearing about his life in India, liked imagining the totally different way he had been raised. It was fascinating, thinking about how the British had transported their culture halfway across the world and clung to it, all the while letting just a little of the local customs slip in.

Josh stepped away and sat down on the pebbles and

Beth was about to join him when he began pulling at his boots.

'What are you doing?'

'Taking off my boots.'

'I can see that. Why?'

'I've never been able to go to the beach and resist a paddle in the sea.'

'This is a bit different from one of your Indian beaches.'

'It's still the sea.'

'A much colder sea.'

He looked up at her, an encouraging smile on his face, and Beth had the realisation that she would do anything this man suggested. It wasn't logical, but it was a fact. He could persuade her to climb a tree in just her undergarments if he wanted to.

'Come on. The others will still be a while. There's no one else here. We can paddle our feet and still have time to sit in the sun and dry off before they arrive. No one will ever know.'

Beth had loved dipping her toes in the sea as a girl and had often enjoyed swimming from one of the safer beaches in the area when she was a child, but as she had grown older it had been drummed into her that daughters of earls did not take their boots off in public no matter how inviting the sea looked.

Glancing over her shoulder, she tried to calculate how long it would be before Annabelle and their guests arrived in Seaford. It was quite a detour up the river to get to the bridge and she thought Josh was probably right—they would have plenty of time to put their boots back on before anyone appeared over the crest of the hill. For a moment longer she hesitated, wondering what Leonard Ashburton would think if he found her barefoot on the seashore. She didn't think he would approve.

Let him disapprove, a rebellious voice in her head protested. If he was that bothered by her enjoying the cool water on her toes on a deserted beach, then perhaps he should find himself another wife.

'Just for a minute,' she said, sitting down next to Josh and pulling at her boots.

The water was cold, icily so, and Beth was reminded that, although the air temperature was unseasonably warm, it was still only May. The sea hadn't had the chance to warm up yet and as the gentle waves lapped at her toes she felt them start to tingle before going ever so slightly numb.

'This is glorious,' Josh declared, happily splashing along in the sea. He had rolled up his breeches to just below the knee but she could see splashes on the material as high up as his thighs. It didn't seem to bother him.

'Do you swim in the sea in India?'

'Oh, yes. There is a beach about a half an hour's ride away with the most beautiful golden-white sand and the sea is so clear you can see the bottom even twenty feet from the shore. I try to get there at least once a week for a swim and sometimes just sit on the beach, contemplating the view.'

Josh always seemed animated, always active but, as with his taking time with the sunsets, she liked that despite his hectic life he still managed to find time to pause. It was something she was bad about, something she didn't do enough. There always seemed to be something to fill her time: dresses to be altered, the garden to be tended, appearances to be kept up. A hundred different little jobs that meant she hardly ever just sat and enjoyed the moment.

'I wish...' she began and then trailed off. She was at risk of saying something she shouldn't.

'You wish...?' Josh prompted her, his hand reaching out reflexively for hers. He didn't take it, instead brushing the tips of his fingers against hers, which somehow felt more intimate than if he'd simply taken her hand. Beth swallowed, forcing herself to focus on the conversation lest she say or do something she might regret.

'I wish I could see this beach of yours. And the home you speak so fondly of, the rolling hills and the lush landscape. It all sounds so exotic, so wonderful.'

'Perhaps you will one day,' he said.

'As your sister-in-law.'

They both fell silent.

'Annabelle is annoyed with me. She said I was being a martyr too.'

Josh smiled at this, and Beth found herself smiling too. She *could* be stubborn sometimes.

'Why did she say you were being a martyr?'

'She doesn't want me to marry for her sake. She would rather I wait for someone I care more for.'

Josh nodded slowly, his eyes fixed out to sea and his expression suddenly serious.

'She said Mother could sell the house, cover the debts that way, and that they would have enough for a modest yearly income and a small house.'

'So you agree your mother is choosing maintaining appearances over you.'

'No.' Beth felt the need to defend her mother. Josh had not seen her in a good light, and Lady Hummingford could be single-minded, but she did love her and Annabelle, as well. Her mother was concerned with maintaining the pretence that they were still wealthy, still one of the lucky few families to be in the upper echelons of society.

Turning to study her, he shook his head slowly, reaching out and this time taking her hand before raising it to his lips.

'It is possible to be too good, too selfless, in this world, Beth. Not everyone is as kind as you and they will often take advantage of that.'

His eyes were warm and dark and she could see herself reflected in them. She wanted to ask him if there were even the possibility of a chance for them. *If* she refused his brother, *if* she defied her mother, *if* she chose her own happiness over anyone else's…but there were too many obstacles in the way.

'Perhaps—' he began, but cut himself off with a frown on his face.

Beth spun to see what he was looking at.

On the beach just a few feet away was a seagull, one of the hundreds that soared and glided through the sky in the area. This one was squawking and flapping about on the beach in distress, one wing caught in a scrap of a fisherman's net. It kept trying to fly away but the net hampered its ability to get off the ground and with every attempt it just entangled itself even further.

Josh approached the bird slowly, taking his time to make it aware of his presence. As he reached out the bird went for his fingers, pecking and nipping, but Josh was too quick. Carefully he took the bird in both hands, holding the dangerous beak away from his body whilst he deftly unwrapped the fishing net. Once the bird was freed he quickly inspected the wing and then held the bird up to the sky to let it fly away.

They both watched until the bird was no more than a speck in amongst the gathering clouds.

Beth turned back to Josh but as she did so a movement at the periphery of her vision caught her eye. With disbelief she watched as Annabelle, Leonard Ashburton and their other guests came into sight along the beach. They had covered the distance quickly, either that or she had lost track of time here in the sea with Josh. She looked down at the wet hem of her dress and her sandy toes and felt her heart sinking, momentarily wondering if she was subconsciously trying to sabotage her chance of marrying Leonard Ashburton.

'Lady Elizabeth,' Leonard Ashburton said, looking her up and down as he dismounted. He was the first across the sand and all the time she could see his eyes flitting between her and his brother. 'I see you are enjoying the sea.'

'It is quite refreshing. Perhaps I can tempt you to join us?'

'No,' he said curtly. 'I do not paddle.'

'Oh?' She couldn't think of anything else to say.

'No.'

'Come on, Leo, the water is lovely.'

Leonard Ashburton frowned at his brother.

'I think we need to talk, Josh,' he said in a way that allowed no argument. Beth felt as though all the air had been knocked from her chest as she saw the two brothers communicate silently, both glancing at her. He knew; he must do. Leonard Ashburton had guessed that the woman who was meant to be trying to become his wife had fallen for his brother.

All of a sudden she felt light-headed, but knew she couldn't reach out and clutch at Josh's arm. That would only make things a hundred times worse.

'Leo…'

'It's important, Josh.'

Josh nodded, his face serious. 'Shall we meet you back at the house?'

The words stuck in Beth's throat, her reply coming out as a croak. Josh peered at her but didn't say anything, sparing any more attention being directed towards her. She watched as Josh pulled on his boots and took his horse by the reins and set off with his brother away from her along the beach.

'Perhaps it is for the best,' Annabelle murmured quietly in her ear. Her sister had dismounted and squeezed Beth's hand, before turning to the rest of the guests and suggesting they spend an hour or so relaxing on the sand before they returned to Birling View.

Chapter Fifteen

'I don't profess to know much about love,' Leo said quietly, his eyes fixed on a spot in the distance. Josh waited for him to continue but for now nothing more was forthcoming.

'You're thinking of your impending marriage.'

Leo grimaced. 'I think it is quite clear to the both of us *that* won't be happening.'

'What do you mean?'

'I'm not going to marry the woman you're in love with.'

Josh laughed, but the laugh trailed off as he realised his brother was being serious.

'I'm not in love with her.'

'I know most people find it strange, this bond we have despite not seeing one another for twenty-five years, Josh, but you are my brother and I know you. Don't ask me to explain how, but I do. I see how you look at Lady Elizabeth, how you smile when she is around. There is something between the two of you.'

Opening his mouth to protest again, Josh instead forced himself to take a moment. He needed to con-

sider if what his brother was saying was true. There was
something between him and Beth, something more than
the desire that seemed to simmer between them whenever they were within one another's sight. He liked her,
liked the way she took a moment to consider her words
before speaking, the way her face was transformed by a
smile. He liked how she really listened when he spoke
and how she couldn't help but reveal her inner thoughts
when he asked.

'I admire Lady Elizabeth,' Josh said slowly and then
shook his head violently. 'Damn it, Leo, I can't lie to
you.'

They were walking along the beach on the wet sand
a few feet from the sea, away from the cliffs they had
ridden over half an hour previously. Somewhere behind
them Beth and her sister would be doing their best to
smile and entertain the other guests, all the while wondering what Josh and Leo were discussing and what
implications it had for their future.

The tension in his neck and shoulders was giving him
a headache and although he knew he was holding every
muscle in his body tense he just couldn't seem to relax.
It was laughable really—he'd calmed unhappy workers, negotiated with the toughest businessmen in India
and carved out a future for his guardian's company in
the international market but he couldn't find the words
to express how he felt for Beth.

Leo placed a gentle hand on his shoulder and waited
for Josh to look up.

'Sit with me. Let's talk. Properly talk.'

Josh nodded. He knew he was the only one to see
this side of his brother, that most of society thought

Leo was abrupt and unfriendly, but to him he was exactly what a big brother should be: full of kindness and wanting to guide him.

'I kissed her, Leo,' he said, making sure the words were clear even though his voice was quiet. He didn't want to have to repeat the statement. 'I should have told you. I'm sorry.'

'I expect it wasn't yourself you were thinking of.'

Josh nodded. He'd kept the secret for Beth and felt as if it was a betrayal telling his brother now, but there was a difference between omitting telling Leo and lying to him. He couldn't lie to his brother.

'Tell me what has developed between you.'

'She's a very special woman. Kind and funny and great company.'

'It isn't just physical attraction, then?'

Josh shook his head. 'No, although...'

'Lady Elizabeth is a pretty young woman.' Leo said it in a disconnected sort of way, as if he could appreciate her beauty but was not affected by it.

'We've spent a fair bit of time together, at the pleasure gardens and at the opera. I bumped into her in the park.' It sounded to his ears as though he were trying to justify his feelings for her. In reality he didn't know what the outcome of this all would be. Leo didn't seem angry though, more concerned about Josh than anything else.

'Yet she still arranges this house party to try to further the prospect of our engagement. Does she feel the same way about you as you do about her?'

Josh held out his arms in a gesture that was supposed to mean he was unsure, but after a moment he dropped them to his side. If he stopped and thought about it, he did know.

'Yes.' The attraction between them had always been mutual, from the very first time they'd set eyes upon each other in Leo's garden to the kisses they'd shared just yesterday. It hadn't been one-sided, hadn't been him pushing the issue. She had felt it just as much as him. 'She knows her duty, but she doesn't like it.'

Leo smiled wryly then, one of the first self-deprecating smiles Josh had seen on his brother's face since his return to England.

'I never thought I would be such an unpalatable choice for a husband.' In anyone else Josh would think the words carried bitterness, but Leo was so detached from the idea of his marriage that he sounded more perplexed than anything else. 'Surely the answer is that I discreetly withdraw and you two marry.'

If only it were that simple.

'I understand they are relying on your status and wealth to appease their debtors. Unfortunately an unknown second son just will not do.'

'Ah. I think I'm starting to understand. Lady Hummingford has impressed the importance of duty on Lady Elizabeth.'

'Exactly, and Beth feels a responsibility towards her sister. She doesn't want her to lose her home.'

'What do you want, Josh?' Leo asked suddenly, turning all the intensity of his gaze on his brother.

Josh ran his hand through his hair and looked out over the sparkling blue-grey water.

'Aside from the impossible?'

'She's the daughter of an earl, albeit an earl who was in severe debt. You cannot have a dalliance with her.'

'I know. I know respectable young ladies do not have short affairs with second sons about to leave the country for good.'

'They don't have short affairs with anyone.'

'It's impossible.'

'You have two choices,' Leo said in the infuriatingly calm and sensible way of his. 'Either you marry her or you forget about her.'

'What if I can't do either?' He couldn't forget about her, even if he tried. Beth was firmly lodged in his heart and mind and never would he forget her. That left marriage, and even if you took away all the obstacles that prevented her from saying yes to him he still wasn't sure that would be the right thing for them.

'Why can't you marry her? Aside from the fact her mother wants my money, my reputation?'

'Aside from that?' Josh had to laugh at the easy way his brother dismissed the main factor driving Beth's actions these last few weeks. 'I have to return to India.'

'I know very well men have wives in India.'

He couldn't argue with that. Of course they had wives, English wives. Perhaps not daughters of earls, but gently bred women.

'I need to focus on the business. My guardian…' It wasn't fair to use his guardian as a reason. Mr Usbourne cared about his business, but he also wanted Josh's happiness and had often remarked Josh might be happier with a wife by his side. It was more complicated than that, more nuanced.

Josh fell silent, watching his boots as they walked

across the beach, feeling the faint suck each time he lifted his foot up from the wet sand.

'It wasn't what I pictured for myself,' he said eventually, feeling like a cad. He wanted Beth but he wasn't prepared to change his own image of the future for her.

Leo nodded, his expression remaining serious. 'It isn't what you expected, what you thought would happen. When you have planned your life, planned your future, for so long it can be difficult to accept when something comes along unexpectedly and makes you consider your choices.' He paused, coming to a stop and facing Josh. 'Let me make this easy for you. I will make some excuse, leave the house party for a few days. You consider whether you want to try for a future with Lady Elizabeth.'

'What will you do about a wife?'

'I'm sure I'll find one before Lord Abbingdon shuffles off to face his maker. The man is remarkably robust for an invalid. And if you decide Lady Elizabeth is not the woman you wish to spend your life with—' he shrugged, looking at the horizon '—I still have a debt to settle.'

Chapter Sixteen

'What have you said to him?' Lady Hummingford was red in the face and Beth knew it was taking all of her mother's self-control to whisper the words instead of shout and scream as she really wanted to.

'Nothing at all, Mother. He apologised and said he needed to travel urgently to see Lord Abbingdon. I don't think it was an excuse.'

'Of course it is an excuse. You have spent no time with him. You have ignored him, neglected him. A man wants to feel valued, the centre of your world. This is the most important thing I have ever asked of you, Elizabeth, and you've treated it with contempt.'

'That's not fair.'

'Do you know what will not be fair?' Her mother leaned in close, her mouth drawn into a tight line and her forehead puckered with a frown. 'It will not be fair when your sister is turned out onto the street. No one will marry *her*. She will be penniless and homeless and you could have prevented that.'

Beth felt the tears well up in her eyes. When she had

been with Josh or Annabelle she had begun to believe they were right. It wasn't fair to blame her five-year-old self for the accident that had disfigured her sister, but standing here with her mother she felt the familiar guilt, the familiar sense of duty.

'Go,' her mother said harshly. 'I need to try to see what I can salvage from this mess.'

Beth pressed her lips together to stop her from saying something she might regret. However cruel her mother's words, there was truth in them. Beth hadn't committed fully to making Leonard Ashburton want to marry her and the consequence was his lack of interest. The lack of interest that would see them lose their family home.

With as much dignity as she could muster Beth fled her mother's private drawing room, hoping none of their guests were in the hall as one kind word, one friendly smile, and she would dissolve in a mess of tears.

She'd almost made it to the stairs, head down and teeth biting her lip so hard it was nearly drawing blood, when she barrelled into Josh.

'Slow down,' he said, gripping her by the upper arms to steady her as she bounced off him. She looked up, which was a big mistake. The concern blossomed on his face as her tears began streaming. 'Don't cry, Beth,' he said softly, and even though they were in the middle of her mother's house, even though anyone could walk past, anyone could see, he drew her into his chest and held her.

His arms were strong and reassuring wrapped around her and the thump of his heart in his chest soothed her and after thirty seconds she felt strong enough to pull away.

'It's all over,' she said quietly, hearing her voice catch in her throat. Even now, even with the feeling of devastation at what she had caused, a small part of her still felt relief, and that was probably the worst part. She would always have to live with knowing she could have done more, could have put more effort in.

For a long moment Josh didn't say anything and then he took her by the hand and pulled her silently through the house. It was only luck they didn't see anyone else as they left through the open doors in the library, skirting round the edge of the terrace into the garden. Josh remained quiet as he led her zigzagging backwards and forwards over the scraggy garden paths to the summer house.

Once inside they sat side by side on one of the benches, facing the direction of the house to better see if anyone was approaching their private sanctuary.

'I hoped to catch you before you spoke to your mother.'

'You knew?' It was a pointless question. As enigmatic and aloof as Leonard Ashburton was, he had an undeniable soft spot for his brother. He might leave with only a cursory explanation to her, but Josh would have received much more from his brother.

'Yesterday...' he began, looking out of the summer house into the distance '...on the beach after we...' It was unlike him to struggle to find the right words.

Yesterday Leonard Ashburton had summoned his brother for a private talk as they walked along the beach. Beth had yearned to know what they had discussed but she'd had to return to Birling View with the rest of the guests and then Josh had been surprisingly absent for the evening meal and after-dinner card games.

'When Leo arrived on the beach yesterday what he saw between me and you confirmed what he has suspected for a while.'

Beth felt some of the blood drain from her face and leave her with a horrible sick feeling in the pit of her stomach.

'What did he suspect?'

'That I care for you. That there is something between us.' He reached out and placed his hand on the wooden bench next to hers so their fingertips were just touching. 'He asked me directly what was going on with us, and I couldn't lie to him.'

Beth shook her head. She knew how it was with a sibling you loved dearly. She could never lie to Annabelle, not if asked a direct question. Her conscience allowed her to omit a few details here and there, but never to lie outright to Annabelle. She couldn't ask any more of Josh than she could give herself.

'I told him about the kisses, about how I care for you.'

'Was he angry?'

'Not at all.'

Beth grimaced but found she was too interested in what had happened next to dwell on Leonard Ashburton's indifference to her.

'So he's gone.'

'Yes. Temporarily at least.'

'Temporarily?' None of it was making much sense.

'He wants me to be happy.' Josh sighed heavily. 'Sometimes I think he's more concerned with my happiness than his own. I don't know if it is guilt that he got to stay here after our parents died, that he is the one who will inherit, that he has had the life that should have been both of ours, but he is very invested in my happiness.'

Beth looked up sharply. She felt her heart start to pound in her chest and her skin begin to tingle. This sounded like a build-up to a declaration, a declaration that could change her whole world, her whole life.

'He didn't want to be an obstacle between us, if we had a chance at happiness together. I told him I couldn't give you what you really needed, the funds to save your family home, but he insisted I consider my future anyway.'

Her lungs began to burn and she realised she was holding her breath.

'I've never felt this way about anyone, Beth. Never.' Josh picked up her hand and she knew that if he told her he loved her then she was lost. She might hate herself for failing to do her duty, for failing her sister, but she wouldn't be able to resist him if he promised her love. 'I know you are determined to marry for duty, to marry someone who can take your family out of debt. I'm not that man. I'm well off, but all my money is tied to the business. One day I will have funds, but not for a few years. If we decided to be together your family would probably lose Birling View.' He paused as if waiting for her to say something, anything, but Beth's head was swimming. It wasn't a declaration of love, but it sounded very much as though he was proposing a future together. Marriage, a whole life by one another's sides.

'I don't know what to say.' Her head was spinning,

her heart surging at the thought of spending a lifetime with Josh but her mind telling her not to be selfish, not to forget her mother and sister.

'Don't say anything, not yet. Let me have today. One day with you to myself and perhaps at the end things will be a little clearer for both of us.'

It didn't seem that much to ask, although Beth couldn't see how anything would be clearer after one day.

'What will we do?'

'Anything we desire. With one another. Up until now everything we've done has felt illicit, tainted by the knowledge that it should be Leo you're spending time with. Let's have one day without any guilt, without any expectation, just to enjoy one another without thinking too much about the future.'

It wasn't something she could say no to. It sounded so perfect, so exquisite, and whatever they decided at the end of the day at least they would have had this one day together.

'You should know Leo said if we decided we did not have a future together and you are still keen for your marriage to him to go ahead he will honour his promise to your father. You should know you have that option.'

Silently Beth nodded. She couldn't imagine marrying Leonard Ashburton, not now.

'Where are we going first?' Beth asked, resolving not to think of the future until much later today. For now she was going to enjoy herself.

'First we need to raid the kitchen. It is going to be a long day and we will need sustenance.'

'Mrs Turner will chase us out.'

'Nonsense. If I can't charm your cook, then I'll eat some of the horse's hay for lunch instead.'

Beth laughed. It felt good just to let go even if she knew all of her problems would still be there this evening.

They half walked, half ran back to the house, ducking behind a scraggly hedge when they spotted Mr Ralph strolling leisurely through the garden. Bursting into the kitchen breathless earned them a sour look from Mrs Turner, and Beth was certain however charming Josh could be wouldn't be enough to convince their grouchy cook to spend precious time packing them provisions for their day of freedom.

'You weren't lying, Lady Elizabeth. I take it back.'

He winked at her, prompting her to play along.

'A lady never lies, Mr Ashburton.'

'This must be the industrious Mrs Turner.' He took her flour-covered hand and bowed over it as if she were the queen of Spain.

'Indeed,' Mrs Turner said, as yet unimpressed by Josh's charm.

'Lady Elizabeth told me you ran the kitchen all by yourself and I refused to believe her. Not after those exquisite soufflés last night.'

Somehow he'd picked exactly the right thing to compliment Mrs Turner on and before Beth's eyes the older woman visibly softened.

'They were far from my best. The kitchen is too far from the dining room to do them justice. A soufflé should be served straight from the oven.'

'If they were not your best, Mrs Turner, I do not think the world is ready for your best. I for one would refuse to leave Birling View, waiting each day for one of your delicious soufflés.'

It was too much, surely it was too much. He was being too effusive, too over the top, but to Beth's amazement Mrs Turner was actually blushing. This was the woman who had chased her and Annabelle from the kitchens even as grown adults, muttering that it was her domain and they should stick to waltzing around upstairs. Now Beth was wondering if she was about to start fluttering her eyelashes at Josh.

'I wonder, Mrs Turner,' Josh said, leaning in conspiratorially, 'if I might ask a favour.' He held his hands up quickly, continuing to talk before she had a chance to answer. 'I wouldn't dream of asking you to pack a picnic for us, I know how much you have to do cooking for all the other guests, but would you mind terribly if Lady Elizabeth and I took an apple or two and perhaps a few slices of bread for our picnic?'

There was a long silence and Beth thought she was going to throw them both out of her kitchen.

'I can't have just anyone rummaging through my kitchen.'

He flashed her his most charming smile.

'But if you sit down I'll pack you a little basket you can take out with you.'

Josh sat, taking a biscuit from the tray fresh out of the oven when offered and making all the right noises. Mrs Turner offered Beth one as an afterthought and Beth had the sense to munch on it quietly, being as unobtrusive as possible.

Ten minutes later, heavy picnic basket in hand, they

left the kitchen. It felt illicit, exciting, and Beth felt her heart lightening as they slipped through the hall.

'Enjoy yourself,' Annabelle's soft voice called out from the shadows of the hallway. Beth spun and smiled at her sister, feeling the familiar guilt as she realised that once again she was going to enjoy the day whilst Annabelle stayed cloistered inside. Quickly Beth turned back and grasped her sister's hand.

'Go,' Annabelle urged.

'I'll stop by the village before the shop closes tonight and pick you up that book I promised you,' Beth said, leaning in and kissing her sister on her cheek.

'Thank you.'

Beth turned and stepped away, casting one final look back over her shoulder at Annabelle.

Chapter Seventeen

They didn't take the horses, instead choosing to walk over the grassy cliffs, heading east from Birling View up the steep hills that climbed towards Beachy Head. It was another warm day but there was a pleasant light breeze that stopped it from feeling unbearable as they strolled arm in arm.

'I remember coming to the seaside in England when I was a boy,' Josh said as they stood at the top of the cliffs, looking out over the sea below. As always it was crashing against the cliffs here; even on a completely calm day the waves were impressive around the point of the coastline. 'I don't know where it was but, given our family home was in Kent, it makes sense it would have been somewhere not that far from here.'

'I can't imagine only remembering fragments of my time in the country where I was born.'

'I don't think of it as home, just a distant memory of somewhere I used to live.'

'Are you glad you came back?'

'Yes.' It was said without hesitation, and he realised

he didn't have to think about it. There had been so many good things about coming to England, so many important things. It was worth the six-month voyage in both directions, worth a year of his life spent at sea even for a few short months in the country. 'I would choose to do the same again in a heartbeat.' He offered Beth his arm and they continued their leisurely stroll before he continued. 'Before I left India I was aware how lucky I was. I had the business waiting for me, a future. I had people who loved me, friends, a life. Despite all that I felt as though a part of me was missing.'

'Your family.'

He nodded. There had always been a hole; no matter how happy and fulfilling the other parts of his life, he had always been acutely aware of the people who were missing.

'I can't ever know my parents, and I was so young when they died the memory of them is hazy, but Leo was here. Alive and living the life we both should have had if fate hadn't intervened.' He smiled at Beth. He didn't want her sympathy; he didn't want her to feel sorry for him. His life had been blessed in many ways and now he had reconnected with Leo he felt more complete. 'I may not see Leo for another ten years but at least now I know him as an adult, as a man, not the boys we were when I last saw him.'

'I'm really pleased you have reconnected with your brother.'

'There has been another good thing about this trip to England.'

She looked up at him, the sun glinting off her hair and making her blue eyes sparkle, and Josh had to stop himself from taking her in his arms there and then and kissing her until they both forgot where they were.

'What's that?'

'You.'

Reaching out, he brushed her cheek with his fingers, knowing soon they would be forced to make decisions about the future, and those decisions might prise them apart. He might not get the chance again to touch her velvety soft skin, to look into those pale blue eyes, to enjoy her smile.

'Me?'

In answer he took a step towards her, taking his time to memorise each and every feature, each and every detail of this moment. He felt the surge of desire coursing through him as her lips parted, inviting him in. He kissed her, slowly at first, tasting the sweetness of her lips and enjoying the little jolt of pleasure that ran through his body.

Up here on the clifftop it was quiet but not private. Anyone could see, anyone could be passing, but Josh couldn't find it in himself to care. So what if they were spotted in an embrace? He would just marry Beth and be done with it, whisking her back to India far away from any scandal or gossip. The thought was liberating and he pulled her body closer to his, deepening the kiss and encircling her waist with an arm.

'We shouldn't,' Beth murmured, only half-hearted in her protest.

'Why not? I want you. You want me.' It was hardly the most persuasive or eloquent of arguments but it was enough for Beth. She relaxed back into his arms, her lips brushing against his again.

Eventually Josh pulled away, knowing if he didn't he wouldn't be able to resist tumbling Beth down into the grass, and although the clifftop was an acceptable location for a kiss, it wasn't anywhere near private enough for anything more than that.

'I've fallen for you, Beth,' he murmured in her ear, placing a kiss just below her earlobe and loving the little shiver of pleasure he felt run through her body.

She smiled at him, her eyes still a little glazed from the intensity of the kiss moments before.

'You've bewitched me. I can think of nothing but you.'

'Don't be silly.'

'I'm not. You're the first thing I think about when I wake and the last thing before I go to sleep. My days are filled with thoughts of you and my dreams...' He grinned wickedly. 'I shouldn't tell you what happens in my dreams.'

'What happens in your dreams?'

He leant in closer, so his lips were touching her ear. 'Very pleasurable things.'

Ever so quickly her tongue darted out between her lips and the colour started to rise in her cheeks.

'You're imagining it too, aren't you?'

The shake of her head was unconvincing and Josh grinned.

'Liar. You're imagining what might go on under the covers if we found ourselves in bed together.'

'A gently bred young lady would never imagine anything of the sort.'

'You're thinking how it would feel to have my hands on your bare skin, to have my lips kissing you here.'

He placed a finger on the exposed skin of her chest, just under her collarbone. 'And then trail down to kiss every single inch of you.'

'I'm thinking nothing of the sort.'

He leaned in closer again. 'You should. Even the imagining is quite pleasurable.'

She closed her eyes for a moment and the thought that she was imagining them together in her bed was enough to send Josh wild with desire for her.

'You're making this hard for me,' Beth said, her eyes still closed. 'These last few weeks all I've been able to think about is you, and now you're going to invade my dreams, as well.'

'Are you saying you haven't dreamed about me already?'

She gave him a little secret smile and Josh knew she had fantasised about him just as much as he had about her.

'You're not going to make this easy for me, are you?' They began walking again, arm in arm, their bodies brushing against one another as they moved.

'How do you mean?'

'Today we said we'd have one day to enjoy, one day before we decide what we want to do with our futures, but everything you do makes me want you more.'

'Good.'

'But do you mean that? Is it a good thing?'

Josh hated himself just a little in that moment. So much of the hurt and uncertainty Beth was feeling was his fault. If he had been able to commit to her earlier, to come out and tell her he loved her and didn't care about the obstacles in their way, then the decisions they were facing would have been easier to navigate. The truth was he was scared of rejection, scared that, even though she looked at him with love in her eyes, she would choose Leo over him. He knew the fear came from the rejection he'd experienced as a child, the feeling of always being second best, but even though he had that insight he couldn't banish it.

'There's something I need to say to you. Something very important.' Firmly he quashed his doubts and the roil of nerves deep in his belly. He gripped her hand and pointed at the steep path that led from the cliffs to a sheltered little beach nestled in a cove below them. 'Let's go down to the bay, sit and talk.'

Her eyes searched his face as if she was trying to work out exactly what he wanted to say to her, but eventually she nodded and arm in arm they started the climb down to the beach.

The sand was fine and soft and as soon as they reached the beach on the rocky coastal path from the cliffs above Beth paused to pull off her boots and stockings and feel the sand beneath her toes.

In a way she wanted to put off the moment when they sat and Josh told her how he felt. She wanted him to say he loved her, that he would do anything for them to be together, but if he did she knew it would mean she would then have to make some very difficult decisions. If he didn't say he loved her, if he said instead he cared for her, desired her, she knew her heart would break just a little. There wasn't a perfect solution.

Josh quietened all her concerns by gently taking her hand and leading her to a spot where the sand met the

grass behind. They sat, their legs pressed together, their
backs to the cliffs and looking out to the sea. It was a
secluded spot and only someone standing on the very
edge of the cliff above would be able to see them.

'I promised myself I wouldn't do this today, that this
would be about enjoying ourselves, but I think I need
to tell you how I feel.' He took her hand and Beth had
to work on controlling her breathing, forcing herself to
inhale and exhale in rhythm as she waited for his words.
'I love you, Beth. I've loved you these past few weeks
but I was too much of a fool to see it. I couldn't admit
it to myself, couldn't acknowledge how much you've
come to mean to me.'

Beth's smile was instantaneous and her heart soared.
He loved her. Whatever came next, whatever difficult
decisions they had to make, he loved her.

'I honestly never thought I would fall in love. I've
spent much of my adult life avoiding getting too close
to people, worrying I might lose them like I lost my
parents, like I lost Leo.'

She placed her hand on his and he smiled at her,
pulled back from the melancholy.

'There have been so many obstacles, so many reasons I've told myself not to fall for you, but I just haven't
been able to help myself, Beth.'

'I feel the same,' she said quietly, biting her lip. This
shouldn't really be happening. They needed to be sensible about the future, about their different lives and
what was expected of them. Mutual declarations of love
weren't going to be helpful if they had to go their separate ways in a few weeks.

'I don't think you understand,' Josh said, gripping her

hand tighter. 'I love you so much I burn for you when we're not together. The idea of being a single county away makes me feel bereft, let alone half a world.'

She remained silent, waiting to hear what he said next, knowing that she felt the same.

'I love Leo, but the thought of you becoming his wife makes me feel sick. Not because he would mistreat you, not because you would be bad for him, but because I want you all to myself.' He ran a hand through his hair, his face serious now. 'I want you to be mine, only mine, for the rest of time.'

'I want that too.' They might want it but Beth knew desiring something wasn't always enough. 'I love you too, Josh. I love every last thing about you.' She was about to say more but he kissed her, a kiss full of promise and expectation but Beth still felt the uncertainty dragging at her stomach.

'I love you, you love me,' he said as they broke apart. 'The rest is just practicalities.'

She didn't say anything, her head still reeling from his declaration and the half-formed hope that maybe, just maybe, everything might work out.

'I promise I will make this work for us,' he said quietly. 'Just give me a little while to figure it all out in my head.'

Beth knew she should protest, insist they work it out together, but she was tired of trying to come up with solutions to save her family and willing to let Josh try for once. If he didn't manage anything suitable they could put their heads together then.

'While I'm thinking do you fancy a swim?'

'A swim?' Beth laughed. It was warm, but it wasn't swimming weather.

'It's a beautiful day, why not?'

'It'll be freezing. It's not like your Indian Ocean.'

'How cold can it really be?' He pulled her to her feet and she watched in amazement as he began to shed his clothes, dropping his jacket to the ground and pulling his shirt up over his head. Beth found she couldn't look away, her eyes locked on his skin as he placed his shirt on top of his discarded jacket. The heat rose from her core to her skin as he tucked a hand into his waistband and began to loosen his trousers.

'You're going in naked?'

'It's not as though there is anyone else around to see us.'

'Someone could see from the cliffs.'

'Then run fast into the water.' He held her eye as he unfastened his trousers and stepped out of them, then turned and walked briskly to the sea. She watched as he took three great strides into the water and then dived under a wave, surfacing on the other side. 'It's barely even chilly.'

Beth glanced at the empty clifftop and then back to where Josh was kicking his legs on his back in the water. She wanted to throw caution to the wind, then strip down and follow him into the sea. To entwine her body with his and decide once and for all that she was going to *be* his.

All the years of conforming, of following the rules, of doing what she was told flashed in front of her and before she had even consciously made the decision to change she felt her fingers tugging at her dress, loosening it enough to wriggle out of. She was still clad in her chemise and petticoats, although the petticoats quickly followed the dress onto the pile of clothes discarded on the sand. Her chemise she kept on, knowing it would turn transparent in the water but unable to shed the last of her protective layers.

Josh swam towards her as she dipped a toe in the sea, rising from the waves like something out of a Greek epic. It was fresh and she had to brace herself to not run up the beach.

He advanced, holding out a hand, and Beth couldn't help but rake her eyes down his toned body. He was tanned all over and she wondered how much time he spent with his top off back home as his chest had that bronzed glow that hinted at months of summer sun, even though it was a little faded now.

Gripping her hand, he tugged her gently into the water, smiling as she gasped in shock as the first wave splashed above her knees.

'It's really not that bad once you're in.'

Beth rose up onto her tiptoes, holding her body rigid as the water lapped at her and then, steeling herself and taking a deep breath, she dived under the next big wave.

The shock of the cold took her breath away and she struck out in a fast swim to try to warm her protesting muscles. From swimming in the sea as a child she knew it was better just to submerge and swim as fast as you could until your body started to warm from the exertion. Annabelle had always stood on the shoreline, unable to force her body to commit to the water, and Beth always thought she stayed colder that way than Beth when she dived in.

She was halfway along the length of the beach, swimming parallel to shore, before she stopped and glanced behind her. Josh was keeping up with long, easy strokes and seemed to like chasing her through the water. Quickly she struck out again, laughing as his fingertips touched her toes before she pulled away.

The chill had left her skin by the time he caught her, looping an arm around her waist and pulling her to him, their feet scrabbling on the sandy floor. Beth's chemise was floating in the water, only clinging to her skin on the part of her chest that was above the waves. It felt heavy and she longed to have the courage to fling it off, but her upbringing won out and she instead tried to put it from her mind.

'The water is glorious,' she said as they bobbed in the salty water.

'I love the freedom of swimming in the sea, of being able to float and ride the waves with so little effort.' Josh was relaxing with his head back as if reclining in an armchair. One of his arms still rested underneath her back and the movement of the water meant it brushed lightly against her skin, sending wonderful shivers down her spine.

'I like that when I was swimming in the sea here off the coast of Sussex you might have been swimming in your ocean in India.'

He turned to her, straightening and putting his feet on the ground so he could move closer.

'Never again,' he said quietly. 'We will either be swimming in the sea together in Sussex or the ocean in India, but never half a world apart.'

'How?' Beth knew he had asked for time to work

things out but she needed to know. She wanted to be sure of the practicalities before letting herself get carried away with the fantasy.

'If your mother and sister were taken care of, if you knew their futures were secure, would there be any other barriers to you coming back to India with me?'

Beth considered for a moment, knowing this was one of the most important conversations of her life. It was perhaps not ideal to be having it floating in the sea, but they needed to have it now before she was torn apart by worry over the future.

'No. If they were provided for, if I knew they were not going to be thrown out of the house, if they were safe, their futures were safe.'

'I do not have the available funds to pay off your family's debts, Beth,' he said quietly. 'If you marry me then I do not think we will be able to save Birling View.'

She nodded, expecting to feel as though she had been punched in the stomach but in reality it was what she knew was coming. Josh wasn't the heir. From everything she had heard he was going to take over a very successful business, but that didn't mean he had a lot of disposable income just lying around.

'But there is still a way. If Birling View was sold it would pay off most of the debts. I'm sure my funds would stretch to a modest annual income for your mother if she didn't have enough left over from the sale of the house.'

'What about Annabelle?'

Josh shrugged. 'She could choose. We could provide a small property for her and your mother if she preferred or she could come to India with us.'

Beth felt the relief wash through her. There was a way for everyone to be, if not happy, then at least looked after. Her mother would grouse and moan at having to sell Birling View, but Beth was starting to realise that she hadn't put her family into debt, it wasn't solely on her shoulders to get them out. Her responsibility was to look out for her family, and that could be achieved without entering a loveless marriage just to save the family home.

'Annabelle could come with us,' she repeated, feeling her heart soar. She loved her sister dearly and couldn't imagine starting a new adventure in her life without Annabelle there to enjoy it with. In India she could make sure Annabelle was happy and even slowly encourage her to build on her recent forays out of the house. It might be a fresh start for both of them away from their mother's critical eye.

'Of course. I have a house high in the hills. It has eight bedrooms in addition to the master suite, plenty for her to choose from.'

'You wouldn't mind?'

He looked at her then, staring into her eyes until Beth felt as though he could see her soul.

'I wouldn't mind in the slightest. I would invite the devil himself to stay if I thought it would mean I was even a fraction more likely to persuade you to come with me. And your sister is certain to be a better house guest than the devil. I barely know her, but how can I fail to care for someone you love so much?'

Beth let out a squeal of delight and launched herself at him, kissing him and looping her arms around his neck and legs about his waist. He tasted salty and fresh and as his hands drew her closer to his body she wondered if she could ever be happier than in this moment.

They kissed with the waves lapping at their bodies and the air above them cooling and Beth wanted this moment never to end.

After a few minutes she felt Josh's hands tighten across her buttocks as he picked her up, carrying her out of the surf, water dripping from them both and leaving a trail across the sand. He carried her all the way to the top of the beach to a spot in the sunshine where they couldn't be seen by anyone on the cliffs above, then he laid her down and lowered himself down next to her.

Beth's skin felt chilled as the water cooled in the air until Josh began running his hands over her. On her body her chemise was almost see-through where it clung to her skin but Beth had finally lost her inhibitions and didn't care.

'Marry me, Beth,' Josh whispered as he kissed her neck, trailing his lips down over her collarbone to her chest.

She managed to nod before he moved lower and caught one of her nipples in his mouth through the material of her chemise and then the only sound that she could make was a low groan of pleasure.

He teased her, nipping and kissing, dancing his fingers across her skin until she felt as though her skin were on fire and she longed for the weight of him above her. At some point he gripped the hem of her chemise, lifting it off over her head and murmuring in appreciation as he took in the sight of her before his body covered her own.

Beth felt her hips rise to meet his, as though her

body was instinctively primed for this moment, but he hovered just out of her reach, a mischievous smile on his face.

'You only get one first time,' he whispered in her ear, his breath tickling her neck. 'Let's enjoy it.'

Beth almost shouted out loud as she felt his fingers dance across the skin of her thighs, moving ever upwards and inwards. When he brushed against her she felt a jolt pass through her body and every muscle stiffened, but then as he gently stroked and teased she felt herself begin to relax.

All the time her hands were exploring his body, trailing over his shoulder, his back, reaching down to where his spine met his buttocks. Then he shifted, pulling out of her reach as he lifted his body and dropped his head lower so his lips could pepper kisses across her abdomen, circling her navel and making something tighten inside her as he slowly moved lower.

She hadn't realised her thighs had clamped around his shoulders until he began gently to press them outward, before giving her a wicked smile and kissing her in her most private place. Beth gasped, her hands grasping at his head, but he murmured something she didn't catch into her skin and kissed her until her head arched back and she felt her hair trail through the sand.

'Just imagine,' Josh said as he lifted his head for just a moment, 'when we are married we can do this all day every day if we desire.'

Beth tried to utter something witty about him not being a very good boss if he was secluded in his bedroom with her all day but then he dipped a finger inside her and all conscious thought left her head.

'Every. Single. Day,' he said, and Beth felt her hips arch up towards him, begging him for more even though she didn't know what more would be.

He moved rhythmically, teasing her and kissing her until Beth felt a wonderful tension begin to build inside her. Josh must have sensed it too for he smiled at her and then carefully positioned himself over her, slipping inside and pushing her over the edge. Every muscle in her body tensed and she felt as though she were floating above the ground as wave after wave of pleasure pulsed through her.

Gently Josh pushed into her again and Beth realised he was holding back, giving her time to recover and adjust.

'I want you,' she said, looking up into his eyes. 'All of you.'

Josh groaned and thrust further into her, the force momentarily taking her breath away and then her hips were rising to meet his over and over until they both tipped into oblivion.

He stayed on top of her for a minute then carefully rolled to one side, gently pulling her body close to his in the sand.

For a long while neither of them spoke. Beth was contemplating how her life had changed so significantly in the last few hours and she wondered if Josh was thinking the same.

'Time for lunch?'

She rolled her eyes. 'I was lying here thinking of our future and you're thinking about your stomach.'

'I need to keep my strength up,' he said, kissing her on the nose and reaching for the picnic basket.

'Shouldn't we at least get dressed first?'

He took the opportunity to rake his eyes all the way down her body before answering.

'If you insist.'

Chapter Eighteen

As he took a bite of a delicious cheese scone Josh watched his future wife, smiling at the thought of how their fates had changed in such a short while.

He hadn't planned on proposing to her, hadn't even truly decided what he wanted before they'd set out for their walk this morning. Then all he had known was he wanted to spend more time with her, to banish the horrible feeling that their time was too short.

It was only when they had sat down at the base of the cliff that he had realised he couldn't imagine living a single day of his life without Beth by his side. In the short time he'd known her he had started each day thinking of her and wanting to tell her every interesting thing that had happened to him. Leo's words had resonated, telling him to decide what he wanted and then to go for it.

Even though marriage didn't fit into his plans, even though it would mean big changes in both their lives, he knew the alternative was unthinkable. He wouldn't be able to say goodbye to Beth in a few short weeks. It would kill him.

'You're going to love India,' he said as he dipped into the picnic basket and brought out two rosy red apples, offering one to Beth before biting into his own. 'The climate will take a bit of getting used to, and the culture, but it is such a wonderful country, Beth. I can't wait to show you it.' He watched for any sign of uncertainty in her eyes, any sign of doubt. It was a lot to ask of someone, to give up their home, their country and their family to start a life on the other side of the world.

'You're wondering if I will regret saying yes to you.' Beth regarded him as she bit into her own apple.

'You read me well.'

'I don't know if you're easy to read or if I just *know* you well.' She paused, leaning over and taking his hand. 'I won't regret it. I won't change my mind.'

'You're giving up a lot for me.'

'I'm giving up a future of a loveless marriage for something much more wonderful.'

She leaned over and kissed him just as he bit into the apple, coming away giggling.

'Will your guardian approve of me?'

'He'll be ecstatic. He's always suggesting I might like to settle down. I think he'd almost given up hope I would. Mrs Usbourne will love you too, and she will help you settle in to life in India I'm sure.'

'I'll have you and I'll possibly have Annabelle. Whatever happens, that is all I need.'

They finished their picnic, dipping into the hamper until they were both full and sated and Josh beckoned Beth over to him. He leaned back and she rested her head on his chest. For a long while he was just happy to watch her drooping eyelids as she dozed in the sun, marvelling at how perfect she looked from above as well as every other angle. He felt his own eyelids grow heavy in the afternoon sunshine and allowed himself to succumb to sleep.

They woke with the sun slightly lower in the sky, both unsure how long they had slept.

'We should head back,' Beth said, not looking overly keen about her own suggestion. 'I will have to tell Mother our news and speak to Annabelle.'

'We will tell your mother together,' Josh said, squeezing her hand. Beth nodded, biting her lip. He knew she would be nervous, knew she would want to put off the moment when she had to tell her mother she wasn't going to marry a man who could save their family home, but it would be best to tell her mother quickly. That way the shouting and recriminations could occur, then the dust settle and then they could all begin to move on.

'She's going to be so angry.'

'Remember you didn't put your family into debt.'

'No. It wasn't really Mother's fault either though. Most of the debts were Father's.'

'After she has grown used to the idea, once she's settled into a nice little house somewhere, she might find it liberating to live without the constant worry of debt hanging over her.' As soon as he'd said it he wasn't sure he believed it. Lady Hummingford was a dowager countess, a woman born into the aristocracy who was used to living in luxury and comfort. To someone like her, status and appearance were everything and the thought of living quietly in a comfortable little house would not be palatable.

'Hmm.' Beth didn't sound convinced either. She stood, brushing the sand from her dress and looking down at the crumpled material. It looked as though she had rolled about on a beach in it, which wasn't far from the truth.

Josh helped her straighten her skirts as best he could and then Beth busied herself tidying her hair, laughing as the gentle wind kept tugging it from her fingers every time it was almost pinned.

'Can we detour to the village? I promised Annabelle I would pick her up a new book from the shop when we returned to Sussex and with all the preparations for the house party and entertaining the guests the last few days I haven't got round to it yet.'

'Of course.' He knew she was delaying the inevitable, trying to think of any reason not to return home and face her mother, but he wouldn't say no to a few more hours in Beth's company.

They climbed up the steep cliff path and headed arm in arm away from the sea. The little village of East Dean was only a short stroll away. Josh didn't have his pocket watch with him and hoped they would make it to the shop in time before it closed for the evening. In India he could tell the time by the height of the sun in the sky and its heat on his back, but here in England he was not accustomed enough to its patterns.

The clock on the church tower told them it was half past four and Beth hurried him down the high street towards the little row of shops. Only as they approached did Beth stop in her tracks and grip his arm.

'My mother,' she said, gesturing down a side street. 'And my sister.' Her voice was full of disbelief, as if she couldn't quite trust what she was seeing. 'Annabelle has never been into the village before. Never.'

For a moment Beth didn't move, just stood there clutching his arm as her eyes took in the scene in front of them. Lady Hummingford and Annabelle were walking at a slight angle to them so hadn't caught sight of them yet. They weren't talking, both with their eyes fixed ahead, but were arm in arm and Josh wondered for the first time if he had judged Beth's mother too harshly. Perhaps all the scheming and pushing her eldest daughter towards a match she wasn't keen on really had been to protect her youngest daughter. They certainly looked close as they meandered down the street.

Beth seemed undecided and as her mother and sister turned to walk in their direction she pulled Josh back a few steps. They were about to disappear around the corner when he gripped her hand and bade her not to move.

'What's wrong?'

Josh had seen the group of young men approaching Lady Hummingford and Annabelle from the other side of the street. There were six of them, all in their early twenties, well-built men who could be labourers or sailors. They weaved as they walked and looked as though they had spent the best part of the afternoon drinking.

'They look like trouble.' He watched, not wanting to intervene if the men were just passing by, but some deep instinct told him they were looking for a confrontation.

'Look at that,' one man shouted, raising a weaving hand to point at Annabelle. 'Or maybe don't unless you want to bring your lunch back up.'

The other men laughed, crowding in.

'Hasn't anyone ever told you to wear a veil, *my lady*?'

'Did a demon from hell rise up and scratch you about the face?'

'Now, lads, don't be cruel. She's quite attractive from behind. What do you say? Come with me and I'll tup you as long as I don't have to look at your face.'

There was a blur of movement beside him and he realised Beth was running forward, ready to plunge into the middle of the men to defend her sister.

Cursing, he started after her, grabbing her arm and thrusting her behind him just as they reached the group. He registered Annabelle's shocked face and the falling tears, but forced himself to focus on the men first.

'Shame on you,' Beth shouted, shouldering past him. 'Hounding a lady in the street. What would your mothers say?'

A few of the men looked sheepish and started to back away but two who had taunted Annabelle stayed firmly put.

'What's it to you?'

'Look at them, they're sisters. Only this one has had her face carved up. *This* is what she would look like if she wasn't covered in scars.'

'Get away from her,' Josh said, his voice low but dangerous. There were six of them but they were drunk; still he would prefer the men just to leave before Beth began throwing punches herself. She looked angrier than he had ever seen her, like a protective lioness, guarding her young.

The men hesitated and then one blew Beth a kiss before they turned and staggered away.

'Annabelle,' Beth said, but already her sister had turned and started to hurry away. 'I've got to go after her.'

'Come on.' He grabbed her hand, not caring about the filthy look Lady Hummingford gave him, and together they ran after Annabelle. She was fast, her upset and shame fuelling her, and by the time they reached the gates to Birling View Annabelle was still a hundred feet ahead of them. Beth slowed on the approach to the house, letting her hand slip from his.

'I must go to her.'

Josh nodded, watching his fiancée disappear into the house with an inexplicable feeling of dread in his stomach.

Chapter Nineteen

'Please, Beth, just leave me alone.'

Beth felt her heart swell and pulse in her chest as she looked at her sister's crumpled form on the bed. No matter what happened, no matter how upset, Annabelle never sent her away.

'No.' She entered the bedroom they shared and closed the door behind her, turning the key in the lock, and then approached the bed and wrapped her arms around her sister whilst she sobbed. For a long while neither said anything at all, even once the tears had dried up and Annabelle had stilled.

'What happened?' Beth asked eventually.

Annabelle sniffed and allowed herself to be manoeuvred up into a sitting position. Her face was red and blotchy, the scars angry and dark against the surrounding normal skin. Her eyes were puffy but at least the tears had stopped falling.

'Mother suggested a trip to the village. She said I'd done so well going out with you and the other guests.' Annabelle sniffed and wiped away the fresh tears that fell onto her cheeks. 'I was surprised. I thought she was angry at me for showing myself, for making a spectacle of myself, but then she said we should try going out again this afternoon.'

Beth rubbed soothing circles on her sister's back with the palm of her hand. Every so often Annabelle would let out a little shudder that shot through her whole body.

'I felt nervous. I wanted to wear my cloak—you know the one with the big hood—but Mother said it was too hot and she was right, really. It was too hot.' The cloak had a deep hood that could shadow the face and hide Annabelle's scars and her sister always wore it about the estate if she thought there was a chance of meeting anyone.

'So you went to the village…' Beth prompted as her sister fell quiet.

'It was busy and I could see people looking at me, staring.' She swallowed and closed her eyes for a moment.

Beth felt a surge of annoyance at her mother. It was good to encourage Annabelle to get out, but the village was hardly the most gentle of places to choose for her second outing. People knew their mother and she was sure there were rumours of the second Hummingford daughter secluded on the estate. Everyone would want to catch a glimpse of her when she stepped out into the world.

'I could take their stares. It made me feel uncomfortable, but I did what you always say. I squared my shoulders and straightened my back and pretended I was walking a little taller.' She broke off and fresh tears were accompanied by a little sob. 'But then we were surrounded by that group of men. They were drunk, they stank of stale beer, and I knew they were trouble as soon as the first one began to approach.'

Beth squeezed her sister's hand and then leaned in and hugged her, trying to convey all the love she felt for Annabelle in one embrace.

'You heard what they said.'

Silently Beth nodded. It had been unnecessarily cruel. Unprovoked. Beth knew people could be that horrible, but in her sheltered life she hadn't often come across it.

'There was nothing to draw their attention?'

'No. Nothing. They just saw me, saw my face, and it disgusted them so much they decided they just *had* to say something.'

'Oh, Annabelle.'

'I'm never leaving the house again. Never ever. I'm staying right here in this room where my horrific face can't revolt anyone.'

'Don't—'

'You don't understand, Beth. Of course, you don't understand. Look at you, you're beautiful. People look at you and smile. They look at me and…' She broke off and buried her face in the pillow.

Beth knew she had to let her sister cry her tears to work through the hurt and anger at being treated so badly, but she wanted to shake her, to tell her that appearance didn't matter, that Annabelle was sweet and kind and wonderful, but she kept her mouth closed. It was fine to think appearance didn't matter when people didn't point and stare at you in the street. Annabelle was entitled to her hurt. And in a way she was right.

Beth didn't doubt that her blonde hair, clear blue eyes and sweet smile conferred certain unseen advantages. People treated attractive people in different ways, better ways.

'I love you,' she whispered into Annabelle's hair.

'I don't want to ever leave this house again,' Annabelle repeated quietly, and Beth heard the resolve in her voice alongside the sadness.

Pushing away the thought of what that meant for her, Beth concentrated on trying to comfort her sister, all the while knowing her whole world had shifted again.

'I'm sorry,' she murmured quietly, repeating it again and again. Her own tears mingled in with Annabelle's on the bedclothes as she felt the weight of responsibility for Annabelle's pain, mixed with the familiar recriminations. If only she'd watched her sister better, if only she hadn't been so selfish and engrossed in her play, if only she had seen the vase, if only...

Beth crept silently from the bedroom, closing the door behind her. Finally Annabelle had settled, at first dropping off into a fitful doze but now she was in a deeper sleep, her arm thrown across her forehead and legs curled to one side.

In the hallway she paused, not knowing whether to go straight to see Josh or whether to get her thoughts straight first. He had this way of persuading her things would work out all right and she needed to be firm to make sure she did the right thing.

Instead of heading over to the part of the house with the guest bedrooms she slipped downstairs in the darkness. It was late, perhaps eleven, and the neglected house guests had long since retired. Beth supposed her mother had hosted the dinner that evening. After popping her head around the door to check Annabelle was being comforted, Lady Hummingford had disappeared and must have been seeing to the other guests. It had always fallen to Beth to comfort her sister whenever she became upset. Their mother wasn't the maternal or openly affectionate type and so the sisters had always turned to one another if they needed a hug or kind words.

At the end of the hall Beth made her way down the narrow servants' staircase to the kitchen below and took the key from the hook that opened the door. It was a matter of seconds before she was standing in the cool evening air, having turned the key in the lock behind her.

She moved quickly, cursing herself for failing to bring a shawl or cloak. The days were mild but it was still only May and at past eleven there was a definite chill in the air. Rather than go back for something to cover her shoulders, Beth picked up her skirts and ran across the grass, hoping the burst of activity would warm her from the inside. Above her the moon was shining, almost full, seeming to guide her to the cliffs beyond the estate. She had a hankering to see the sea, to feel the salty wind on her face, to be far enough away from anyone else that they wouldn't hear her scream and rail and cry at the unfairness of it all.

The paths were familiar even in the darkness and she never once missed a step, but Beth had grown up knowing how dangerous the cliffs could be. A stumble too close to the edge and you would plummet down to the rocks below. Even without missing a step sometimes chunks of the crumbly chalk would just give way, and you only had to be standing at the wrong place at the wrong time. It meant she always stayed back from the edge, choosing paths a few feet from the drop as she climbed the steep hill.

Only once she was at the top did she stop, inhaling great gasps of air as she tried to catch her breath. It was about a mile from Birling View to where she was standing now, a mile uphill she had run without stopping. Still, even though her chest burned and her heart was hammering in her chest she felt the same freedom she always did up here.

After a minute Beth let herself sink down to the ground and as she sat there was a wave of emotion and she felt herself begin to cry. Her tears earlier had mainly been for her sister. For the cruelty of the men, and how they had taunted her at the worst possible time—just when Annabelle was beginning to venture out. Now Beth doubted she would ever be persuaded to leave the house again.

The tears that fell now were for herself. For a few wonderful hours Beth had really believed she could marry Josh, that she could choose the man she loved over duty, but still provide a safe and happy future for her sister and support her mother. For the first time in her life she'd been completely and utterly happy, and for the first time she had felt the guilt that was always hiding somewhere inside her float away.

'Stupid,' she muttered to herself. She should have seen it would never be that easy.

Beth allowed herself to cry for a few more minutes,

feeling the dampness from the grass soak into her skirt. Then, with one last firm strike of the back of her hand across her cheek, she wiped the salty tears away and took a few deep breaths.

'Enough.'

Tonight she would go to Josh, make him understand that she could not marry him. Then tomorrow she would ask her mother to write to Leonard Ashburton, seeking confirmation of their engagement and to set a date for the wedding. Beth didn't think she would be able to write the letter herself, but her mother would be only too happy to oblige.

With the wind whipping her hair, she stood and started the walk back home. The descent was at a much slower pace than her frantic rush up to the clifftops but even so she was back at Birling View long before she was ready.

As she slipped the key into the lock and opened the door she glanced up, noting the candle burning in Josh's room. He was waiting for her.

Chapter Twenty

The tap on the door was so light he wouldn't have heard it if he hadn't been sitting silently waiting for Beth. There was a book by his side on the bed, abandoned long ago when he'd realised he'd read the same page three times and still couldn't recall what it had said.

As he padded across the room, his socked feet not making a sound, he felt a sensation of mounting dread in his stomach. Something was wrong.

'Beth.' She was standing in the shadows and slipped into his room like a ghost when he opened the door. He could tell she'd been crying by her red-rimmed eyes and her flushed cheeks, but when she brushed against him her skin was cold. 'You're freezing.'

She nodded, starting to shiver despite the heat of the room.

Without thinking he embraced her, pulling her closer and holding her silently until her body had stilled and some of the warmth had returned to her skin.

'How is your sister?'

'Sleeping. She was very upset. Understandably.'

'Did she tell you what happened?'

Beth nodded, anger flashing on her face for just a moment. 'It was completely unprovoked. Of course, she didn't know the men, they just saw her and saw a chance to belittle a woman with scars.'

'It's just strange they came up to her for no reason...' Josh trailed off, knowing it wasn't the right time to debate human nature with Beth.

'She's sleeping now.'

'Good.'

'I needed to talk to you,' Beth blurted out. For the first time since they'd met she seemed nervous around him.

'Why don't we sit down?'

She looked around the room. It was comfortable, not the finest guest room—that had been given to Leo—but still it had space for a small desk and an armchair alongside the bed. After a moment's hesitation Beth picked the upright desk chair, perching on the edge. With that decision Josh knew she'd come to discuss something bad, otherwise she wouldn't have been able to resist choosing a spot on the bed where they could sit with their fingers entwined.

The armchair made a scraping sound on the floor as he pulled it over to face her. As he sat down he caught a glimpse of the despair on Beth's face.

'Whatever it is, whatever is wrong, we can fix it. Together.'

'No.' She shook her head. He could see she wanted to cry but she sniffed back the tears and set her mouth into a firm line. 'I can't marry you, Josh.'

Even though he'd half expected something similar

ever since she'd walked through his door looking so serious and upset, hearing the actual words was like taking a knife to the heart.

The silence stretched out between them as Josh groped for the right words to change her mind. He understood, she would be falling back into her normal spiral of guilt over her sister, thinking that she needed to put her family first and sacrificing her own happiness. He understood all of it, but he couldn't accept it. Somewhere he must have the words to make her change her mind, to make her see that she didn't have to live in misery.

'They taunted her, teased her mercilessly about her appearance. It was only her second trip outside the estate and that is what she is faced with.' She was speaking quickly now as if trying to get him to understand something that he could never accept. 'She was devastated, Josh. I've never seen her so upset. She said she is never going to leave the house again…'

There it was. Probably an innocent enough remark on Annabelle's part, said in the midst of her despair, but the one thing that was guaranteed to make Beth turn away from him and back to a wealthy suitor who could provide the funds to keep Annabelle's sanctuary.

'I understand she is upset,' Josh said, trying to be reasonable. Nothing would be gained if he showed quite how much he was hurting. For Beth to give up on them so easily, to reject their future together without even coming to him and trying to see if there was another way.

The feelings of abandonment were surfacing, alongside the sense of being second best. Long-forgotten feelings, ones that had been repressed since childhood, since Leo was chosen to stay and he was last to be claimed. Quickly he pushed them down. The time for emotion would come later; right now he needed a clear head.

'She's more than upset.'

'I understand that. And I understand her not wanting to venture out in public again, at least not for a while. What I don't understand is why we can't be together.'

Beth raised her eyes to his and he saw the pain there; he knew this was hurting her as much as it was him.

'The house.' She sniffed again, still just managing to keep the tears under control. 'She has vowed never to leave *this* house.'

'Surely it wouldn't matter if it was this house or another house. The cottage we spoke about—'

'No, Josh.' Beth's voice rose almost to a shout and she quickly clamped her hands over her mouth as she remembered they were surrounded by the other guests, hopefully sleeping peacefully in the neighbouring rooms. 'No. She has *nothing*. No future prospects, no hopes of a husband or children. No friends even. All I can give her is this house, her home.'

'I know you want to look after her, but you don't owe her your own happiness.'

'I owe her a little security.'

'For an accident that happened over fifteen years ago?'

Beth closed her eyes, her face pale and drawn, the sadness evident in every movement. He knew she wasn't making this decision lightly, but he also knew she was wrong.

'Give it a few days at least. Annabelle might feel differently once the worst of the humiliation has passed.'

'She may do, but I won't. I'm sure Annabelle would urge me to marry you, to live my own life, but I can't do that, Josh. Don't you see?'

He stood, running a hand through his hair. 'I love you, Beth. I love you more than I've ever loved anyone else. Give us a chance. I promise we will not abandon your sister. We will ensure she is contented.'

It seemed as though the silence stretched out for ever whilst Beth sat with her head buried in her hands. He hoped she was contemplating his words, realising that they could work this out together, as they had planned.

'I'm sorry, Josh. I should never have dreamed.'

He reached out for her, wanting to comfort her even if she was pushing away their hope of a future together, but she stood and slipped past him, opening the door and running down the hall. As he listened he heard her let out the sob that she'd held in all the time she'd been in the room.

Chapter Twenty-One

It was the last day of the house party and when Josh emerged from his bedroom servants were bustling up and down the stairs with trunks and boxes. He doubted the other guests would stay long after breakfast; he couldn't imagine it had been the most diverting few days for them when it had clearly been engineered solely to put Leo in the same place as Beth without much thought to the other guests.

He didn't fancy breakfast, but was determined to see Beth one last time before he left, planting himself in a chair close to the door in the library in a position from which he could see the foot of the stairs. As soon as she descended he would be able to swoop out and show her he wouldn't abandon her.

The minutes ticked past into hours and he had just started the sixth chapter on a particularly dull book about English marsh birds when the door to the library was pushed fully open and Lady Hummingford stepped inside. He stood, feeling the cool animosity emanating from her and realising he felt the same way about her.

Lady Hummingford closed the door behind her with a firm click, but Josh quickly stepped past her and re-opened it.

'I'm watching for someone,' he said, making it impossible for her to close it again.

'For my daughter.'

He inclined his head, wondering what Lady Hummingford was doing here. He knew she didn't like him particularly, but he wasn't sure if she was aware of his entanglement with Beth.

'She won't be coming down today.'

'I would like to see her before I leave.'

'Unfortunately that will be impossible.' She didn't offer any excuses, any lies about a headache or a summer cold. Instead she held his gaze as if baiting him to argue.

'I will send her a message. Then she can decide.'

'Mr Ashburton, my daughter will not receive any message you send to her. None of my servants will deliver it.'

'I will slip it under her door myself.'

'I have advised the footmen that you are not to be allowed back upstairs.'

'That is foolish, Lady Hummingford.'

'On the contrary. I need to protect my daughters and I am doing just that.'

'You still hope she will marry Leo.'

Lady Hummingford didn't answer but Josh could see he was right.

'Leo respects my opinion. One word and he will step away, withdraw his offer.'

'Your brother is a man of honour. He might not want

to marry Elizabeth, but he is bound by the promise he made my husband. I do not think a few words from you will change that.'

'How could you do this to Beth?'

'Lady Elizabeth to you.'

'She will always be Beth to me.' He knew he shouldn't bait her but couldn't help letting this slip out.

'Leave. Return to India and let your brother and my daughter get on with their lives.'

'She could be happy with me, really happy. Isn't that what a mother should want for her daughter?'

'How naïve you are. I want security, not happiness. *That* is what matters in this world. And not just for Elizabeth.'

'I may not be as wealthy as Leo, but I can give Beth a good life.'

'But what about Annabelle? What about me?'

'You'd lose the house, but we could find you a nice cottage. It would be a comfortable life.'

Lady Hummingford sneered at him. 'I'm a countess—the wife of an earl and the daughter of a viscount. Someone of my status does not live in a *nice cottage*.'

'They do if they're in as much debt as you are. Why make Beth pay for your husband's mistakes?'

'Why should I pay for them?'

Josh blinked, surprised by the venom in her voice. He'd never liked Lady Hummingford, but Beth had convinced him she was only looking out for the welfare of both her daughters. Now he wasn't so sure.

'Elizabeth will marry your brother and he will pay our debts. We keep the house. Annabelle gets to hide in her bedroom for ever and I...'

'You can live in a house fit for a countess, knowing you've sold your daughter's happiness for it?'

Lady Hummingford didn't react to his words, instead pushing open the door to the library and motioning for two of the footmen to approach.

'Think what you like of me, but Elizabeth has made up her mind. She is doing her duty and that will give her comfort in the years to come. She has sent word to your brother that she is keen to accept a proposal and I will push for the wedding to be as soon as possible. Within the month she will be married.'

He felt as though he had been punched in the gut and actually took a couple of steps back. Even after what Beth had said last night Josh had thought he could persuade her there was another way, a way that protected everyone but still let them be together.

The idea that Beth had already sent a note to Leo, had already given up on them entirely, was too much.

'Leave. Leave Elizabeth in peace. Let her get on with her life without any further distractions.'

'I will leave, but only once I have spoken to Beth.' He eyed the two footmen. 'And you're a fool if you think these two boys can stop me.'

Lady Hummingford considered him for a moment and then nodded.

'Stay here. I will bring her down.'

It seemed only a few seconds between Lady Hummingford disappearing and her return with Beth in tow. Josh was shocked at how pale she looked, how drained and upset. Her clothes were crumpled, her hair a mess and her eyes had dark rings around them, making them look sunken.

'Beth,' he said, stepping towards her, but Lady Hummingford intercepted him.

'Sit there, Elizabeth. You have one minute.'

Beth stayed standing, her one little rebellion, but Josh could see there was no real fight left in her.

'We can still do this, Beth, we can still be together,' he said quickly, knowing these were the most important words of his life.

'I'm sorry, Josh.' Her voice was flat, as if she'd used up all her emotion.

'Have you written to Leo? Told him you will be his wife?'

There was a second's hesitation and then a nod. Josh felt all the hope leave his body in one burst. She'd given up on them.

Not caring that the door was still ajar, not caring that Lady Hummingford was likely still outside, he stepped closer and gently took Beth's face in his hands. He kissed her, knowing it would be the last time he kissed the woman he loved.

'Goodbye, Josh.' Her voice cracked and as soon as she'd said the words she turned and fled from the room.

'Goodbye, Beth.'

Six hours later he was sitting in Leo's study staring morosely into a large glass of brandy. He'd ridden straight to Leo's Kentish residence, a nicely proportioned house just outside Tunbridge Wells.

'What will you do?'

Josh didn't answer for a moment. He felt as though his brain had slowed and thinking was like moving through treacle.

'Return to India. I don't think I can stay and watch her marry you.'

Leo leaned back in his chair and regarded Josh for a long moment.

'I don't have to marry her, not if you don't want me to.'

'No, marry her. At least that way I know she's safe and you haven't broken your promise. I know that means a lot to you.'

'It's a bad situation.' Even Leo was showing a hint of emotion. 'Stay around for a little longer. She may yet change her mind.'

Josh shook his head. She wouldn't change her mind. Of course, he wanted her to, wanted her to come bursting through the doors declaring she'd made the worst mistake of her life, begging him to give her a second chance. He couldn't wait around for it though; the sting of rejection was fresh and he hadn't realised how deep that had cut. It had opened the old wounds that he'd thought healed but instead were just lurking under the surface.

'I'll catch an earlier ship back to India. If I leave for London tomorrow there will be a ship I can book passage on by the end of the week.'

'If that is what you think best.'

Nothing felt right, but he knew he couldn't stay around and watch Beth marry his brother. That would be devastating. Travelling to half a world away it would still be upsetting, but at least he wouldn't have to witness it, wouldn't have to see them do what he had hoped for himself.

'I'll miss you, Leo.'

'And I you, Josh. Perhaps in a year or two I will be able to come and see you in India. Until then we will have our letters.'

Josh could picture Leo stepping off the gangplank of a ship just docked in the clear blue waters of the Indian Ocean. In the picture Beth was on his arm, parasol held above her head to protect her from the strong Indian sun, her hair blowing in the warm breeze. He would have to insist Leo didn't bring his wife on any trips.

They both lapsed into silence, Josh taking a gulp of brandy and appreciating the burn in his throat, anything to distract him from his morose mood.

Half an hour later Josh collapsed into bed, squeezing his eyes tight and hoping that his sleep wouldn't be filled with images of Beth, but knowing he would be disappointed. There hadn't been a night in the last month he hadn't dreamt of her.

Chapter Twenty-Two

You've made the worst mistake of your life, the little voice in Beth's head kept telling her spitefully.

It was only a few hours since Josh had ridden away without a backwards glance and already she was pining for him. The thought that she would never see him again made her feel as though her heart were ripping in two.

You sent him away.

And she had, cruelly and without any hint of emotion. She'd had to make him leave, knowing her resolve could crumble at any moment, knowing one kind word from him and she would collapse into his arms.

Beth closed her eyes and tried to shut out all the self-recriminations and doubts. She'd done it for Annabelle, for her mother. She had done her duty. In years to come, surely she wouldn't regret that.

She was sitting in the summer house on one of the wooden benches, trying to block out the memories of being in here with Josh. When she trailed her fingers along the wood of the seat she felt as though he were there with her, about to materialise with that easy grin and tease her about something.

She remembered all of their conversations, from the first time they'd met at his brother's party when she had mistaken him for Leonard, as they'd got to know each other little by little in London, to the times she'd bared her soul to him down here on the Sussex coast. He'd loved her, knowing exactly who she was, knowing every last flaw and secret.

Wrapping her arms around herself, she hugged tight, trying to fool herself it was Josh holding her. Despite her words, despite pushing him away so completely, Beth realised she was having doubts.

'It's too late,' she murmured to herself. Too late to change her mind, too late to change her future.

She wanted to do her duty, to see her family looked after, but as her mother had watched Josh ride away with a satisfied smile on her face Beth had seen for the first time what others might see, looking in. She'd remembered Josh's protestation that she couldn't blame herself for something that happened when she was five years old, that their mother should be the one to feel responsible for leaving Annabelle unsupervised and five-year-old Beth wasn't at fault. In all the years that had passed, years filled with guilt and regret, it had always been Beth's fault. Annabelle had never placed the blame at her door, but their mother had, and now Beth was realising that it just wasn't fair. It shouldn't be solely her responsibility to provide for Annabelle's future. Of course, she wanted to look after her sister, but it shouldn't be that she *had* to; that should fall at their mother's feet.

'I thought you might be hiding out here,' Annabelle said, pulling the light shawl up around her shoulders as she stepped into the summer house. It was still a bright day but not as warm as the last few had been and there were clouds gathering in the sky.

'How are you?'

'Better, thank you. I'm sorry for being so self-indulgent.'

'Don't be silly. It was a horrible ordeal for you.'

Annabelle came and sat down next to her, taking the spot Josh had sat in only a few days earlier.

'I think you might have done something stupid, Beth,' she said quietly.

'I think I have.'

'I saw Mr Joshua Ashburton riding off at quite a pace earlier today. He didn't look like a man who had got what he wanted.'

Pressing her lips together to hold in the emotion, Beth shook her head.

'He asked me to marry him.'

'Why did you say no?' Annabelle sounded shocked, her fingers clutching at Beth's.

'I didn't, not at first. He asked me to marry him and I said yes.'

'But…?'

'We had it all planned out—how you would come with us to India if you wanted, and Mother would have to sell the house, but we could set her up in a modest residence. It wasn't perfect but it allowed me to follow my heart and not feel completely guilty about leaving you and Mother behind.'

'Oh, Beth, please tell me you didn't give it up for me.'

'I was rushing home to tell you, I couldn't wait, and

then we saw what happened in the village with those horrible men. You were so upset...'

'Beth.' Annabelle shook her head, looking much older than her twenty-one years.

'And then you said you could never leave the house again and I knew I couldn't force you to come to India with me, or even leave Birling View, not when it is where you feel safe.'

'Why didn't you just ask me?'

It was a good question. For so long she had tried to protect Annabelle from the world, without acknowledging that she was now a young woman with her own thoughts and opinions.

'I knew you would have said to marry Josh and not worry about you, but of course I worry about you.'

'I'm an adult, Beth. I know I might not go out, I might not have the chance of a family of my own, a house of my own, but I still can make my own decisions about my future.'

'I just wanted to protect you.'

'I know. You always do. And you have done so well all these years, but now isn't it time for you to reach for your own happiness?'

'Mother doesn't think so.'

Annabelle scoffed. 'Mother has become so consumed with money and the debts Father left that she doesn't remember you are a person too, entitled to hope for more for your own future.'

It was true. Their mother had never been the most maternal of women and over the years she had become more distant, but it had become much worse since their father had died, leaving her to deal with his debts.

'I just wanted to protect you,' Beth repeated, the knowledge that she had made a big mistake taking hold deep down.

'I know, but I don't want your protection at the price of your happiness. Not when the alternative is entirely acceptable. I'll take a pleasant little cottage from Mr Ashburton and will be just as happy there as I am here. Happier, even, as I will know you are contented.'

'I pushed him away, Annabelle.'

'Do you think you can get him back?'

Beth considered for a moment. He had been unable to hide the hurt in his eyes when she'd rejected him, but he did love her.

'I have to try.'

'You should go before Mother finds out your intentions.'

'No,' Beth said decisively. 'I'm not creeping around any more. I will tell her what I plan to do and she will just have to accept it.'

Annabelle squeezed her into a hug and Beth felt her resolve hardening. She would go after Josh and show him how sorry she was and hopefully that would be enough.

'Ah, Elizabeth—good. I wanted you to see the letter to Leonard Ashburton before I send it.' Her mother passed over the neatly written note, staying seated at her writing desk and straightening her stationery as Beth read the words.

Dear Mr Ashburton,
After careful consideration, Lady Elizabeth is eager to settle the details of the arrangement be-

*tween you. She is keen to announce the engage-
ment as soon as you are happy to do so and would
like a date in the coming few weeks set for the
wedding.*

*I know you will honour your promise to my late
husband and hope you will be in contact shortly
to finalise the details.*
Yours sincerely,
Lady Hummingford

It was short, to the point and left no room for doubt.
Beth held the note out so her mother couldn't miss what
happened next and then promptly tore the paper in half.

'Elizabeth, what are you doing?'

'I am not going to marry Leonard Ashburton, Mother.'

'Don't be silly, Elizabeth. I don't want to discuss
this again. That other man has left, never to return,
and now it is time to forget all that silliness and think
of your future.'

'I am thinking of my future. I am going to marry
Josh.'

'Don't be selfish, Elizabeth. Think of your family,
the debts.'

'They're not my debts, Mother. I will not leave you
destitute, but I am not going to give up my chance of
happiness just for the sake of keeping up appearances.
Sell the house, the debts will be settled.'

'And your sister? You would see her out on the
street?'

'She won't be on the street. She can come with us
to India or she can stay here with the modest yearly income Josh can provide.'

'You think that's enough?'

Beth forced herself to remain calm. Normally this was the point when her guilt would start to kick in and she would concede because she felt so responsible for Annabelle.

'Yes. It is.'

Her mother looked at her long and hard, a flicker of contempt in her eyes.

'You know I would never blame you for what happened to your sister...' she began.

'You always blamed me.'

'That's unfair, Elizabeth. You were only a child, of course. But it is indisputable that you have certain advantages, chances that your sister will never have. If you choose to throw that away on a man who cannot support you and your sister in the appropriate manner...'

'Yes, Mother?'

'Well, it is selfish.'

Beth took a deep breath and steadied her nerves. Her mother had always been strong and impossible to argue with, but she had to do it now or risk a lifetime of regret.

'You and Annabelle will be provided for,' she repeated calmly. 'And I get to be happy. Surely you must want one of your daughters to be happy.'

'Happiness is fleeting. Security is not.'

'You speak as if Josh was a labourer or a poor sailor. He has good prospects and is from a good family.'

'I cannot let you marry him.'

Beth remained silent for a moment, holding her mother's eyes.

'If you marry him I will have no more to do with you.'

Even though Beth knew her mother was just pushing her, testing her limit, she felt the pain of the betrayal.

'So be it,' she said calmly, hoping her voice wouldn't catch on the lump in her throat. She turned to go, aware they wouldn't get any further, when a thought struck her. 'Tell me, Mother, why did you choose to take Annabelle out yesterday? After all those years of encouraging her to stay inside, why yesterday?'

'I don't know what you mean.'

Beth saw the flicker of unease in her mother's eyes and felt sick at the implication.

'For seventeen years you've kept Annabelle hidden, then yesterday you pressed her to go to the village.'

'If you have an accusation to make, just say it. I am too weary to be trying to guess what you mean, Elizabeth.'

'You organised it, didn't you? The young men in the village—you paid them to insult Annabelle, to ensure she was so upset she would ask me to save Birling View, to marry Leonard Ashburton.'

'Don't be ridiculous.' The words were a denial but Beth knew with a sickening certainty that she was right. Her mother had set the whole horrible experience up.

For a moment she was too shocked to move and then she knew she didn't want to be in the same room as her mother a single second longer.

Quickly she ran upstairs, throwing open the door to her and Annabelle's bedroom to find Annabelle at the writing desk.

'Come with me,' she said, crossing the room and crouching down in front of Annabelle. 'I can't leave you here with her.'

'Don't be silly. You've got your new life to start. You don't want me holding you back.'

'I do. Come with me. Please, Annabelle.'

Annabelle leaned forward and kissed Beth on the forehead.

'For once stop worrying about me and go live your life.'

'You don't know what Mother has done.'

'It doesn't matter. I'm staying here. I will help Mother deal with selling the house and we can find a suitable house somewhere. Perhaps our cousin will assist us.'

'You could come to India. It would be an adventure.'

'Your adventure, Beth, not mine.' Annabelle smiled softly at her. 'I won't have you stay for me, and I'm not coming with you. Just promise me one thing—that you'll write every single week so I can hear of all the exciting things you'll be doing.'

Beth hesitated, but then nodded. Annabelle had the right to make her own decision, and the offer to come join her and Josh in India would be an open-ended one. If she felt the time was right in a month or a year, then she could make the journey.

'I love you.' Beth gripped her sister in a tight hug.

'I love you too. Now go get your Mr Ashburton.'

Chapter Twenty-Three

It was almost mid-morning by the time the carriage was approaching Leonard Ashburton's country residence. She had moved quickly at Birling View, instructing the footmen who were still there from the house party to ready the hired carriage before her mother could think to forbid it. Without even packing a change of clothes she had departed, knowing she needed to catch up with Josh as soon as possible. Even so she had been forced to stop in a coaching inn as the light failed and the coachman insisted they wait for dawn before continuing as he didn't know the roads. At the inn she had sent the coachman to enquire about Leonard Ashburton's exact address as she didn't want to waste a minute driving round the area surrounding Tunbridge Wells searching for the estate.

Now she had pressed the coachman into starting just as the first light peeked above the horizon, meaning they had made good time, but still she felt as though she were too late.

'This is the last day Lady Hummingford has paid me

for,' the groom said as he helped her down from the carriage. 'The carriage is due back in London by nightfall. Do you wish me to wait?'

'Yes, please. I may need to travel to London myself.'

'Very well.' He stepped back, leaving her very much alone on her approach to the house.

It had a pretty brick façade with climbing flowers covering the lower half and large windows that must let in a lot of light. It was large without being imposing and looked surprisingly welcoming.

Beth wondered how much influence over the appearance of the house Leonard Ashburton had. She knew it was one of his uncle's properties, all of which would be inherited by Leonard, but she didn't know if he was allowed to treat this as his own house already. It seemed too pretty, too frivolous for the stern and sober man.

Knowing she was trying to delay the moment she had to knock at the door, Beth forced herself forward and picked up the heavy knocker.

'Lady Elizabeth Hummingford to see Mr Joshua Ashburton,' she said to the elderly butler who opened the door.

'You'd better come in,' Leonard Ashburton said, not waiting for the butler to speak, as he emerged out of a room off the main hall.

It was bright and airy inside and Beth felt the urge to dawdle and gawp, but she quickly followed after Leonard Ashburton, perching on the edge of the seat he indicated in his study.

'Is your brother here, Mr Ashburton?'

'No.'

She felt her hopes fizzle and die. Josh might have

gone straight to London instead, straight to the docks if she were unlucky, to find a ship to book passage on back to India. To get as far away as he could from her.

'He left about two hours ago.'

Damn coachman insisting they stop overnight. She would have caught Josh if they'd pushed on.

'Did he say where he was going?'

'What business do you have with my brother, Lady Elizabeth?'

Beth swallowed. She wondered how much of the last few days Josh had told his brother and knew by the suspicious look in Leonard Ashburton's eyes it must have been a good proportion of it.

'I need to see him urgently.'

'I see. Am I to understand you've made a mistake that you wish to rectify?'

Beth nodded.

'Thank goodness for that. I was worried you were really dense. And, of course, then I would have had to marry you and I find it hard to tolerate stupid people.' It was the longest sentence he'd ever said to her and Beth was struggling to work out just how many times he had insulted her in it.

'I do not wish to marry you,' she said sharply. 'I just want to find your brother.'

'And marry him, I hope?'

'Yes. If he will have me.'

'Hmm. Perhaps he will. Josh isn't good with rejection, not after what happened when we were children, but if you can catch him before he sails hopefully you can show him it was just blind stupidity on your part.'

Beth clenched her jaw and ignored the fresh insult.

'Where has he gone?'

'To London, to the docks, to seek passage on a ship back to India.'

'When is he planning on leaving?'

'As soon as possible.'

Standing abruptly, Beth felt some of the blood drain from her head. She needed to get moving, to start the journey up to London. No doubt Josh would be on horseback rather than in a cumbersome carriage, so he had that advantage over her as well as a two-hour head start. She would need some luck to find him.

'Do you know which docks he will head for?'

Leonard Ashburton quickly wrote down an address for her and together they moved into the hall.

'Good luck,' he said. They were the friendliest words he'd ever uttered to her. Perhaps with the knowledge he wasn't going to have to marry her he was able to warm to her a little more.

'Thank you.'

Beth hurried down the steps and gave the address to the reluctant coachman. He grumbled something about needing to be back in Southwark by five o'clock sharp, but climbed up to his seat at the front of the carriage anyway and, once Beth was settled, urged the horses down the driveway.

Glancing back, Beth saw the stiff figure of Leonard Ashburton watch her go and wondered if he was truly keen for her to reach his brother before he departed for India.

'Friday is the earliest? Nothing before then?' Josh wasn't sure why he felt in such a rush to leave England, but waiting three whole days before his ship departed for India seemed like far too long.

'Nothing earlier. Do you want the passage?'

'Yes.' He handed over the money, trying to ignore the regret at the way his stay in England had been cut short. There was no way he could remain and witness what was to come next so he wouldn't waste time pining for longer in his birth country.

'Back home,' he murmured as he left the cramped little office. The thought of the hot sun on his face and the familiar sights and smells only lifted his spirits a fraction.

The docks were busy with men hurrying to and fro, loading and unloading the big ships that sat moored in the water. His trained eye could tell their cargos immediately and most of their countries of trade and origin. His guardian's business had started as a shipping company many years ago and that was still the core activity, but over the years they had expanded to include a branch of the company that dealt with transportation of goods throughout India. Josh loved the logistics of it, the detailed calculations needed to work out how to move a product from the verdant interior, to the docks at the coast then across the world to the half a dozen countries their ships sailed to.

This was what he needed to focus on. The last few months had been a distraction, nothing more. Now he needed to get back home and put all of his energy into making the business thrive. He had heard of the steam trains gaining popularity in mines and ironworks in parts of England and knew in his heart this was the future of travel and transporting goods. Quietly he had been buying up stretches of land and researching what would be needed to bring the steam train to India.

Even as he tried to concentrate on his plans for the business thoughts of Beth kept creeping in. A swish of a woman's skirt reminded him of the evening he and Beth had strolled through the pleasure garden, a hint of lavender scent made him think of her fresh and fragrant skin. Everywhere there were reminders of her.

He knew he needed to accept her rejection of him and move on, but even when he was trying not to think about it, it still hurt.

'Josh.' He heard her calling his name even before he saw her standing on the docks, looking completely out of place.

At first he wasn't sure if she was real. Lady Elizabeth had no reason to be alone and unaccompanied on the dockside of London, but as he stepped closer he could see the rise and fall of her chest, the soft movement of her lips as she breathed. She was real.

'What are you doing here?' He guided her out from the main thoroughfare, away from the men heaving heavy loads of cargo across the docks into the warehouses that towered high above them.

'Josh, I'm so sorry.' Her words came out in a rush and he had to put a hand on her arm to get her to stop and slow down.

'What are you doing here, Beth?'

'Is there somewhere we can go? To talk?'

He thought about sending her away, rejecting her as she had rejected him, but he knew he could never do it. It might hurt him more in the end, but he needed to know why she was here.

'I'm finished here. We can go back to my brother's town house. Where is your carriage?'

'The coachman had to leave. It was a hired carriage and our time was up.'

Josh felt a surge of protectiveness for Beth, alongside anger at the coachman who had left a young lady in an unsavoury area of London with no means of getting away.

'You're alone.'

'Yes.'

'Your mother didn't accompany you?'

'No.'

He hated the surge of hope that flared in him at her answer.

It took half an hour to weave their way through the docks back to a street where they could hail a carriage. He could see Beth was eager to get whatever she had to say off her chest but he didn't want to discuss things out here in the open. She had been so definite when she had sent him away that he couldn't see anything good coming out of her following him to London, and he wasn't about to have his heart broken for a second time whilst stuck in a carriage with her with nowhere to go.

Only once they were sitting in the comfort of Leo's study, the servants instructed not to disturb them under any circumstances, did he motion that he was ready to hear what she had to say.

'I'm sorry, Josh. I never set out to hurt you.'

'That I believe.'

'When we were on the beach on Saturday, when I said I would marry you, I truly thought I would. I thought we could work everything out.'

He stayed silent. He'd believed that too. For a short while he had convinced her to let go of her guilt and to let go of the belief that she was solely responsible for what happened next to her sister and her mother. For a few short hours she had believed she could marry him.

He clenched his jaw, trying not to let the pain show on his face. Her rejection of him still cut like a knife and he was finding it hard to focus on her words.

'Then when I saw Annabelle so upset all my old guilt and feelings of responsibility came rushing back.' There were tears in her eyes and Josh had to restrain himself from reaching out to her. It was important she said whatever she had come to say. Then they could both move on with their lives. 'I felt like what we had planned was just a fairy tale, a dream. Something that was too good for me. So I pushed you away.'

'You did.'

'I'm sorry,' she said again, shaking her head and looking just over his shoulder. 'I wish I could turn back the clock.'

Josh waited, forcing himself not to guess what she was about to say. She had sought him out for a reason, and by her tone so far it would appear that reason was regret. Whether it was regret purely at the way they had parted, or regret for the decision she had made, it was not yet clear.

His mind was racing, trying to work out what he would do if she begged him to give her a second chance. He just didn't know, so instead pushed himself back to the present rather than spending his energy on speculation.

'After you left, I felt miserable. I couldn't imagine

my life without you.' She shook her head. 'No, that's not true. I could imagine it and it was horrible.' Beth slipped from her chair and knelt in front of him, reaching out for his hand. Her skin was warm and soft against his and he could feel the flutter of her pulse under his fingertips. 'I already knew I loved you, but I realised I had made the worst mistake of my life. I was sitting there in the summer house, pining for you, and I realised once again I had allowed my guilt to rule my life.'

She bit her lip before continuing. 'I am not solely responsible for my mother and my sister. They are both adults, they can make their own decisions, live their own lives.'

'Do you actually believe that?'

She nodded. 'I think you said words like those to me so many times it must have burrowed into my consciousness. I realised that you were right—I could be a loving sister without sacrificing my own happiness.' The words were coming out in a rush now. 'And I spoke to Annabelle and she said she just wanted me to be happy and would be quite content in a little house somewhere rather than me trying to save Birling View.'

'And your mother?'

Beth grimaced. 'Do you know she set up that whole thing with Annabelle? Somehow she knew we would head back through the village, probably because I promised Annabelle I would pick up her book, and she paid those men to be there just at the right moment to taunt her own daughter.'

That was unexpected. As much as he disliked Lady Hummingford he wouldn't have thought she could do something so harmful to her own daughter. He remembered the sense he'd had that something was wrong, something was staged or unnatural about how the group of men had approached her sister, and realised this must have been why. Lady Hummingford had arranged it all along.

'Beth, why are you here?'

'I want to be with you, Josh. I want to marry you and come with you to India, to be your wife, to have your children.'

She looked up at him with her blue eyes sparkling, a mixture of hope and trepidation swimming in their depths.

'We had the chance of all that and you pushed me away. What's to say you won't change your mind again?'

Part of him wanted to swoop her onto his lap and kiss her senseless, but there was something holding him back. That fear of her changing her mind again, of him letting her in and then getting his heart broken all over again.

'I won't. I made a mistake, Josh, but I love you. Please.'

Slowly he shook his head, not meaning to reject her completely, but unable to believe that she could put them, their relationship, first.

'I love you, Beth,' he said slowly, his voice sounding harsh to his own ears, 'but I don't think I could survive you leaving again.'

She nodded, biting her lip. 'I know I hurt you, unforgivably so. I know me pushing you away, rejecting you, brought back all those awful memories from your childhood.' She took a shaky inhalation of breath. 'And I know how hard it must have been when it seemed that

I chose your brother over you. I'm so sorry, Josh. The last thing I ever wanted to do was hurt you. I was stupid and selfish, only thinking of my pain and my responsibilities.' Beth clutched at his hand and paused for a moment, needing the time to collect herself. 'I won't promise to be perfect, I won't promise never to do anything wrong again, but I will promise to always choose you. To always make each and every decision with you in the forefront of my mind.'

Josh closed his eyes, trying to make sense of the battling thoughts inside his head. One part of him wanted to embrace her and forget the last two days had ever happened. The other part, the cautious part, warned against opening himself up to heartbreak again.

'I don't know, Beth.'

'Down on the beach, when you told me you loved me and I said I loved you, you said that was enough, the rest was just practicalities.'

He nodded, wondering what she was going to say.

'You were right. I love you, you love me. The rest *is* just practicalities. I let myself lose sight of that, but I know we are meant to be together, Josh. It doesn't matter where in the world we are, as long as we have each other.' She gave him a gentle smile and he felt his heart swell. 'Give me the chance to show you how much I love you.'

He searched her eyes, seeing just hope and love there, and realised he didn't want to live his life without the woman he loved. She had hurt him, but she was here now and he could feel the sincerity in her words. Slowly, unable to repress a smile, he leaned down and pulled her into his lap. She let out a little sigh of relief just before his lips covered hers and they were lost to one another's kiss.

'You're lucky there were no ships leaving today. I was eager to be away.'

'I was worried about that. When I went to your brother's house and he said you'd already left for the docks I had visions of having to chase you all the way to India.'

'Would you have done that?'

'Yes.'

He kissed the tip of her nose, then her cheeks, then her lips, wondering at how quickly his life had changed again.

'I'm going to marry you very soon,' he murmured. 'Then you won't be able to change your mind again.'

'I'm not going to change my mind...' she smiled at him '...but I won't protest about getting married very soon.'

He calculated the timescales in his head. 'We may just be able to squeeze in a wedding before we have to leave for India.' He looked at her seriously. 'You don't have any doubts about leaving the country so soon?'

Beth trailed her fingers across his cheek and kissed him again. 'No doubts at all. I can't wait to see my new home.'

Chapter Twenty-Four

The wedding was a quiet affair, held in the church of St Mary's, close to Leonard Ashburton's town house. Their only guests were Leonard Ashburton and Annabelle, who had made the trip to London for the first time in her life.

Beth felt wonderfully content, as if all the worries of the last few weeks had been swept away with the wedding vows.

'Leo wanted to speak to you,' Josh said, coming over and taking her hand, dropping a kiss on the inside of her wrist.

'Oh?'

'A wedding gift of sorts. I'll let him explain.'

Josh motioned Leo over, grinning as he clapped his older brother on the back.

'Congratulations, Mrs Ashburton.'

'Thank you.'

'I thought I might offer my services in arranging everything here that needs arranging,' Leo said, his expression serious as usual, despite the happy occasion.

Beth must have looked puzzled for he pushed on quickly.

'Josh has informed me your mother will have to sell Birling View, and that he is planning on setting up an annual income to support her and your sister.'

'Yes.'

'I owed your father a debt, a debt I cannot now settle.' He gave a little smile. 'Due to happy circumstances, of course. What I propose is that you and Josh allow me to help your mother and your sister. I will assist your mother in selling Birling View if she needs any guidance and I will set up the annual income payments.'

'That's too much,' Beth protested.

'It is only what I would have done if we had married. It will be hard to manage from the other side of the world. Let me do this for you.'

Beth opened her mouth to protest again but slowly closed it as she really considered the offer. It was beyond generous, but he seemed very keen to do this for them. 'Perhaps you could set everything up, and in a few years, when we are settled in India, we can take over the payments.'

'As you wish.'

'Thank you, it is most kind of you.'

Leonard kissed her formally on the hand, then bowed and excused himself, leaving her alone with her husband.

'Are you ready for your new life, Mrs Ashburton?'

'I am. Let me say my goodbyes to Annabelle and then I will be ready to depart.' The wedding had been rushed. By the time the banns had been read the required number of times it had been almost time for them to leave England and set sail for India. They had found passage on a ship that allowed them to marry first, but it meant their wedding night would be spent at sea. It was all happening so fast, but Beth didn't mind, not now she and Josh were married.

'Don't cry,' Annabelle said, tears streaming underneath the veil she wore to cover her face.

'I'm going to miss you so much.'

'And I you.'

'Any time you change your mind, any time you want to visit, just send word and we will book you a passage.'

Beth had held onto the hope that her sister would agree to leave England with them and come start a new life in India. Although in recent weeks Annabelle had become bolder, venturing out of the estate a few times and even making the trip to London for the wedding, she still preferred to mostly stay indoors.

'I know. Don't worry about me. I have my eye on a pretty little house in Eastbourne. It has a lovely garden and sea views. I think Mother and I could be quite happy there.'

At the mention of their mother they both fell quiet. Her absence was expected but that didn't mean it didn't hurt. Beth had sent her an invitation to the wedding with a note saying she hoped to see her mother one last time before she set sail for India, but Annabelle had come alone.

'Write to me every week. I want to hear all about your new home.'

'Of course. And we will be back to visit before you know it.' Beth felt the lump form in her throat. Even though she knew they would be back, it wasn't likely to be for a few years yet. The voyage took so long and Josh was going to need to be present to take the reins of the business.

'I love you, Beth.'

'I love you, Annabelle.'

They embraced for a long while, only pulling apart as Beth heard the hooves of the horses pulling their carriage slow to a stop outside.

'It's time,' Josh said, taking Beth by the hand and giving Annabelle a kiss on the cheek.

Hand in hand Beth and Josh descended the steps and climbed up into the carriage. They leaned out and waved as they moved away, looking back until they rounded the corner and the house behind them was obscured from view.

'Any regrets?' Josh asked, coming to sit on the padded seat beside her.

'None at all.' She felt sad to be leaving her sister behind, but she didn't regret her decision. They were off to start their new life together and Beth couldn't wait to set foot on the ship that would take them there.

Josh enveloped her in his arms and kissed her, only stopping when they reached the docks half an hour later.

'Shall we, Mrs Ashburton?'

'Lead on, Mr Ashburton.'

Beth felt the slight wobble of the gangplank as she stepped off the solid land of the docks, but she straightened herself and boarded the ship with a steady step. She looked to the horizon, wondering at the change in her fate these last few months, then all thought was swept from her mind as Josh picked her up and twirled her round before murmuring something about their wedding night in her ear.

Epilogue

'Close your eyes,' Josh said, his excitement contagious.

Beth did as she was bid, closing her eyes lightly so her eyelashes brushed against her cheeks. The sun was warm on her face, despite the parasol she held above her head. They were travelling in an open-top carriage; Josh had insisted it was the best way to introduce her to her new country, her new home. So far he hadn't been wrong. The sights of the crowded streets, the colourful clothes of the residents, the scent of the exotic spices, all were better appreciated in the open air.

Now they were approaching their new home, climbing the lush green hills, and with every second Beth felt the anticipation build. Josh had described the estate in so much detail she felt as though she had already walked the cool hallways of the house and explored the lush green rolling hills that made up their land.

'Are you ready?'

Beth nodded, feeling a mix of excitement and trepidation. *This* was her new home, the house she would be mistress of, the place they would start their family and live their lives.

'Open them.'

She did. Slowly lifting her lashes to let her eyes adjust to the bright sunlight, Beth gasped, unable to believe quite how beautiful it was. The house was painted white with grand pillars framing the front door and large windows to let in the sunlight. It was large but didn't lack character as some sprawling mansions did. In front of the house was a pretty little fountain and laid out to each side neat little gardens. The white of the house contrasted wonderfully with the deep greens of the surrounding rolling hills and it was built in such a way that it had uninterrupted views all the way down to the sparkling sea.

'Oh, Josh, it's beautiful.'

'I know.' He kissed her and Beth saw the happiness in his eyes. He might have loved his time in London and enjoyed the voyage, but here he was at his happiest. Here was his home. 'Come on, I want to show you everything.'

He gripped her hand and helped her down from the carriage, pulling her along in his excitement to give her a tour around her new home. Outside the house a small group of servants awaited them, smartly dressed and smiling broadly at their master's return.

'This is Heena. Heena, I would like you to meet my wife. Heena is our housekeeper. She was my nursemaid when I first came to live here with the Usbournes and when I built my own house I asked her to come and be my housekeeper.'

'I could never say no to you,' Heena said, smiling fondly at Josh before turning her attention to Beth.

She was a woman in her late forties, plump and short with glowing skin and one of the widest smiles Beth had ever seen. She stepped forward and took Beth by the hand.

'I am so happy to meet you, Mrs Ashburton. Anything you need, anything at all, you let me know.'

'Thank you.'

Introduction after introduction followed in a whirl and Beth knew it would take her some time to learn all the names and roles. All the staff seemed eager to meet her and friendly, and she could see they were happy to have Josh back home.

'I know everyone is watching,' Josh murmured in her ear once they had finished with the introductions, 'but I'm going to pick you up now and carry you over the threshold.'

He grinned at her, not giving her a chance to reply, and swooped her up into his arms.

Beth wriggled until he gave her a stern look, stilled for a second and then wriggled some more.

'This dress must weigh a stone.'

'Is that your way of telling me I'm getting heavy?'

'Not at all, my lovely wife. Just your clothing must weigh more than when I did this on our wedding night.'

'Hmm.' She couldn't be mad at him. She *was* heavier. They had spent much of the six-month voyage to India in their cabin and at some point something miraculous had happened inside her. By her calculations she was about four months pregnant, her belly just starting to round. She hadn't told Josh yet, wanting to tell him once they were here and settled so he wouldn't spend the whole trip worrying about her.

He carried her inside and Beth expected him to place her down in the hall but instead he kept her in his arms.

'I know I should show you the house,' he said softly in her ear, 'but I really think you would like to see the bedroom the most.'

'For its wonderful view? Or perfect proportions? Or perhaps because the furniture is so well made?'

'All of those things are true, but I have to admit to more nefarious motives.'

'Nefarious? Now I'm intrigued.'

'Intrigued enough to skip the rest of the tour?'

'The rest of the house will still be here later.'

'I love you, Mrs Ashburton.' He took the stairs two at a time and Beth was only able to catch glimpses of the light-filled house as he whisked her up to the bedroom. Once inside he kicked the door closed with his foot and then carried her over to the bed, depositing her on the crisp white sheets.

'The Usbournes will be here later. I sent a message asking them to join us for dinner at seven. By my calculations that gives us three wonderful hours to test the robustness of this bed.'

'I will need to get dressed for dinner.'

'Fine. Two hours and forty-five minutes.'

'And do my hair.'

'The Usbournes will love you even if you greet them with your hair tangled like a bird's nest.'

'I'm not sure that is the first impression I want to make,' she said, laughing.

Josh cut her laugh short with a deep kiss and suddenly perfectly pinned hair seemed less of a priority. With a soft moan she sank back onto the bed, feeling the wonderful weight of her husband's body above hers.

Two hours and forty-five minutes later Beth was rushing to fix her hair whilst Josh muttered as he pulled at the laces on her dress. She had spent the entirety of the voyage without a ladies' maid and as such Josh was now reasonably proficient at fastening her dresses, although not as good as he was at unfastening them. Even so, when he helped her to dress there were always mutterings about the unnecessary complexity of women's garments.

'Do you think they will like me?'

Josh paused, his hands falling still on her shoulders. 'Of course, my darling. They will love you. How could they not?'

'They're such a big part of your life.'

He dropped a kiss on the bare skin of her neck.

'All they've ever wanted is for me to be happy. You make me happy. So they will love you for that even before they get to know you and love you simply for being you.'

'I've got something to tell you, Josh,' she said, spinning to face him. 'I think I'm pregnant.'

His eyes flicked down to her abdomen, a smile spreading across his face. Beth squealed as he picked her up and spun her round, setting her back down gently and placing a hand over her subtle bump.

'Not just six months of fine dinners in there, then.'

She swatted him but the movement was cut short as he leaned in for a kiss.

'I love you, Beth.'

'I love you, Josh.'

His hand was still on her abdomen when there was a soft knock on the door. He moved away to answer it, taking a letter from the person outside.

'It's just arrived. From England.'

Beth smiled, recognising her sister's handwriting. No doubt many letters would arrive over the coming weeks. Annabelle had promised to write weekly, although it would take six months for the letters to cross the oceans to get here.

Eagerly Beth tore open the envelope, tears forming in her eyes as she recognised Annabelle's elegant looping handwriting.

My darling Beth,

How I miss you already. It has only been three weeks since you set sail, but it feels like a lifetime. So much has happened I barely know where to begin.

Mr Ashburton has been true to his word and is helping us sell Birling View. We have been to see a few cottages that would be suitable. Mother finds fault with all of them, of course, but I think once she has accepted that we have to move she will be forced into a decision.

One is just outside of Eastbourne, with beautiful views over the sea. I loved it and liked imagining that you might one day be looking out of your window over the ocean whilst I'm looking out of mine.

I do have some more news, but I hesitate to

*tell you. It isn't anything definite yet, and I can't
quite believe it is happening. In fact I'm not sure
it will happen. Perhaps I will write in a week and
let you know when things are a bit clearer, once
Mr Ashburton has clarified the situation.*

*Do write and tell me all about your new home.
I miss you dearly, Beth, and I hope you are happy.
All my love,
Annabelle*

'Read this,' Beth said, holding out the letter to Josh
after a second read-through. She was frowning, wondering what the news could be that Annabelle was holding back.

'How mysterious.'

'What do you think it could be?'

Josh shrugged, handing her back the letter. 'Perhaps
Leo has found her a position as a companion or something.'

'Perhaps.'

'Or perhaps he means to marry her.'

Beth blinked, looking back down at the letter as if
willing it to divulge some more clues, but the words on
the page didn't offer anything more up.

'Marry her?'

'You're right. Probably a stupid suggestion.'

There was another knock on the door and the maid
informed them Mr and Mrs Usbourne's carriage had
been sighted at the end of the driveway. Beth forced
herself to put down the letter and focus on the evening
ahead, even though her head was spinning from the
possibilities.

'Are you ready?'

She nodded and, arm in arm, they walked downstairs. For a moment she thought of her sister, thousands of miles away in England, and wondered if she was doing something similar and then Josh kissed her on the cheek, distracting her completely as they waited for their guests to arrive.

'I love you,' he murmured to her as his guardians stepped out of the carriage, all smiles and warmth. As they came and embraced her, with Josh by her side, Beth realised she already felt at home here. All she needed to be completely and utterly happy was her husband holding her hand and the little flutter of life inside her.

* * * * *